"It's no mystery why the first Scumble River novel was nominated for the prestigious Agatha Award. Denise Swanson knows small-town America, its secrets and its self-delusions, and she writes as if she might have been hiding behind a tree when some of the bodies were being buried. A delightful new series."

—Margaret Maron

Praise for Denise Swanson

Her "SCUMBLE RIVER MYSTERIES ARE MARVELOUS."
—Jerrilyn Farmer

Murder of a Barbie and Ken

"I was thoroughly entertained by the antics of Skye Denison and company and plan to add the Scumble River Mysteries to my 'must read' list."

—Paula Myers, *Old Book Barn Gazette*

"As with any good mystery, the action starts early and doesn't let up. Swanson deftly blends Skye's compelling personal issues with town gossip and murder clues. Cleverly plotted, subtle and stylish, this one ends with a brilliant bang." —*Romantic Times* (Top Pick)

"The book is well-written, it is humorous in a subtle and self-deprecating way (no slapstick here), and it is eminently readable. I predict you will love a visit to Scumble River."

—*Mystery News*

continued . . .

Murder of a Snake in the Grass

"Swanson's Skye Denison, amateur sleuth, is an endearing and realistic character. . . . A fast-paced, enjoyable read."

—*The Herald News*

"This book is delightful. . . . The characters are human and generous and worth following through the series."

—*Mysterious Women*

"A well-written, nonviolent, enjoyable story that captures the essence of the small Midwestern town."

—*Mystery News*

Murder of a Sleeping Beauty

"A smooth, pleasant, and ultimately satisfying book."

—*Chicago Tribune*

"Another cunning, light-hearted story from Swanson. The book keeps pace, reminding us all over again why we have come to know and love that sly, witty Skye—the paradigmatic sleuth." —*The Sunday Journal* (Kankakee, IL)

"Another delightful and intriguing escapade . . . do yourself a favor and buy it." —*Mystery News*

Murder of a Sweet Old Lady

"Superbly written with emotion and everything a good mystery needs. . . . Shame on you if you miss anything by Denise Swanson." —*The Bookshelf*

"Swanson's writing is fresh and snappy. . . . Skye Denison [is] one of the most likable protagonists in softer-boiled mystery fiction today. *Murder of a Sweet Old Lady* is more fun than the Whirl-A-Gig at the County Fair and tastier than a corndog." —The Charlotte Austin Review

Murder of a Small-Town Honey

"A delightful mystery that bounces along with gently wry humor and jaunty twists and turns."
—Earlene Fowler, Edgar Award–winning author

"A light-hearted, entertaining mystery."
—*Fort Lauderdale Sun-Sentinel*

"A charming, insightful debut mystery." —Carolyn Hart

"A likable new heroine reminiscent of some of our favorite childhood detectives—with a little bit of an edge. . . . A fresh, delightful and enjoyable first mystery."
—The Charlotte Austin Review

"Skye is smart, feisty, quick to action and altogether lovable." —I Love a Mystery

"A charming debut novel that rings with humor, buzzes with suspense, and engages with each page turned. . . . An impressive first novel worthy of praise."
—*The Daily Journal* (Kankakee, IL)

Other Scumble River Mysteries

Murder of a Barbie and Ken

Murder of a Snake in the Grass

Murder of a Sleeping Beauty

Murder of a Sweet Old Lady

Murder of a Small-Town Honey

Murder of a Pink Elephant

A Scumble River Mystery

DENISE SWANSON

A SIGNET BOOK

SIGNET
Published by New American Library, a division of
Penguin Group (USA) Inc., 375 Hudson Street,
New York, New York 10014, USA
Penguin Group (Canada), 90 Eglinton Avenue East, Suite 700, Toronto,
Ontario M4P 2Y3, Canada (a division of Pearson Penguin Canada Inc.)
Penguin Books Ltd., 80 Strand, London WC2R 0RL, England
Penguin Ireland, 25 St. Stephen's Green, Dublin 2,
Ireland (a division of Penguin Books Ltd.)
Penguin Group (Australia), 250 Camberwell Road, Camberwell, Victoria 3124,
Australia (a division of Pearson Australia Group Pty. Ltd.)
Penguin Books India Pvt. Ltd., 11 Community Centre, Panchsheel Park,
New Delhi - 110 017, India
Penguin Group (NZ), 67 Apollo Drive, Rosedale, North Shore 0632,
New Zealand (a division of Pearson New Zealand Ltd.)
Penguin Books (South Africa) (Pty.) Ltd., 24 Sturdee Avenue,
Rosebank, Johannesburg 2196, South Africa

Penguin Books Ltd., Registered Offices:
80 Strand, London WC2R 0RL, England

First published by Signet, an imprint of New American Library,
a division of Penguin Group (USA) Inc.

First Printing, July 2004
10 9 8 7 6

To Joan, George, Beth, Tom, Kathy, Kate, and Emily Stybr; and Lynn, Ralph, Allison, and Adam Vanderhyden. Thanks for allowing me to become a part of your family.

In loving memory of Lisa Stybr (1959–1984). Our time together was too short.

Acknowledgments

Thanks to the "real" Plastic Santas, Al Sefcek, Rick Cole, Tom Johnson, and Greg Votta, who are nothing like the fictional ones—except for their great musical talent. A special thanks to my cousin, Greg Votta, for sharing stories of his band with me.

Thanks also to Julia Alldredge, who told me the story of the rural meth labs and sent me the newspaper clippings to prove it.

Scumble River is not a real town. The characters and events portrayed on these pages are entirely fictional, and any resemblance to living persons is pure coincidence.

CHAPTER 1

Roll Over, Beethoven

The music struck Skye Denison with the force of an ax blow. She stood in the open door of her brother Vince's hair salon with a cooler at her feet and a picnic basket in her arms, trying to determine if her ears would start bleeding if she ventured over the threshold.

When Vince mentioned his band was changing their name from Plastic Santa to Pink Elephant, Skye hadn't realized that they'd be changing the type of music they performed, too. Now she understood why her mother had asked her to drop off the food at the rehearsal. Skye had thought it was odd May didn't want to do it herself. Normally, Skye's mother used any excuse to get out of the house and go somewhere. Evidently May had already heard Pink Elephant rehearse.

A blast of frigid air blew a strand of Skye's hair across her face and reminded her that she was standing outside in the middle of one of the coldest Illinois Februaries on record. Steeling herself to the deafening sound, she kicked the plastic ice chest through the doorway and entered the waiting area.

White wicker chairs and settees, which usually held customers waiting for their turn to be cut, colored, or coiffed, were filled with instrument cases, amps, and cables. The stark black equipment was a jarring contrast to the sofa's garden print cushions, and the glass coffee table that typically displayed *People*, *Cosmo*, and *Glamour* was littered with guitar picks, sheet music, and drumsticks.

Skye moved through the waiting room and paused at the entrance to the styling area. This was the juncture where the noise level went from merely painful to excruciating. She felt as if there should be a sign saying, "ABANDON ALL HOPE OF EVER HEARING AGAIN, YE WHO ENTER HERE" posted among the red hearts and shiny pink-foil garland that decorated the lattice archway.

The band members were scattered among the styling stations, curler carts, and freestanding hair dryers. The smell of testosterone battled with the acrid odor of perm solution, while the stink of cigarettes and beer lost the war to the sweet aroma of floral shampoo and conditioner.

Skye blinked. It wasn't every day that she saw four macho musicians performing against a beauty salon background of delicate mauves and pinks.

Vince was crowded up against the far wall between the front windows, surrounded by drums of all sizes. Whenever he lifted his drumsticks too high they got tangled with the fronds of a fern that hung down from a shelf above his head. There were beads of sweat above his green eyes, and his butterscotch hair was tied back in a ponytail.

Opposite Vince, sitting at one of the freestanding hair dryers and hunched over the keyboard in front of him, was Finn O'Malley, a scruffy carrottop wearing faded jeans and a tattered T-shirt. At some point the dryer's hood had slipped down and covered the top quarter of Finn's head, making him look like an alien from a 1950s science fiction movie.

To Vince's left, Rod Yager concentrated on strumming his guitar. Stringy brown hair obscured his face, and his blue jeans and T-shirt were only slightly less frayed than Finn's. At first glance it appeared that he was performing some strange version of the Mexican Hat Dance, but then Skye noticed that what he was really doing was trying to avoid tripping over the cords of the various hairstyling implements that trailed across the salon floor.

Center stage, platinum blond hair trailing down his back, cobalt blue eyes blazing with emotion, the lead vocalist Logan Wolfe screamed out the lyrics to an acid rock hit from the '90s. His tight black tank top was soaked in sweat and his black jeans rode low on slim hips.

Skye closed her eyes and tried to hear why someone would like this kind of music. As a school psychologist, she often watched television programs, went to movies, and listened to CDs that she would never choose on her own in order to better understand the teenagers she evaluated and counseled. But this noise masquerading as a song was beyond her comprehension.

As Logan's voice trailed off, Vince glanced up and waved Skye over. She put the picnic basket on the counter, hung her jacket up on the coat rack, and walked through the arch toward him.

"What do you think of our new sound?" Vince yelled from across the room.

"It's . . . uh . . . loud." Skye tried to think of a polite lie but ended up saying, "I sort of liked the music you played before better."

"We'll still play that when we do gigs for the older crowd."

Skye gave him a sharp look. Was he saying she was old? She was only thirty-two.

Vince got up from his stool and gave her a quick hug. With his arm still around her, he said, "Guys, you remember my sister, Skye?"

Rod and Finn grunted hellos.

As they wandered away to investigate the food, Finn said to Rod in what was clearly the continuation of an ongoing conversation, "I still don't understand why the chicks don't seem to dig me."

Rod slung his arm around the other man's shoulder. "It's how you talk to them, man. You gotta quit being so sexist. Broads really hate that."

Skye was still shaking her head at Dumb and Dumber's remarks when Logan strolled over, took her hand, and said, "Of course I remember you. You moved back to town a couple three years ago, right?"

Skye shrugged. "It seems longer." She had left her hometown right after she graduated from high school and returned only after finding herself fired, jilted, and broke.

"Nope, it was two years ago last summer." He smiled seductively. "I keep track of all the pretty ladies in Scumble River—especially those with such beautiful emerald green eyes and sexy curls."

Vince frowned and removed Skye's hand from Logan's. "I'm sure your wife would be thrilled to hear that."

Skye shot her brother a puzzled glance. Considering Vince's own reputation as a ladies' man, she was surprised at his censure of Logan's behavior.

The singer shrugged, not bothering to respond to Vince's taunt. Instead he stepped closer to Skye and fingered a ringlet of her hair. "What color do you call this? It's not brown, but it isn't red either."

"Chestnut." She assessed the singer. He was handsome in a pop idol sort of way. She could see the appeal he would have to a lot of women, but he wasn't her type. Piercings and tattoos left her cold. Not that she thought for a minute he was really coming on to her. He was obviously the kind of guy who flirted with every female he met.

Vince moved between them, forcing Logan to step away from Skye.

She could feel the tension between the two men and wondered what was causing it. She didn't flatter herself that it had anything to do with the singer's behavior toward her.

Vince and Logan continued to stare at each other until Skye took each of them by the arm and moved them toward the food. "Mom sent over some supper for you guys. Don't make me tell her you didn't eat every bite."

Skye watched as the men filled their plates, grabbed cans of beer from the cooler, and sat down to eat. It took her a few minutes to realize that they weren't talking to each other. Well, Rod and Finn were still discussing the mysterious ways of women, but no one else was saying a word. Logan had his back to the group and was staring at a poster of Monet's *Water Lilies*, and Vince had retreated behind the reception counter. Was something wrong with the band?

Skye had planned to leave right after dropping off the sandwiches, but the mood among the musicians concerned her. She had recommended the group to play at the high school dance Saturday night. What if they were breaking up? Everyone would blame her if there was no music at the Valentine's Day Ball, and the superintendent would kill her.

Grabbing the manicurist's chair, she wheeled it over to where Vince was sitting and asked in a low voice, "So, what's up?"

"Nothing. What do you mean?"

"You guys seem upset with each other or something."

"Nah, just a difference of opinion." He finished his sandwich and crumpled his napkin. "It'll blow over soon."

"Why were you so mad at Logan when he was flirting with me before?" Skye raised an eyebrow. "You know he wasn't serious, and even if he were, I can take care of myself with guys like that."

"Yeah. I know."

"Besides, he could never compete with Simon." Skye

was referring to Simon Reid: funeral home owner, local coroner, and currently her boyfriend.

"I know," he repeated. "But the guy irritates me sometimes with his never-met-a-mirror-he-didn't-like attitude."

"That's what you're upset about?"

"Nah." He didn't look her in the eye. "We're trying some new music tonight and it's just not sounding good. It makes me jumpy."

"So, why don't you just do the soft rock stuff you've been playing? The band sounded great at the last wedding reception I heard you at."

Vince rolled his eyes. "Let's just say we're tired of playing the 'Chicken Dance.' "

Skye hid her grin and asked innocently, "Why?"

"Because it's the redneck 'Macarena.' " He hummed a few bars and shuddered. "Yech!"

"You could always do the 'Hokey Pokey' instead."

Vince swatted her arm. "Gee. Can we? Please?" Before she could return the conversation to why Vince was upset, he sprang up from his chair and said, "We need to get back to practice."

Skye was forced to let the matter drop. As long as the band showed up and played for the dance Saturday, she'd worry about their interpersonal relationships later. "Are you going to return the basket and cooler to Mom, or should I take them?"

"I'll bring it over to the folks' house tomorrow, before I open the salon." Vince moved back behind his drums, and the other guys took up their instruments. "Want to stick around and listen?"

Skye cringed, thinking, *No, thanks, I could hear you just fine from the parking lot, inside the car, with the heater and the fans running full blast.* Out loud she said, "Darn. I'm expecting an important phone call, so I'd better get home.

I'll see you guys at the school's Valentine's Day Ball. I'm one of the lucky chaperones."

"Right. I just hope we can get it together by then."

Skye put her coat on and moved toward the door. "Don't worry. I'm sure you'll knock 'em dead."

CHAPTER 2

Chain of Fools

The next afternoon, as Skye pulled into the high school parking lot, a Scumble River Fire Department truck roared out. The driver waved as he passed, and she waved back. He looked somewhat familiar, but then in a town of barely three thousand, most people did.

Usually fire drills took place only during nice weather, but today students and staff stood shivering in raggedy lines along the blacktop, and none of the teachers had their coats on, a sure sign of an unplanned evacuation. What in the world had happened?

Skye found an empty spot near the back of the lot. Getting out of the car, she stepped ankle deep into a puddle of slush and swore under her breath. It had been a tough winter. The snow had started in November, and now in February there was no sign of an early spring. After shaking the icy water off her foot, she picked her way carefully across the slick asphalt. The last thing she needed was to perform a pratfall in front of four hundred teenagers with long memories and warped senses of humor.

Homer Knapik, the high school principal, was standing on the school's front steps bellowing through a bullhorn that appeared glued to his mouth. "Everyone may now go back into the building." Homer was squarely built, with a surplus of body hair and a permanent scowl. He reminded Skye of a cantankerous collie.

The kids rushed for the door, while their teachers shouted for an orderly return. Skye lingered outside, avoiding the crush. As the last student straggled in, she followed.

Homer caught her as she crossed the threshold. "Just the gal I wanted to see." He led her into his office and shut the door.

"What happened?" Skye took off her coat before taking a seat, preparing for a lengthy discussion.

Homer dropped into the chair behind his desk. "Arlen Yoder pulled the fire alarm."

"Shit!"

"My sentiments exactly," Homer agreed.

Two years ago Arlen's older brother had been expelled, and in September of this year Arlen had gotten into serious trouble, resulting in his temporary suspension. The boys' parents didn't feel either punishment was justified and were extremely difficult to deal with. Once, months ago, Mr. Yoder had even been physically violent toward Skye during a meeting about his older son. She had always regretted not reporting him to the police at that time.

"Why on earth did Arlen pull the fire alarm?" Skye asked. Unlike his brother, he wasn't a malicious kid. He had fallen into some bad company over the summer, but since that other boy's removal, he'd been toeing the line.

"He claims that someone shoved him against the wall during passing time and one of the flaps on his shirt got caught in the fire alarm mechanism. When he tried to get free he pulled the lever accidentally." Homer folded his hands across his stomach and leaned back.

"Do you believe him?" Skye asked.

"That's the thing." Homer scratched behind a hairy ear. Skye half expected him to dig out a flea. "While we were waiting for the firemen to clear the building and tell us it was okay to go back inside, I looked at his shirt. It was one of those with all kinds of pockets and zippers, and one of the flaps *was* torn."

"What did you do?" Skye asked.

"Before I announced that the kids could come back inside, I called his mother to come and get him."

Skye pulled her appointment book from her tote and made a note. "Maybe I can figure out if he's telling the truth. I'll see him at nine Monday morning."

"That will require that he lives that long." Homer's eye twitched.

The ringing of the phone saved Skye from responding.

Homer snatched up the handset and barked "Yes?" He paused, then said, "No. No. Don't put him through . . . Hello, Mr. Yoder. What can I do for you?" Homer listened before saying, "No, I'm sorry, that would be against board policy." He listened again. "Feel free to call the superintendent. No. I can't change the rules for your son. Look, just have him report to the school psychologist at nine Monday morning, and we'll sort things out from there." He banged down the receiver and told Skye, "Mr. Yoder wants me to let his son attend the Valentine's Day dance this weekend." Homer dug a roll of antacids out of his desk drawer.

"Did you suspend Arlen?"

"Yes, pending a full investigation." Homer had crunched two of the Tums, and the white fizz around his lips made him look like he was foaming at the mouth.

Skye bit back a smile; the situation with Arlen was serious. "So, you can't let him attend an extracurricular function."

Homer nodded and popped two more tablets. "You know his father is going to hound me about it. He'll ruin my Valentine's Day weekend."

"Put on your answering machine."

"He'll come to the house." Homer moaned.

"If that happens, let the police deal with him."

Homer appeared to make a sudden decision. "I've got to make a call." He picked up the phone. "You can go now."

As she was gathering her things, Skye heard part of Homer's conversation. "It's me. I've decided we should go away for the weekend. Make us a hotel reservation in St. Louis. We'll leave tonight as soon as school gets out. I'll tell the superintendent that I have a death in the family, and they have to handle Saturday's St. Valentine's Day dance without me."

Apparently there wasn't room in Scumble River for both Homer and Mr. Yoder, and Homer wasn't taking any chances on who would win that particular showdown at the OK Corral.

Skye shook her head and retreated to her own office. After hanging up her coat, she took out the psychological report she was currently writing. Friday after lunch was a bad time to try and see kids for either evaluations or counseling, so she used those hours to whittle away at the stack of never-ending paperwork that was one of the more irritating parts of her job as a school psychologist.

She was trying to figure out a professional way to state that the boy she had tested did not have a serious emotional problem, and in fact was just a brat, when the dismissal bell rang.

Skye had been roped into being one of the Valentine's Day Ball sponsors, and the student committee was meeting in the gym after school to put up the decorations. It was time to go supervise.

After locking the folders she had been working on in the file cabinet, Skye grabbed her purse and coat. She was on a tight schedule and needed to get home as soon as they finished decorating. She didn't want to have to return to her office and take the chance of being waylaid by an "emergency."

It was three-fifteen by the time Skye reached the gym. Trixie Frayne—Skye's best friend, the high school librarian, and another of the dance sponsors—had already gotten the students organized and working.

The kids represented the full range of the high school social strata or, as the kids called it, the food chain. The female Ultras stood around giggling and tossing their long, straight blond hair, avoiding any activity that might break a nail. Their male counterparts flexed their muscles and flashed blindingly white grins. The Student Body Leaders tried to talk to the Ultras, and when they were ignored, snapped orders at the Brains, who along with the Geeks—those in the band and choir—did all the actual work.

"How's it going?" Skye asked.

Trixie slumped on the bottom bleacher. Her short brown hair, usually a smooth cap, was ruffled as if she had been running her fingers through it, and her normally cheerful brown eyes held a worried expression. She let out a loud sigh.

Skye frowned. This wasn't at all like Trixie, who usually bounced around like a super ball and saw the silver lining even in a tornado cloud. "What's wrong?"

The other woman played with the heart-shaped buttons on her red cardigan. "Everything."

"Could we narrow it down just a little?" Skye leaned forward. "Home, school, the world situation?"

"All of the above." Trixie crossed her legs and dangled a red high-heeled slide from her toe. "The kids have been really hyped up lately."

"Do you think the false fire alarm this afternoon had anything to do with their behavior?"

"No. The grapevine says it really was an accident." Trixie

was one of the few adults the kids felt comfortable confiding in.

"Then they're probably just excited about the ball." Since there was little else to do in Scumble River, a school dance was a big deal to the teens.

Trixie shrugged. "It could be. My gut feeling is that something's going on that the adults don't know about."

"And how is that any different from our standard operating procedure?" Skye joked. Trixie didn't smile and Skye hastily continued in a more serious mode. "I'd be glad to call a couple of the kids in on Monday and try to get them to tell me what's happening, but odds are all I'll get are blank stares and denials. Trying to find out that kind of information from teenagers is like trying to nail Jell-O to a tree."

Trixie's expression became stubborn. "Something's happening, and I want to know what it is."

Skye twisted a curl around her finger. "Well, we've got a meeting with the student newspaper staff scheduled after school Monday. Let's see if they have any ideas."

Trixie nodded. "That's a good plan. If anyone will tell us, it'll be Frannie and Justin and their friends. They have a strong sense of right and wrong."

Skye smiled at Trixie's mention of their two star student reporters, Frannie Ryan and Justin Boward. "And they have an excellent nose for news."

Trixie nodded again, then lapsed into silence.

Skye could hardly believe how down in the dumps her friend seemed. Something else was obviously bothering her.

She opened her mouth to ask, but before she could formulate a question, Trixie said, "What do you think of the mayoral race?"

Skye shook her head. "I can't believe Wally's running." Walter Boyd was the Scumble River police chief, and it had been quite a surprise when he tossed his hat into the ring for mayor. "But then, I've noticed some changes in his personality lately."

"Don't you think he'd do a good job? What changes?"

"I'm sure he'd be an excellent mayor, but I'm surprised he wants the hassle." Skye considered the last couple of months and tried to explain. "Wally seems to have lost his zest."

Trixie shrugged, clearly not understanding. "I'm more surprised that Ace Cramer is running against him." He was the younger of the two male gym teachers and coached the basketball and baseball teams at Scumble High.

Skye jerked a thumb over her shoulder. "Speak of the devil." Ace had just walked into the gym and stopped to talk to the crowd of Ultras. "He seems like a nice enough guy and appears to be pretty smart, which is more than I can say about Coach." Skye had a running feud going with the older P.E. teacher, who was also the part-time guidance counselor.

"Maybe, but he strikes me as mostly glibido."

"Huh?" Skye had never heard that expression.

"All talk and no action."

"Oh." Skye didn't really know him well enough to comment.

"And it seems sort of funny for someone employed by the school district to run for public office."

"Why?"

"I don't know. It just does."

"The kids sure seem to like him," Skye said. "He has a group of them surrounding him whenever I see him."

"True." Trixie abruptly changed the subject. "We got a call from Owen's mother's attorney last night." Trixie's mother-in-law had passed away a few months ago.

"What did he have to say?" Skye figured they were finally getting to the main reason for Trixie's misery.

"That between the hospital, the doctors, and the funeral,

it looks like we're going to owe about twenty-five thousand bucks."

Skye let out a low whistle. "There's no insurance?"

"That's what's left *after* her health insurance paid its 80 percent." Trixie grabbed a tissue from her pocket and blew her nose. "She only had two thousand in life insurance, and her funeral cost nearly seven. It would be even more if we hadn't bought the double burial plot when Owen's dad died last year."

"What about her house?"

"Between the second mortgage and back taxes, there's no equity left." Trixie hunched over. "We're just barely making the payments on the farm as it is. Last season's crops were damaged by high winds, and the price of corn and soybeans is way down. The only way we could get twenty-five thousand dollars would be to sell off some acreage, and Owen would rather sell me than an inch of land."

"Yeah. My dad and uncles are like that, too." Skye patted her friend's shoulder. She knew only too well what it was like to have money problems. She had crawled back home a few years ago after maxing out her credit cards and was still struggling to pay off her debts. She didn't see any easy solution to Trixie's financial woes and couldn't think of anything to say that would make her friend feel better.

The two women sat in silence until Skye reached into her purse and pulled out a Cadbury bar. She handed it to Trixie. "You win the emergency chocolate for today."

Trixie smiled for the first time since Skye's arrival. Just before she bit into the bar she said, "Damn right I do."

Trixie polished off the candy and licked her fingers. "Any more?"

Skye stifled the urge to smack her friend. It wasn't Trixie's fault she could eat her own weight in sugar and never add an inch to her size four figure, while Skye could gain pounds by reading a Godiva ad. "Sorry. That's all I have."

"Oh, well." Trixie glanced at the wall clock. "It's nearly four. We'd better see how the kids are progressing if we want to get out of here by five."

Trixie and Skye went in separate directions. Using tulle and quilt batting, the students had created a cloud scene that could be used for the backdrop of the couples' portraits. Streamers and garlands were draped over the ceiling beams, and murals that the art classes had painted hung along the walls. The only thing left to do was set up the tables.

Skye grabbed a pink linen square from a stack sitting on a chair and had just flicked it open when a scream echoed through the gym. Her head snapped toward the sound, and she saw Bitsy Kessler with her mouth open for another shriek. Bitsy was standing by the storage area under the stage and pointing.

Skye dropped the tablecloth and ran toward the girl.

Bitsy was screaming over and over again, "He's dead! He's dead!"

Skye pulled her out of the doorway. She didn't see a body. She took one wary step into the storage area and pulled the string that turned on the overhead light. A little to the left was a dummy draped over a sawhorse, wearing nothing but a Scumble River athletic jacket. The straw stuffed legs and Raggedy Ann–type head made it obvious that it was only a mannequin. By no stretch of the imagination did it look real.

When Skye emerged from the storage area, Trixie was sitting on the bleachers comforting Bitsy, who was still sobbing. The other kids surrounded them.

Skye loudly cleared her throat. They all looked in her direction and she announced, "Everything's fine. No one is dead. Bitsy must have mistaken an old stage dummy for a real person, but everything is okay. Please go back to what you were doing."

The teens drifted back to their tasks.

Skye sat beside Bitsy and asked, "Are you alright now?"

The girl hiccupped and giggled. "My bad." Her laugh had a hysterical edge to it.

It took Skye a moment to understand that in teenspeak Bitsy had just said she had made a mistake. Skye examined the teen carefully. Something was off-kilter. "Maybe you'd better go home. Is your mother picking you up?"

"Not till five." Bitsy stood up, suddenly all smiles. "Don't worry. I'm cool."

The girl was bewilderingly changeable, and Skye resolved to stick close to her until her ride arrived.

They finished decorating the gym a little before five, and after turning Bitsy over to her mother, Skye got into her own car. She patted the wide leather bench seat fondly. No question, the vehicle was growing on her. When her dad and her godfather, Charlie Patukas, had first presented her with the aqua 1957 Chevy Bel Air, Skye had been none too pleased. She'd had plans to buy a sleek little Miata, and the bargelike Bel Air was the last vehicle she would have selected, given a choice. But the love that the two men had invested in the car made it impossible for her to turn it down.

Now as the engine purred to life, she accepted that this car was probably a better option for her than one that would only seat two people and had a trunk that was smaller than the Bel Air's glove compartment.

As she drove home, her thoughts played tag between Bitsy's odd behavior and Trixie's money problems. What was wrong with the girl? And what would happen to Trixie and Owen if they couldn't pay off his mother's bills?

CHAPTER 3

Does Anybody Really Know What Time It Is?

Skye was smiling as she pulled into her driveway. The sight of her riverside cottage always soothed away the stresses of the day. She loved everything about the house, from its unusual octagonal shape to the small cupola rising out of the center, like a periscope on a submarine.

In the winter the snow and the frozen river created the illusion of a silent world where time stood still. Spring and summer brought rebirth with water trickling along the shore and trees in bud.

Before going inside, Skye walked back out to the road and retrieved her daily dose of bills and advertisements from the mailbox. She started to flip through the stack as she opened her front door and stepped inside but was interrupted by the meowing of her black cat, Bingo. He sat on her foot and leaned his entire fourteen pounds against her shins, demanding his supper.

Skye threw the mail onto the hall bench, scooped him up, and walked into the kitchen. As she tunneled her fingers through his soft fur, scratching behind his ears and underneath his chin, his purring intensified and his eyes closed in ecstasy. She continued petting him until he wiggled out of her arms and went to sit by the cupboard containing his food.

She grabbed a can of Fancy Feast from the bottom shelf and popped the lid, wrinkling her nose at the strong fish smell as she spooned the food into Bingo's dish. She put the bowl on the floor and asked, "How can you eat this stuff? It reeks."

Bingo ignored her question and buried his face in the blob of salmon mush.

Skye shrugged. It was time to get a move on. She had to do a few chores and change her clothes before Simon picked her up at six. Since they both had to work the next evening, they were celebrating Valentine's Day tonight.

She returned to the foyer and hung up her coat, then headed toward her bedroom. After stripping down to her underwear, she slipped on her robe, gathered her checkbook, stamps, return address labels, and a pile of bills, and headed for the great room. She had gotten paid earlier that week and had immediately deposited her check, so the money should be in her account by now.

She settled on the couch and looked through the monthly statements. Mmm, which Peter would she to rob this month to pay which Paul? Or would this be one of the rare times when her income and expenses came out even?

Scumble River was among the worst-paying school districts in the state, possibly the country. Most of the staff worked there because it was too far to drive to a better-paying school district and family situations prevented them from moving anywhere else.

Skye's story was a little different. After being fired for insubordination from her first full-time job as a school psychologist, she hadn't been able to find any other position. It seemed that no one wanted a school psychologist who was willing to oppose an influential adult to stick up for a child.

It was only due to her Uncle Charlie's influence as president of the school board that Scumble River had hired her.

She was writing the last check when she remembered the mail she had dropped on the hall bench. Shoot. She padded out to the foyer and sorted out the junk. Of the remaining two pieces, one was her car insurance premium—there went the last of her money—and the other was hand addressed and the size of a greeting card. Was someone sending her an early Valentine?

She slit the envelope and slid out the stiff white square of paper. It was an invitation to a brunch on Sunday hosted by someone named Moss Gibson.

Could he be a relative? Skye couldn't think of anyone she knew by that name, but distant cousins frequently popped up with no warning. She'd have to call her mom and find out if this Moss Gibson was one of them. But first she'd better get ready for her date.

When she finished dressing, she sat on the edge of her bed and picked up the phone. As usual, her mother answered before the first ring was completed. Skye always wondered how she did that. "Hi, Mom. It's me, Skye."

"Everything okay?" May was a champion worrier.

"Everything's fine." Skye knew she had to go through the ritual. "How are you and Dad?"

"We're fine."

"When I checked your work schedule, I was surprised you weren't on duty tonight." May was a police dispatcher and usually covered the afternoon shift from three to eleven.

"I traded. I'm working tomorrow night, so the new dispatcher can have Valentine's Day off."

"That was nice of you." Skye smiled. Her mom always put everyone else's needs before her own. "But didn't you want to spend tomorrow with Dad?"

"You know he hates going out on the actual holiday. Everything's too crowded. We're going out tonight."

"Oh. Right." Skye contemplated sharing her own plans with May but decided against it. She didn't want her romantic evening with Simon to be turned into a foursome. "Hey, the reason I called was to ask you if we're related to a guy named Moss Gibson. I just got an invitation to a brunch he's hosting this Sunday and I've never heard of him."

"We got an invitation, too. I checked with Grandma Denison to see if he was someone from your father's side of the family, and she said no. And he's not a relative of mine that I know of."

"I wonder if he's selling something." Skye'd had her fill with home product parties a few months ago, when she'd been forced to attend one every week for several months. "Are you and Dad going?"

"Sure, why not? It's something to do." May was not a homebody, and even though her husband was, Jed would go to keep his wife happy. "How about you?"

Skye thought quickly. If her parents were attending, she'd better be there, too. They tended to be a little too trusting and this might be some sort of scheme to bilk them out of their savings. "Sure. Is Vince invited?"

"He didn't say anything about it," May answered. "You don't think his feelings will be hurt if he wasn't invited and we all go, do you?"

"No. I doubt he'd care." Skye scanned the invitation. "Mine says 'and guest,' so he can come with me if he wants."

"That's a good idea. You ask him." May sounded relieved. "Hey, someone just pulled into the driveway. I've got to go. Dad and I'll see you Sunday."

As Skye hung up, the doorbell rang. Six on the dot. It had to be Simon. Occasionally she wondered if he circled the block waiting for the precise tick of the clock before pressing the bell.

She slipped on red high heels and went to let him in. In the foyer, she paused to look out the window, just to make sure it was indeed the man of her dreams and not a Nightmare on River Drive.

Although many people in Scumble River still didn't lock their doors, Skye was a lot more wary. Experience had taught her that things weren't always what they seemed in the idyllic small town.

Simon's golden-hazel eyes twinkled at her through the glass. She opened the door and stepped aside, admiring him as he paused on the mat and stomped the slush from his shoes.

No question about it, he was one sexy, handsome guy. Ice crystals melted in his short auburn hair and his tall, lean physique reminded her of Gary Cooper. Although his features hinted at a refinement that was rare in Scumble River and his elegant black wool overcoat would have fit right in at a Broadway opening, he seemed happy in the small town and was well liked by its residents.

Simon finished wiping his feet and gathered her into his arms, thoroughly kissing her before letting her go. "You smell great."

"Thanks." Skye laughed. "It must be my fabric softener. I'm not wearing any perfume."

"Ah, clean clothes," Simon teased. "The only thing that smells better is freshly baked bread."

"For that you'll have to hug my Grandma Denison." Skye rested her hand on his arm. "How's the bowling alley coming along?" Simon had purchased the business in November and had been having it remodeled since then. When it reopened, his mother would manage it for him.

"Good. We should be ready next Friday as planned."

Skye almost hated to ask the next question. "How are you and Bunny getting along?" His mother had appeared out of the blue a few months ago, and relations between her and Simon had been rocky at first.

"Not too bad. She's worked hard and seems to have a knack for the business."

"That must be a relief." Skye half turned toward the living room. "Do we need to leave right away, or do you want to stay for a while?"

"Our reservation is for seven-thirty and the radio just said traffic going north on I-55 is heavy, so we'd better get started." They were going to Chicago for dinner, and ninety minutes of travel time was cutting it close.

"Okay."

Simon helped her put on her coat, then guided her down the icy sidewalk and tucked her into his car. The Lexus was still warm from his drive over. Skye snuggled into the soft leather seats and made a vow. Tonight she would concentrate on Simon and their relationship.

She wouldn't worry about Vince and why his band members were acting strange. She wouldn't think about what Mr. Yoder might do in retaliation for Arlen's suspension or how Trixie would pay off her mother-in-law's debts. Tonight she would concentrate on having a romantic evening with the love of her life.

Skye frowned and chewed her lip. Of course, Bitsy's strange behavior that afternoon was cause for concern. She had to remember to look into that on Monday.

CHAPTER 4

Break It to Me Gently

The telephone shrilled next to Skye's ear and she moaned. Why had she ever thought she wanted a phone in her bedroom? She should have left well enough alone and stuck to having just the one on the kitchen wall.

It rang again and she squinted at the clock radio. Eight a.m. on Saturday—not early for most Scumble Riverites, but Skye was not a morning person. Reluctantly she reached for the receiver. The caller had to be her mother; all her friends knew better than to phone before ten on a weekend.

May's voice blared from the earpiece. "Do you know what happened last night?"

Skye straightened and clutched the receiver. "No. What happened?"

"That's what I want you to find out," May answered. "Vince has a bruise on his forehead the size of a pie plate."

"Did you ask *him* how he got hurt?" Skye hated it when her mother tried to get her to snitch on her brother.

"How could I? I haven't seen him, and I don't want to call him at work. Saturday is his busiest day." May never let logic stand in the way of her goal.

"If you didn't see him, how do you know he's bruised?"

Skye'd had way too little sleep to be able to handle this conversation.

"Uncle Emmett had a seven o'clock hair appointment. He told Aunt Minnie as soon as he got home. She called me."

Skye should have known. Her Aunt Minnie, May's middle sister, had the best sense of rumor in town.

May's voice interrupted her thoughts. "Are you still there?"

"Yes, I'm here." What was Vince doing cutting hair at seven a.m.? She'd have to have a talk with him about opening up so early. He was making her look bad.

"You need to find out what happened to your brother."

Skye closed her eyes. "It's really none of our business. He could have run into a door or slipped in the shower."

"Maybe I should go over to the salon and bring him chicken soup or some cookies." May solved most problems with food.

"No!" The last thing Vince would want was their mother showing up and treating him like a baby in front of his customers. Skye gave in. "I'll stop by when I run my errands, and if he needs anything, I'll call you."

"Well, I do have a couple of pies in the oven for the church bake sale and I really can't leave them, but call me the minute you find out what happened. You know how I worry."

"Yes, I do and I will. Bye."

"Bye."

Skye replaced the handset in the cradle and sank back on the pillows. The rustling of sheets next to her drew her attention, as did the hand caressing her thigh. She and Simon had finally figured out a discrete method of spending the night together.

Skye had met Simon when she returned to Scumble River nearly three years ago. They had dated for almost a year, broken up over Skye's unwillingness to take their relationship to the next level, and then started seeing each other again nine months ago.

In September, they had finally taken the big step and spent a weekend in a Chicago hotel. It was only after they returned from that idyllic interlude that they realized how hard it would be to keep the intimate side of their relationship secret.

Scumble River was a small town with old-fashioned morals and sensibilities. Unmarried couples did not openly sleep together, although what went on behind closed doors was another matter. But Skye's mother was a police dispatcher, both Skye and Simon had jobs that put them in the public eye, and they each drove distinctive cars. For them, privacy was hard to come by.

They had tried several different ways to spend the night at each other's houses without advertising their activities. Currently they were testing Plan D—Operation Drop-Off.

At the end of their "official date" Simon dropped Skye at her cottage. She then got into her car and followed him to his house, where he put his Lexus in the garage and rode back to Skye's cottage with her.

Since it was only a five-minute drive round-trip, it wasn't too tiresome a scheme, especially when one of the rewards was waking up the next morning beside each other in a warm bed. Not to mention what took place once they were awake.

Much later, after they had showered and while Skye was combing out the wet tangles in her hair, Simon abruptly left the bedroom. He came back a minute later, handed her a small velvet jeweler's box, and said, "Happy Valentine's Day."

Skye became instantly wary. Could it be an engagement ring? Did she want it to be? What should she say if it was? She had no idea and didn't really want to figure out the answers to those questions at this point in their relationship. After what felt like an eternity but was probably only a second or two, she managed to choke out, "Uh, thank you. What a surprise."

"Aren't you going to open it?"

"Sure." He wasn't getting down on one knee, which had to mean something, right? "I, uh, was just trying to remember where I put your present."

"Never mind that; open your gift."

She eased the lid up with the same caution she would have used unwrapping a package from the Unibomber. A green sparkle made her relax for a moment, and she flipped the top all the way open. A beautiful pair of antique emerald earrings was nestled on a cushion of velvet.

Skye threw herself in Simon's arms, raining kisses on his face and neck. "They're wonderful. They match the emerald ring Grandma Leofanti gave me. How did you find them?"

"I remembered your cousin Gillian got the earrings when your grandmother died, and I asked her if I could borrow them to have them copied."

"That is so sweet. Thank you."

"You're very welcome." His hands moved gently down her back. "You said something about my Valentine's Day gift."

"Oh, right. I'll go get it." She made a move to slip out of his arms, but he tightened his grip and kissed her.

As his lips traced a fiery trail down her neck, he murmured huskily, "Don't bother. I think I can find it myself."

It was nearly ten-thirty by the time they finally made it to the kitchen for breakfast. Simon was drinking his first cup of coffee and admiring the digital camera Skye had given him for Valentine's Day when he asked, "Was that your mom on the phone earlier?"

"Yes, Uncle Emmett had his hair cut this morning and

noticed a bruise on Vince's forehead, which was all it took for the family to go on red alert."

"What happened to Vince?"

"I have no idea." Skye took a sip of her tea. "My orders are to find out and report back to headquarters."

Simon buttered a slice of toast and handed it to her. "It's pretty hard to keep a secret in this town."

She planted a kiss on his bare shoulder. "We seem to be doing a pretty good job of it."

"Maybe. But I bet a lot of people know exactly what we're up to and are just letting us think we're getting away with something."

"That's fine with me, as long as no one says anything to my face. I blush way too easily to discuss this." She slipped a hand beneath the towel he wore around his waist. "Or this either."

After she dropped Simon off at his house, Skye drove to her brother's salon. It looked completely different in the daytime, especially without four grungy musicians spread throughout the room and loud music reverberating off the walls.

Vince was just handing a customer her change when Skye entered, and she waited for the door to close behind the woman before speaking. "Hi. Mom called me this morning."

Vince touched the bruise on his forehead. "Uncle Emmett?"

"Yep. He spilled the beans to Aunt Minnie, who immediately called Mom."

"And she wants you to find out what happened?" Vince started to sweep the snips of hair littering the floor.

"Got it in one guess." Skye held the dustpan for him as he pushed the pile of hair into it. "I told her maybe you had hit your head on a door or slipped in the shower."

"Hey, I like that last explanation. I think that's the one I'll go with."

"Fine. How did you really get hurt?"

"It's not important." Vince went behind the counter and starting counting money from the cash drawer into a vinyl pouch.

"Why don't you want to tell me? You know I won't tell Mom if you don't want me to."

"You'll want to *do* something about it."

"If I promise not to care, will you tell me?" Skye frowned. The last time Vince kept something important from her, he was in major trouble.

"You'll want to sit everyone down for a counseling session."

"Fine. Be like that." Skye started toward the door. "But someone in this town knows and will eventually tell me."

Vince sighed. "Logan and Rod had a fight last night after our gig at the Dew Drop Inn. I stepped in to break it up and got sucker punched. It's no big deal."

"What were they fighting about?"

"Nothing important. Logan was drunk, and Rod should have just walked away. He knows you should never argue with an idiot. They drag you down to their level and beat you with experience."

"Then why the big secret?" Skye asked.

"It's not good for the band's rep for people to think we aren't pals."

Skye thought that over before saying, "That makes sense. People like to hold on to their illusions, and one of the bigger fantasies is that playing in a rock and roll band is all about buddies having a good time and hanging out together."

"Exactly." Vince smiled thinly. "And most of the time that's what it is, but then something comes up, and wham, there goes the fun."

"So what came up between Rod and Logan?"

Vince shrugged. "It's settled. Forget it."

Skye decided to back off for now. Instead she asked, "You guys are still playing tonight for the high school Valentine Ball, right?"

"Sure. Everything's cool."

"What time do you have to get there?"

"About five to set up."

"It takes you two hours to get organized?" Skye asked.

"Not exactly. We'll be mostly ready in an hour; then we'll do a sound check and make the adjustments. After that we take a dinner break before we start playing."

"I never realized how much time you guys put into it before you even officially start." Skye hadn't really paid much attention to Vince's band before. She kissed her brother on the cheek and said, "I've got to go. I have a ton of errands to run, and I have to be at the school early, too. I have to supervise the last minute details for the dance." She was halfway out the door when she said, "I sure hope Rod and Logan behave themselves tonight. Fighting in front of the kids would be a problem."

"If Logan pulls a stunt like last night's again, there won't be any need to fight because I'll kill him."

When Skye arrived at six that evening, the high school lot contained two cars. The one wedged between the Dumpsters she recognized as the night custodian's, but the bright red Town Car parked in the handicapped space was unfamiliar. Skye frowned. No one was supposed to be in the building yet. She nosed the Bel Air into a slot, grabbed her purse and tote bag, and walked over to the Lincoln.

It didn't have handicapped plates or a tag hanging from its mirror. Her irritation grew. This type of flouting of the rules was one of her pet peeves, and she felt the need to take some action. She wished she could give the idiot a ticket.

Suddenly an idea came to her and she pulled a pen and pad of paper from her tote bag. On it she wrote STUPIDITY IS NOT A HANDICAP. PARK ELSEWHERE! and tucked the note under the windshield wiper.

Turning, she strode up the front steps, unlocked the door, and went inside. The interior was dark and there was an odor of chalk and sweat as she walked between the beat-up yellow lockers edging the hall. Although she wore sneakers—she'd change into dress shoes once the dance started—she could still hear the echo of her footsteps on the threadbare lime-green carpeting.

A metal gate that folded out of the wall separated the gym from the rest of the school. Students attending the dance would enter through the gym door, and the rest of the building would be off limits. Skye inserted her key into the lock and slipped past the barrier, carefully refastening it behind her.

The gymnasium was dark when she entered, and she immediately began to flip on the lights. She could see that Pink Elephant had been and gone, since there were instruments and amps spread across the stage at the back of the gym. The night custodian must have let them into the building to set up.

Skye was hanging up her coat on one of the portable racks set against the front wall when she heard knocking. She crossed the polished wood floor and opened the outer door, fixing it so it would remain unlocked. The student dance committee poured through the entrance, talking and laughing.

Skye greeted them. "Hi, guys. It looks like we're the early birds." There were supposed to be four chaperones besides Skye. She wondered whom the superintendent had ordered to take Homer's place. "Why don't you hang out for a few minutes, and I'll see what we need to do?"

The kids nodded and drifted off into a corner, chatting.

While Skye was scanning her list, Trixie came in. The usual bounce was lacking from her footsteps, and she sighed as she hung her jacket next to Skye's.

Trixie said, "Owen decided not to come tonight. He's got all our financial papers spread out across the dining room table, and he's trying to find the money we need to pay his mom's bills."

Skye murmured how sorry she was for her troubles, then added, "Simon won't be here either. He has a wake scheduled for tonight. Who buries their loved ones on Valentine's Day?"

Trixie shrugged. "I see the other chaperones aren't here yet. I guess we better get the kids organized."

Skye took charge of the refreshments. Justin Boward was among the kids who had volunteered for that job, and she wondered what he was up to. A school dance was not something he would normally choose to participate in, but Justin often managed to surprise her.

He had changed a lot since the first time she saw him for counseling in eighth grade. He was now nearly six feet tall, and although still skinny, he showed signs of growing into a more solid build. He had recently gotten new wire-rimmed glasses, so his expressive brown eyes were no longer hidden behind the thick lenses of his old horn-rimmed pair.

Nathan Turner had also signed up to help with refreshments. Skye'd had a few run-ins with his obnoxious father that past November, but things seemed tolerable between them now. She really didn't know Nathan beyond the superficial facts that he was a handsome, athletic boy who seemed to have the world in the pocket of his school letterman's jacket. He, too, was not the usual committee volunteer.

Skye put the kids to work setting out cups and napkins and arranging cookies on the silver trays the PTO mothers had lent them. Next on her to-do list was the punch.

Technically, one of the other chaperones, Ace Cramer,

was assigned to the drinks. He was supposed to bring the bags of ice in his cooler, since there was no freezer readily available. But since he hadn't arrived yet, Skye figured they might as well get started. They had stored the other ingredients in the P.E. teachers' office.

Skye said, "Justin, Nathan, how about helping me carry some stuff?"

Both boys nodded and followed her to Ace's office. She tried to turn the knob but it was locked. Suddenly a large hand covered hers and she jumped.

Ace Cramer wore his usual genial smile, but his cobalt blue eyes were cold. "Whoa there, Ms. D.," he said. "What can I do for you?"

Skye managed to smile back, although her heart was still racing. "We were just coming for the punch ingredients. It was getting a little late, and I thought we should get started since there is so much of it to make."

"Sorry." He ran his hand over his white-blond buzz cut. "They were out of ice at the Brown Bag, and I had to go to the gas station by the highway to find enough sacks."

"No problem." Skye stepped aside. "But let's get going."

Ace fumbled for his key, then unlocked the door. "Sure."

Justin and Nathan began hauling out cans of fruit juice and bottles of ginger ale. Skye started to return to the gym to see how the other committees were doing but glanced back into the office. Ace was sitting at his desk watching the boys work. She shrugged; maybe not pitching in and helping was a coach thing.

Trixie had assigned the other kids to various tasks around the gym. A couple of girls were on duty at the photo backdrop. They would collect the money, keep a record of the names, and help position the couples getting their pictures taken. Others were putting fresh flower centerpieces donated by Stybr Florist on the tables.

Seated by the door, ready to sell tickets, was Bitsy

Kessler. She looked like her normal self tonight, and Skye wondered if she had been mistaken about the girl's altered state Friday afternoon.

Next to her was Frannie Ryan. She was the daughter of Xavier, Simon's assistant at the funeral home, and she and Skye had been through a lot together in the past year. Skye was exceptionally fond of both Frannie and Justin.

Regrettably, Frannie and Bitsy did not feel that way about each other. Frannie was extremely bright and had difficulty tolerating those who were less intellectually gifted. Bitsy, on the other hand, could flirt the net off a basketball hoop and had recently been targeting Justin as her next beau. This did not sit well with Frannie, who also had her eye on Justin as boyfriend material.

Trixie had probably put the girls together thinking they would sort out their differences if they worked side by side. Skye wasn't as optimistic, but it was too late to change things now.

Skye checked the clock. Five to seven. Just enough time to visit the bathroom to comb her hair, freshen her makeup, and change her shoes before the hordes arrived. She was applying a coat of red amber to her lips when she heard a dull thud, a loud boom, and then angry voices. She dropped the lipstick tube into her purse and hurried out into the gym.

Logan Wolfe and Finn O'Malley were standing at the bottom of the steps to the stage shoving each other and swearing. Sheet music and other gear were scattered at their feet.

As Skye stepped forward, intending to try and calm down the vocalist and the keyboard player, Rod Yager and Vince came around the corner and waded into the fray.

The band had arrived.

CHAPTER 5

What's Love Got to Do with It?

"What were they fighting about?" Skye asked Vince. He and Rod had managed to separate Logan and Finn, and the musicians were now busy making last-minute adjustments to their equipment on the stage.

Without looking up, Vince shrugged, then continued to tweak his drum set.

"Don't shrug at me, Vince Denison. Last night, Logan and Rod got into a scuffle and you ended up getting hurt. Now he and Finn are seconds away from coming to blows. What's going on with the band?" Skye put her hands on her hips. "And don't tell me it's nothing."

"It's fine." Vince didn't meet her eyes. "I'll take care of it."

The thought of trying to explain to the superintendent, who already didn't like Skye, why her brother's band had started a brawl at the Valentine's Day Dance made her tremble. "Vince, I recommended your group to the school. If there's a problem, I'm the one who will have to face the wrath of Superintendent Wraige."

"Don't worry. Everything's fine." Vince flicked a look at

the other musicians. "Ready to start?" They all nodded and he raised his drumstick.

Skye turned on her heels, exasperated by her brother's refusal to blab. Even though Vince was the older sibling, Skye had always been the one to help him out of his messes. His closed-mouth attitude about the band worried her. What had Vince gotten himself into?

She moved toward the tables scattered around the gym's perimeter. It was seven-fifteen, and the Valentine's Ball had officially begun. Teens thronged the entrance and poured inside. Many came in couples, dressed in long dresses and nice suits. Others arrived in groups, wearing less formal attire; and a few turned up by themselves, slinking in and not venturing much past the entrance.

Skye found Trixie at a table talking to one of the other chaperones. She joined the two women and said, "Anyone have an idea of what we could do to include the kids who are currently trying to pretend they're wallpaper?"

"Could we ask some of the other kids to invite them to join their groups?" Trixie suggested.

Will that make things worse or better? Skye wondered. It would depend on the group. They'd have to choose carefully. "Okay, let's try a couple. It isn't as if we have anything else to do for the next several hours, unless you two were planning on dancing."

The three paused a moment and listened to the music. It was shockingly loud, and the lyrics to the song were indecipherable, which was probably just as well. Both women shook their heads. They wouldn't be dancing to *that*. Shouting to be heard above the din, they agreed on a plan, and each set out to see if they could persuade a more popular teen to invite one of the outsiders into their group.

Skye had noticed a boy who had approached her recently about joining the newspaper staff, so she went to find Justin and see if he'd cooperate in Operation "No Teen Left Standing Alone."

The lights were down low, which made it difficult to locate people, but Skye finally spotted Justin and explained her request as best she could over the pounding bass. He nodded and headed toward the boy she pointed out.

As Skye was making her way back to the table, she saw her godfather, Charlie Patukas, standing with his arms crossed staring at the dance floor, a scowl on his face. At six feet tall and three hundred pounds, he was an imposing figure.

She tapped him on the shoulder. "Uncle Charlie, what are you doing here?"

Charlie swung around, his thick white brows meeting in the middle of his forehead. "That dang fool Homer called in sick, and the superintendent was out of town, so as president of the school board I was next in line."

Skye debated a second, then pulled Charlie aside and told him what had caused Homer's sudden illness. She hated to be a snitch, but in case Mr. Yoder tried to pull something in retaliation for his son's suspension, Charlie needed to be forewarned. The last time a Yoder offspring had been suspended, graduation had almost been ruined.

"If brains were dynamite, Homer wouldn't have enough to blow his nose," Charlie said, his scowl deepening. "Yoder better not try anything. I still owe him for hurting you when his other no-good kid got into trouble."

Skye tried to defend the principal and the younger Yoder boy, but Charlie interrupted her, shouting, "The music's too damn loud. I can hardly hear you. They need to turn it down."

He took a step toward the stage, but Skye grabbed his arm. "It is too loud, but the kids like it that way. Let's talk out here." She tugged him toward the door to the hall, searching for a topic to distract him. "Do you know anything about Logan Wolfe?"

Charlie scratched his head. "He lives on Hines out between the Leofanti property and the Fraynes' farm on the next road. His father died when he was young and left him the house and forty acres. Why?"

"I'll explain in a minute." Skye didn't want to tell Charlie about the band fighting, but her godfather knew almost as much as her mother did about everyone in town, and Skye wanted to know more about Logan. She'd have to come up with some excuse for her curiosity. "How does he make a living? Does he farm?"

"He puts in a crop, but on a good year he'd only make about ten thousand before expenses."

Skye thought of Logan's rock-star appearance and tried to imagine him dressed in overalls and a straw hat. "So, then, does he have another job?"

"Nothing steady." Charlie leaned against the wall. "He gives guitar lessons, and I've heard recently he's been doing some solo singing appearances."

"Mmm." Maybe that was what the band was fighting about. Did the group have some sort of agreement not to perform without the other members?

"Why all the interest in Logan? He's married, you know."

"Great, because I'm not looking to date him." Skye searched for a reason to explain her sudden interest. "It's just that Vince is spending a lot of time with this band, and I wanted to know a little about the kind of people they are."

Charlie didn't look convinced, but before he could question her further, the door swung out and Frannie Ryan burst through.

"Ms. D., Mrs. Frayne says for you to come right away. There's a problem." The girl whirled around without stopping to see if Skye was following her and disappeared back into the gym.

Immediately, Skye pushed through the doors, intent on not losing sight of Frannie. For a moment, the dimness of the gym compared to the bright hallway, coupled with the earsplitting music, made Skye feel disorientated, but she took a deep breath and kept moving.

Frannie was heading toward the back of the gym. Skye caught up to her just as she reached the entrance to the boy's locker room where Trixie was standing.

Skye said breathlessly, "What's up?"

Trixie put her lips near Skye's ear and said, "Nathan Turner is in there."

"How'd he get in? The door's supposed to be locked," demanded Charlie who'd caught up with them.

"I don't know." Trixie leaned closer to Skye and explained, "I was patrolling the edge of the dance floor and saw him go in, but when I tried to follow, the door wouldn't budge."

"Have you tried knocking?" Charlie's face was getting red. He didn't take frustration well.

"Of course." Trixie shot the older man a scathing look. "But we don't want to be too obvious, since we'd rather the other kids don't find out about this."

"Good thinking." Skye was almost afraid to ask her next question. She had never seen Trixie in such a bad mood. "Uh, you've probably already called for the night janitor to bring his key, right?"

Trixie nodded. "He doesn't answer his phone."

Skye thought quickly. "Ace is the gym teacher. He would have a key. Where is he?"

Trixie took off at a run. She returned a few seconds later gripping Ace by the arm. They explained the situation and he unlocked the door.

As it swung inward, they all lurched into the room. Skye regained her balance and looked around. There was no sign of Nathan Turner, but she could hear water running.

Ace said, "Let me look around first. Mr. Patukas, you take care of the ladies."

"I'll go." Charlie glared. "You stay with the girls."

Skye let the testosterone battle it out. It sounded to her like the kid was taking a shower, and she really had no desire to see the teen naked. Trixie obviously felt the same way, since she didn't protest the men's macho attitude either.

Both men stomped off, and a few moments later Ace and Charlie emerged from the back area gripping the arms of a sopping wet Nathan Turner between them.

Skye stared for a second, then asked the first question that popped into her mind. "Why did you take a shower with your clothes on?"

"I was hot."

The adults exchanged looks. Was this a prank, or was something wrong with the kid?

They all looked to Charlie for guidance. He sat Nathan on the wooden bench and said, "Wait here while I call your folks."

"Not home." The teen giggled as if Charlie had suddenly started performing stand-up comedy. Nathan made kissing sounds and said, "They went away for a romantic weekend."

Ew! Skye's mind flashed to an orgy she had accidentally witnessed that past November involving Nathan's father, mother, and several other prominent Scumble River citizens, but she pushed that picture firmly away, and said, "Who are you staying with?"

"You mean like a babysitter?" He let out another high-pitched giggle. "I'm seventeen, man."

"Does anyone know if he has an uncle or aunt or grandparent in town?" Skye asked the group.

Everyone shook their heads. She squatted down in front of the teen, trying to get him to focus. "Do you have any relatives around here?"

Nathan gave an exaggerated sigh. "My grandma lives in Laurel."

Laurel was the county seat and about forty-five minutes from Scumble River. The boy had begun to shiver. It was clear he couldn't sit around dripping wet for three quarters of an hour.

Ace Cramer stepped forward. "Mr. Patukas, why don't you help him change into his P.E. clothes, and I'll go call his grandmother from my office."

Charlie nodded and hauled the teen upright. "What's your grandmother's phone number?" After Nathan answered, Charlie demanded, "Which one's your locker?"

Skye, Trixie, and Ace left the locker room. Trixie and Ace hurried away, but Skye paused.

Frannie was lingering near the door and asked, "What happened?" as Skye stepped out.

"It's being taken care of." Skye was sorry she couldn't satisfy the girl's curiosity, but Nathan had a right to his privacy. "How's everything out here?"

"Fine. They're so lame. No one's noticed anything." Frannie brushed back a strand of long, wavy brown hair.

Skye fingered the sheer sleeve of Frannie's patchwork lace top and, hoping to change the subject, said, "I like this." Frannie had a more rounded shape than the current style allowed, and took a lot of teasing from the size twos and fours. Having a similar curvaceous figure herself, Skye had been making gentle wardrobe suggestions to the girl for several months.

"Thanks." Frannie preened. "Dad let me order some stuff from the Avenue, and today at school one of the Ultras said I looked nice."

Skye grinned. "That's awesome." She had given the teen several catalogs that featured fun and fashionable plus-size clothing and was glad to hear Frannie was getting some positive feedback from the more popular girls.

"Not that it matters what they think."

"Of course not." Skye looked around. "Where's Justin?"

"How should I know?" Frannie snapped. "Was it my day to keep tabs on him?" She rolled her eyes, then finally answered the question. "He's dancing with Bitsy. Didn't you know they were an item?"

"An item item or . . . ?" Skye didn't know how to end her question so changed tactics. "A single dance doesn't mean anything."

Frannie's brown eyes shimmered with unshed tears but she swallowed and said in a steady voice, "Who knows? It's not like I care."

Skye and Frannie had been talking in loud voices to be heard over the music. When it suddenly stopped, it caught them both by surprise. Skye looked at her watch. It was eight o'clock, time for the band's first break.

She watched the musicians leave the stage. A sexy twenty-something female dressed in a red micro mini and halter top intercepted Vince as he headed toward the refreshment table, but he shook his head and eased past her. Skye frowned. That girl was not a high school student. How had she gotten into the dance?

Next the girl approached the keyboard player, Finn O'Malley, who glared and plucked her hand from his chest. Rod Yager had already maneuvered around her, but she caught Logan as he came off the last step.

Skye was too far away to hear what was said, but after several minutes of heated conversation, the vocalist took the girl by the arm and pulled her up the stairs, across the stage, and behind the curtain. What was up with that?

"I need to check on how the refreshments are doing," Skye said to Frannie.

"Okay." Frannie waved. "See you later."

Skye walked over to where her brother was waiting in line for a glass of punch. From behind him, she put her arms around his waist and whispered in his ear, "Buy a girl a drink?"

He whirled around, scowling. "For crying out loud, Heather, I already told you to f . . ." His words trailed off as he recognized Skye.

"Who's Heather?"

"No one."

"So you're telling no one to f . . . ?"

Vince didn't answer; instead he grabbed two glasses of punch. When he handed Skye hers she said, "Is Heather the girl Logan left with?"

Vince's face turned red, he swore, shoved his cup at Skye, and dashed away.

Shoot! What had she said? Skye plunked the glasses down on a nearby table and hurried after him. She could only remember seeing Vince this angry one other time, and in that instance he had busted the other guy's nose. Vince rarely lost his temper, but when he did, all hell broke loose. She had to stop him from doing something he'd regret later.

Vince had disappeared via the same route Logan and the girl had taken. When Skye pushed through the stage curtains in pursuit of him, she paused. The passageway created by the curtains was narrow and dark and smelled of sweat. She knew they were using one of the rooms backstage as their dressing room, but which one?

The first room she came to was full of sets, costumes, and props. As she backed out, she heard hollering and headed in the direction the shouts were coming from. Shoving open the door, she burst in just in time to see Vince punch Logan in the face.

Out of the corner of her eye she saw the girl she assumed was Heather huddled on an old sofa clutching a ratty blanket to her bare breasts. A strange half-smile played around her lips.

The girl caught Skye's disapproving stare and said, "I

know what you're thinking, and I'm not cheap." She giggled. "But I am on special this week."

Skye didn't have time to respond. Logan had staggered backward from the force of Vince's punch, but he righted himself before falling and snatched a folding chair that he smashed over Vince's head. Vince crumpled to the floor, but Logan kept bashing at him, holding the legs of the chair and using the rigid metal back as a club.

Skye screamed and grabbed the vocalist around the chest, trying to pull him away from her brother. Her heart was thumping in her ears. Logan was too strong for her to stop him completely, but at least she had momentarily drawn his attention from Vince. She shouted to the girl, "Go get some help."

Heather looked at her impassively and didn't move.

Skye kept yelling—first at Logan to stop, then at the girl to get help, and finally at her brother to run away. Not one of them followed her directions, although Vince struggled to his feet and stood swaying. His eyes were unfocused and he appeared dazed.

Just as she was losing her hold on the singer, the other two band members charged through the door. Finn grabbed the chair from Logan, threw it out of reach, and then wrapped his arms around the enraged vocalist. As soon as Finn had Logan restrained, Skye backed away. Finn wrestled the smaller man out of the dressing room, hollering at him to calm down. Skye closed the door behind them, wishing it had a lock.

Rod had moved Vince to a chair and she ran to her brother's side and squatted next to him. "Are you all right? Do you need a doctor?"

Vince leaned forward, resting his elbows on his knees and his head in his hands. She could barely hear his muffled answer, "I'm fine."

Skye gently probed his scalp. He wasn't bleeding, but

lumps and bruises were already forming. "Let me call Doc Zello."

Vince grabbed her wrist. "No. Don't."

She looked at Rod, who stood behind Vince. The guitar player shrugged. "His choice, man."

"Fine." Skye crossed her arms and glared at her brother. "Then tell me what that was all about."

Vince started to shake his head but obviously thought better of the movement, answering instead, "Her." He jerked his thumb toward the girl, who had finally moved off the couch and begun to get dressed.

Rod looked at Vince and Skye, then walked over to Heather, took a firm grip on her arm, and escorted her from the room. The girl's protests could be heard even after they were in the hallway.

Once she and Vince were alone, Skye said with a note of skepticism in her voice, "You were fighting over a groupie?" Her brother never fought over women. He always said there were too many flowers in the garden to care that much about any particular blossom.

"It's a long story."

Why do people always say that? "Tell me anyway." Skye's lips tightened. "Or I'm going to go call Dr. Zello or better yet, Mom."

He flinched, clearly deciding on the lesser of several evils. "It's not what you think."

"I don't know what I think, except that you've lost your mind," Skye snapped. "Your taste in women has always been iffy, but this is ridiculous."

"I am *not* involved with her that way."

"So, you haven't slept with her?"

"I didn't say that." Vince sagged back in the chair and stared at the ceiling. "Okay, here's the whole story. You're right. Heather is a groupie. She's been following us since we first started playing. She made it clear she wanted to do the whole band, and none of us was saying no." Vince snuck a quick peek at Skye.

Skye's disgust was written clearly all over her face. "So you all took a turn with her."

Vince nodded. "But then she wanted more."

"What a surprise."

"Yeah. Well." He had the grace to look sheepish. "Anyway, it turns out what she really wanted was to sing with the band."

"And?"

"We didn't think that would be a good idea, considering everything."

Skye shook her head, astounded at his logic. "So, what were you and Logan fighting about?"

"We all agreed to stop . . . uh, you know . . . paying attention to her, and the rest of us have, but Logan keeps giving in and uh . . . you know . . . uh . . ."

"Boinking her?"

"Yeah." Vince scratched his chin. "She's sort of like a stray cat. If you keep feeding it, it will never go away."

"It's probably because Logan's married."

Vince looked confused at the non sequitur. "Huh?"

"Heather is probably threatening to tell Logan's wife if he doesn't keep on with the relationship."

"Maybe. But I think his wife knows he fools around." Vince shrugged. "Anyway that's not the band's problem. Our problem is getting rid of Heather."

"Is she any good?" Skye saw the flabbergasted look on Vince's face and hurried to clarify her question. "I mean as a singer. Does she have a good voice?"

"Yeah. As a matter of fact, at one time Rod, Finn, and I thought maybe we should let her sing with us, but Logan had a fit when we suggested it."

"Why?"

"Said he was the star of this band, and no girl singer was going to take his place."

"What a lovely man."

Vince slowly got up from the chair and tested his head by moving it from side to side. "He's a little self-centered, but you gotta be, in this business."

"I suppose." It was Skye's turn to shrug. "You'd think that if that were the case, he'd have more at stake in getting her to quit following the band and thus would stop having sex with her."

"That's what I was trying to explain to him when you walked in."

"Really? Does he speak sign language? Because all I saw was your fist moving, not your lips." Skye turned her back on her brother and walked away. She had spent enough time on the groupie problem; she had a Valentine's Dance to chaperone.

Once she reached the front of the stage, she took a moment to look around the gym before climbing down the steps. The kids were sitting and standing in groups talking, drinking punch, and eating cookies. No one seemed to have noticed anything wrong.

Skye joined Trixie at a table in the rear and explained what had just happened. She concluded with, "Can you believe how stupid four grown men can be? You would think in this day and age, with all the diseases and everything, they'd be more careful about sex."

Trixie smirked. "But that's just it. When they get excited, they can't think. There's only so much blood in the human body, and when it all surges below their waist, there isn't enough left to run their brains."

Skye laughed until she noticed the band mounting the stage. "Phew. I was afraid they weren't going to come back and play."

"What would we have done?"

"I guess we'd have had to lip sync to *South Pacific*," Skye deadpanned. "It's the only musical I know all the words to, and I have a tape in my office."

Trixie snorted.

Skye studied the musicians. Except for Logan's swollen lip and a bruise on Vince's cheek, no one would ever guess they'd been fighting. She sagged in her seat. At least the dance was half over. Surely nothing else could go wrong.

CHAPTER 6

Great Balls of Fire

Ten after nine. The band was playing some long instrumental piece with a lot of drum solos, and Skye's head was throbbing in time with the beat. She wondered if her eardrums had been punctured. Now she understood why the speech therapist refused to chaperone dances. She didn't want to risk damaging her hearing.

Nathan Turner's grandmother had picked him up fifteen minutes ago. The woman had seemed upset over his being sent home but never questioned why he was wearing gym shorts and a T-shirt in the middle of February. As Skye's mother would say, Grandma Turner was clearly a cucumber slice short of a salad.

After Nathan's departure, Charlie had dragged a chair out into the hallway, stating that he would chaperone the rest of the dance from there because he couldn't stand any more of the loud music.

Ace Cramer and a female chaperone were doing a sweep of the bathrooms, looking for kids who were smoking, sick, or using one of the stalls as a private bar.

Trixie had volunteered for make-out patrol—inspecting the gym's darker nooks and crannies. All they needed was one of the girls to have a baby nine months after the dance and claim the conception site was somewhere in the high school.

Skye checked her watch. Wasn't it time for the band to take a break? She looked longingly at the door. Could she step outside for a second, just until her head stopped vibrating? As she contemplated her escape, a commotion near the stage drew her attention.

What now? Skye was halfway across the dance floor when she heard a shriek. A quarter second later her brain had translated the shriek into a single word—FIRE! Simultaneously the fire alarm sounded.

There was a stunned moment, as if someone had hit the pause button on a VCR, then the crowd started to scream and run toward the front exit. Skye stood her ground, trying to direct the teens toward the side emergency exits—there were two along the left wall and one on the right. There was no need for the kids to go all the way to the front to get out.

Skye was able to grab Bitsy Kessler and a couple of other girls and thrust them out the side exits, but as she tried to herd others out that way, it became more and more difficult for her to remain upright against the surging mob. It took her less than a heartbeat to decide what to do. She had to get to the rear of the gym and make sure no one back in that area was injured and unable to escape.

Skye pushed and shoved her way forward. As she got closer, her eyes began to tear, and the acrid odor of smoke made her cough. It seemed to be billowing in huge clouds from the storage area under the stage.

The stage was set into the center of the back gym wall and was accessible by center stairs. The door to the storage area under the stage was a little to the left of those steps and that was where the smoke was coming from.

As Skye watched, a line of fire materialized from beneath the storage area door, raced to the side, and cut off the area to the right. She rushed forward only to be driven back by the heat. She didn't see anyone on the dance floor, but when the smoke cleared for a moment she spotted Vince and Finn up on the stage. Vince was gathering his drums and Finn had his keyboard under one arm and was holding a bass guitar in the other. Rod and Logan were nowhere to be seen.

Skye hurried over to the left of the stage and yelled, "Leave your instruments. You have to get out now."

Neither musician paid her any attention.

How could she get to them? Flames blocked the center steps. She looked around wildly and spotted a side door that opened into a concrete stairwell leading to the backstage area. Skye raced over, flew up the inner steps, and onto the stage. Grabbing Finn by one arm and Vince by the other, she tried to drag them toward the stairs, shouting, "The fire's spreading; you have to get out now!"

Vince shoved a drum at Skye, who took it automatically; he then took a drum in each arm and along with Finn followed her down the steps. Both men were coughing, and the smoke had thickened so much she could no longer see in front of her. She paused to get her bearings and try to remember where the fire exits were.

Picturing the gym layout in her mind, Skye led Vince and Finn to the right and using the wall, felt her way to the door. She used her body to push the emergency bar and the door swung open. The three of them stumbled outside.

The fire department was already on the scene. Flashing lights, sirens, and excited voices filled the frigid night air. A firefighter came up to them and demanded, "Did you see anyone else inside?"

"No." She set down the drum she had been clutching and pushed hair from her eyes. "The kids all ran toward the front as soon as someone started screaming 'fire.' " She was interrupted by a bout of coughing, then asked anxiously, "Didn't everyone get out?"

The man shrugged and stepped aside for the EMT.

Skye called after him, "Is anyone making a list of the kids who are safe? Parents will start coming here soon."

He shook his head. "Not that I know of."

While the EMT examined Finn, Skye asked Vince, "What happened to Logan and Rod?"

Vince had commandeered a couple of blankets and was wrapping his drums in them, but he spoke over his shoulder. "Logan wasn't on stage when the girl yelled 'fire.' Rod grabbed his guitar and took off down the right side steps as soon as the alarm went off."

Then they were probably safe. "Are you okay? Do you need anything?"

"I'm fine. How about you?"

"Fine." Skye hugged him. "But I have to go see about the kids and start making a list so we know who's accounted for." She looked at the havoc around her and shuddered. Kids were scattered everywhere, many wearing oxygen masks and lying on gurneys. What if everyone hadn't made it out of the building?

No, she couldn't let herself start thinking that way. The students would need her to be calm. "Can you get to a phone and call Mom, Dad, and Simon, and let them know we're okay?"

"Sure."

She needed to find Charlie and Trixie and Justin and Frannie and . . . her mind overloaded. So many. Skye heard herself moan and realized she was dangerously near a total breakdown. She bit the inside of her cheek until it bled. The coppery taste shocked her back into focus. She didn't have the luxury of giving in to her feelings. She had things to do, but what first?

She needed paper and a pen. Her small evening bag, its strap draped across her chest, contained only a comb, lipstick, keys, a few tissues, and her wallet.

Her car. She ran across the lot to the front entrance. On

her way she spotted the police chief, Wally Boyd, but didn't slow down. When she reached the Bel Air, she unlocked the door and grabbed a pad and pen from the glove compartment, then went around to the trunk and exchanged her dress shoes for the boots she kept there for emergencies. Now she was ready to start making a list of those present.

Skye started toward a group of teens sitting on the front steps, shivering in the cold. People hadn't been able to grab their coats before getting out. She scanned the area for another adult and spotted one of the chaperones, who appeared to be wandering around in a daze.

Skye yelled, "Over here."

The woman looked at Skye without seeming to see her. Skye sprinted over and took her arm. "The kids need your help." She tugged the teacher toward the front steps. "Take these kids and any others you can round up over to the junior high." Scumble River Junior High School was located just across the athletic field from the high school.

"How will I get in?" The woman's voice quavered.

Skye reached into her purse and pulled a key from the ring. "Here. This opens the front door. Take the kids into the office and have them start calling their parents."

As a backup, Skye took their names, parents' names, and phone numbers, too. A lot of parents had police scanners and would already be on their way to the school.

Skye found another bunch of students sitting on the hoods and trunks of the parked cars, Justin and Bitsy among them. "Have any of you seen Frannie Ryan?" Skye asked.

They all shook their head. Justin, a sheepish look on his face, offered, "I think I saw her on the other side of the building when we first got out, but then we got separated."

Skye noticed that the boy had dropped Bitsy's hand as soon as she asked about Frannie and was now swallowing hard and fighting back tears. "Thanks. I'll keep an eye out for her and send her over here if I see her."

Bitsy tried to retake Justin's hand, but he pulled out of her reach and said, "I'll come with you." Skye started to shake her head, but he coaxed, "It'll be faster with two of us."

"Okay." Skye nodded. "Show me where you saw Frannie last."

Justin gestured with his thumb. "This way."

As they walked away, she caught sight of Simon getting out of his Lexus. She waved and yelled, "I'm fine. Vince is fine. We're looking for Frannie. Talk to you later."

She and Justin continued to make their way to the edge of the parking lot and onto the snow-covered ground. They crossed to the opposite side of the gym, where the boys' and girls' locker rooms and indoor swimming pool were located.

Skye was extremely familiar with this area, since she used the pool nearly every morning to do laps. There were only two ways out on this side. One was an emergency exit and the other was through the swimming pool enclosure. The only way into the pool area was through the locker rooms.

Justin cleared his throat and pointed to the pool exit. "There. I'm pretty sure I saw Frannie right here when we came out the emergency door."

Skye scanned the vicinity. Except for a few bare trees, there was nothing but snow-covered ground. If she had fallen or was lying unconscious, they would see her.

Where could Frannie be? Surely if Justin had seen her outside the gym, she was okay. Skye turned to him. "She's not here, so she must be back where we came from."

As they stepped around the corner, Skye heard Charlie's booming baritone. He was standing next to his Cadillac, yelling orders that no one was listening to. Cars were screeching into the lot, and parents were shouting and crying for their kids.

She told Justin to go to the junior high, then hurried over

to Charlie and tugged on his sleeve. A grin of relief spread across his face. "Skye, you're okay." He swept her into a bear hug. "How about Vince?"

"He's fine. He went in search of a phone to call Mom and Dad." Skye hugged him back. "One of the chaperones took a bunch of kids over to the junior high to start calling their parents. I think that's where we should set up our base, since it's so cold out and most of the kids don't have coats."

"I'll tell the fire chief and then start spreading the word. You should go over there too. You're shivering."

"I still haven't found Frannie or Trixie. Have you seen them?"

"No." He frowned. "But I'm sure they're around here somewhere."

"I'll meet you over at the junior high as soon as I find them."

Charlie reached into his car and threw a neon orange hunting jacket at Skye. "If you're staying out here, put this on."

"Thanks." She shrugged into the huge padded coat and snuggled into its warmth, not caring that she looked like an oversized traffic cone. The odor of Charlie's cigars was reassuring. "See you at the junior high."

Skye decided to walk the perimeter of the school grounds. As she passed one of the athletic equipment sheds, she heard voices and looked inside. Trixie was huddled under a tarp with a group of teens. Skye hugged her friend as they both cried.

Trixie hiccupped. "I thought you were dead. The last anyone saw of you was when you headed toward the fire."

"I'm fine." Skye patted Trixie's back. "But I was so scared when I couldn't find you."

Trixie sniffed. "It was so cold out, and the firefighters wouldn't let us into the rest of the school in case the fire spread, so I wasn't sure what to do. Then I thought of this shed and herded as many kids as I could inside with me."

"I sent one of the chaperones over to the junior high with my key." Skye gave Trixie one last hug and let her go. "You'd better take these guys over there and have them start calling their folks."

"Aren't you coming?"

Skye lowered her voice. "I still haven't found Frannie. Have you seen her?"

"No. How about Justin?"

"He's safe. I've seen Vince, Charlie . . ." Skye continued to name everyone she had accounted for so far as she walked Trixie and her group toward the junior high. She stopped at the edge of the athletic field and waved them on, then turned back to search for Frannie.

An hour later, Skye looked around the parking lot and bit her lip, fighting tears. All the teens had been taken over to the junior high and the parents who showed up had been directed there too. The only people who remained in the high school parking lot were the firefighters, the police, and Skye.

She approached the police chief. She and Wally had an unusual history but were currently pretending they were just friends. Skye asked him, "Do we know anything yet?"

"It appears to be a relatively small fire, more smoke than flame, and it was contained in the gym. Best of all, people got out fast, so smoke inhalation shouldn't be too much of a problem. A few kids were taken to the hospital to be checked out, but the EMTs didn't seem too concerned."

"That's good news. Have they found any . . . ?" Skye trailed off, unable to force herself to put her thoughts into words.

"No." Wally put his arm around her. "But they haven't been able to get to the stage area yet, since that seems to be the center of the fire and burned the hottest. They don't have the equipment for that kind of search. They had to radio Laurel and ask to borrow theirs. It should be here soon."

Skye hid her face in his chest. "Frannie Ryan's missing."

"I know. Xavier is going nuts. He keeps trying to sneak into the building. Simon has him locked in his car to keep him from slipping past us and getting hurt." Wally sighed. "The firefighters have searched the gym and the surrounding area twice. They don't know where else to look. They hope she went home with someone. The only other possibility is—"

Skye cut his words off with a shake of her head. She refused to think that Frannie might be dead.

Wally said, "Go over to the junior high. Maybe they have some news over there."

Skye nodded but decided instead to take one more look around the building.

At some point in the chaos, she had acquired a flashlight, and as she rounded the corner, she thumbed it on. The snow, a hodgepodge of hundreds of footprints, held no answers. She aimed the beam at the door of the swimming pool enclosure since that was where Justin had last seen Frannie.

Almost the entire wall of the enclosure was made up of nearly opaque blue safety glass. As she swung the ray of light away from that wall, she caught sight of something. Could it have been a human shadow or was that just wishful thinking?

She ran toward the door and grabbed the knob, fearing it would be locked, but it turned easily under her hand. The firefighters must have opened it. She flung the door wide and stepped inside, sweeping the enclosure with the beam of her flashlight, but saw nothing other than the pool, a couple of safety rings, and a pole with a hook on the end. The area appeared exactly as it did every morning when Skye swam laps. It was difficult to believe a fire had occurred a few feet away.

She took a step backward; she must have mistaken the pole for a person. No, wait. What was that sound and where was it coming from? Skye moved toward the doors leading to the locker rooms. She heard another faint noise and this time could tell it was coming from the boys' side.

Skye pushed open the door. Surely the firefighters had checked this area, although it appeared untouched by the fire, so maybe not. The Scumble River Fire Department was staffed by volunteers and didn't have the manpower of the bigger crews.

"Help!" The word was muffled nearly beyond recognition.

Skye followed the sound toward the shower area. Had another teen decided on a spur-of-the-moment bath?

To the right of the showers were rows of lockers. One was rattling, and Skye wrenched open its door. Frannie burst out of the locker screaming.

CHAPTER 7

Dark Side of the Moon

Frannie's hands were tied behind her back with a jockstrap, and her face was covered with a pair of gym shorts, one of the legs having been forced over her head. Skye snatched away the shorts, and the scream died on Frannie's lips as her eyes locked onto Skye's. Whimpering, Frannie's lashes fluttered and she slumped in Skye's arms.

She staggered backward, smacking into a wooden bench bolted to the floor. The edge caught her in the back of the knees, making her stumble. She tried to regain her balance, but Frannie's weight was too much, and Skye fell, hitting her head on the seat.

The world went black for a second, then she became aware that she was flat on her back, and there was a heavy mass on her chest, hindering her breathing. Skye focused. Frannie was out cold and lying on top of her.

She gently rolled the girl off her and freed Frannie's hands from the jockstrap. Struggling to her feet, Skye wondered, *How will I get Frannie out of here?* She needed a wheelchair or . . . Skye looked around. The coaches' office was connected to the locker rooms. Thankfully, the normally locked door was ajar. She ran inside and snatched one of the desk chairs, pushing it beside the unconscious teen. Frannie moaned but didn't open her eyes as Skye heaved her onto the seat.

Skye gripped the back of the chair and started to push. Which way should she go? If she tried to go out the pool door, she wasn't sure she'd be able to maneuver the chair over the snow-covered grass. It would have to be the gym. She hoped it was safe.

As she wrenched the chair to the left, Frannie moaned again and Skye increased her speed. Her flashlight had broken when she fell against the bench, and the room was dark except for the dim emergency lights.

Once she entered the gymnasium, she yelled, "Help. I have an injured girl here."

Her words echoed off the walls and no one answered. As far as she could see, the room was deserted. Pools of water lay everywhere, and the stage was nothing more than a chunk of glowing wood. The air was still smoky, and Skye coughed repeatedly as she pushed the chair through the debris.

Where was everyone? She was nearly to the front door when she heard a soft thud coming from the back of the room. She kept going. Frannie was her main concern. One of the firefighters could investigate the noise.

Skye barreled through the exit, cold wind and stinging wetness slamming her in the face—it had started sleeting. She looked around for help. The firefighters were standing around their truck, loading hoses and other equipment onto the vehicle. Wally and one of his officers were stringing yellow police tape around the burned portion of the school. No one noticed Skye or the injured girl.

Suddenly Frannie roused and started to sob. She jumped out of the chair and tried to run, but Skye grabbed her and wrapped her arms around the girl. Her attempt to comfort Frannie was futile. The girl just cried harder and struggled to break free.

"Help!" Skye yelled as she tried to move Frannie toward the fire truck. "Over here." She was out of breath. "Someone, I need help."

Finally, the fire chief noticed her and came rushing over. "What the f . . ."

Skye cut him off. "We need some help. There may still be someone inside. I heard a noise in the backstage area. And I have an injured girl here."

The chief spoke into his radio. "We have an injury at the high school parking lot. Send the bus."

"Ten-four." The radio crackled.

Next he alerted the firefighters about the possibility of someone still being in the building. The equipment they needed had just arrived from Laurel, and two of the men suited up and went inside.

Finally, the chief turned to Skye and tried to help her with Frannie, who was still crying and trying to break away from Skye's hold. "Let me take her."

Frannie stiffened when he touched her. She stopped struggling against Skye and now clung to her.

Skye smoothed damp hair from the girl's face. "It's all right, honey. The chief just wants to help you."

Frannie whimpered and clung tighter. The chief seemed unsure what to do next, and Skye was out of bright ideas herself. The wail of the ambulance prodded them back into motion. He waved the paramedics over to them, and the EMTs peeled Frannie off Skye, loaded her onto a stretcher, and adjusted an oxygen mask over her nose and mouth.

The chief asked, "Where did you find her?"

As Skye and the chief followed the group to the waiting ambulance, she explained.

He scowled. "My men checked that area. No one was there."

Skye shrugged. She didn't know if the firefighters had failed to open every locker or if Frannie had been put inside after they had searched the area. Right now she didn't care. Instead she said, "Her dad is Xavier Ryan. We need to get hold of him."

"He and the coroner were here a few minutes ago. I'll call Reid's cell phone. They won't have gone far."

The chief made the call, and seconds later, Simon's white Lexus screeched into the lot and fishtailed to a stop. Xavier and Simon burst from the car and raced toward the open back door of the ambulance.

Skye joined them in time to hear one of the paramedics say, "She has a nasty lump on the back of her head and appears to be disorientated. She needs to go to the hospital. Laurel, St. Joe's, or Kankakee?"

Xavier hesitated and Simon said, "Laurel's the closest. We can always transfer her to Chicago if need be."

Xavier nodded. "Laurel. I'll ride with her."

As Frannie's father climbed into the ambulance, Simon clapped him on the back. "I'll be right behind you."

"I'm going with you." Skye started toward Simon's car.

The fire chief grabbed her arm. "You can't leave. You have some questions to answer first."

Simon paused. "Do you want me to wait?"

Before she could answer, a firefighter ran up to the chief and announced, "We found a body."

The chief turned to Simon. "Looks like you're stuck here too."

Simon scowled. "I'll go get the hearse." He turned to Skye. "Are you okay?"

When she nodded, he kissed her on the cheek and hurried off.

Skye sat in a classroom at the junior high, huddled under a blanket sipping oversugared coffee, watching the fire chief and Wally argue. Her eyes kept drifting closed, only to jerk awake as her head sagged forward onto her chest. It was three o'clock in the morning, her head hurt from her fall, and they wouldn't let her go home. Even worse, no one would tell her the identity of the body or how he or she had been killed.

First she had told her story of finding Frannie to the fire chief, then to Wally, then to the fire chief again. Neither man seemed satisfied with her explanation of why she went back into the burned building, but at least Wally wasn't looking at her like he thought she might be an arsonist. Of course, Skye and Wally had a past; she and the fire chief didn't.

Skye and Wally's complicated history included a teenage crush on Skye's part and an ex-wife on Wally's. But for the past six months, since Skye and Simon had hooked up, she and Wally had maintained a façade of friendship.

Wally must have won the dispute, because the fire chief stomped away and Wally rejoined Skye. Before he could open his mouth she asked, "Any news on Frannie?"

"No. I sent someone to talk to her, but the doctor isn't letting anyone except her father see her." Wally pulled up a student desk and sat on the table part. "What made you think Frannie was still inside the high school? You knew the firefighters had checked out the building."

"Desperation." Skye shrugged. "Matter of elimination."

"Huh?"

"Frannie was not at the junior high with the other kids who made it out safely. She hadn't gone home; her dad had checked. She hadn't been one of the few hurt and taken to hospital by ambulance. Where could she be?" A stubborn look settled on Skye's features. "And I knew she wasn't dead."

"So why didn't you ask one of the firefighters to look again?"

"I did." Skye got up and stretched. "They wouldn't listen to me. I'm sure they all thought they'd eventually find her body."

"What made you go into the boy's locker room?"

"I thought I saw something through the windows of the pool enclosure so I went inside. Then I heard a muffled voice and followed it. The locker was rattling, so I opened it and there was Frannie." Skye crossed her arms. "What I want to know is *who* put her into the locker and *why*."

"Good questions." Wally rotated his neck; furrows of exhaustion were etched in his handsome face. "Any guesses?"

"I think she must have seen something she shouldn't have and got knocked on the head and put in the locker to keep her quiet."

"I was thinking along those lines, too," Wally agreed.

"Is the police officer that's at the hospital aware she may be in danger?"

Wally nodded. "He knows she's a potential witness." Wally flipped open his notebook. "And speaking of that, when you were pushing her in that chair across the gym, you said you heard a noise backstage, but that wasn't where the body was found. Any idea why that might be?"

"How in the heck should I know?" She was tired and cranky and had had enough. "You won't tell me who the dead person is or where he or she was found. What do you want me to do, read my crystal ball?"

"We have to notify next of kin," Wally said evasively, ignoring her bad temper. "What type of noise did you hear?"

"A noise. Maybe a thump." Skye scrunched up her face and tried to recreate the incident in her mind. "I just don't know."

"Did you see anything?"

"No." Skye hesitated. "But if Frannie was in the locker, who or what did I see earlier by the pool?"

"My question exactly."

"I'm too tired to think." Skye glanced down. "My dress is in shreds, I'm wearing a filthy hunting jacket, and I reek of smoke. Maybe if I had a shower and some sleep I'd be more helpful—or at least coherent."

"You're right." Wally sighed. "Come talk to me tomorrow morning."

"It is tomorrow morning." Skye took her keys from her purse and moved toward the door. "And I have a feeling we're in for a bad time. People are going to freak out at the idea of someone trying to burn down a school with a couple hundred kids inside."

"How do you know it wasn't an accidental fire?" Wally's face was expressionless.

"I heard the firefighters talking about finding cans of starter fluid."

"That doesn't necessarily mean the fire was deliberately set."

"Right. And there really is an Easter Bunny that lays colored eggs." Skye added over her shoulder as she left, "If that's the story you're going to tell people, tomorrow should be an extremely interesting day."

CHAPTER 8

Whole Lot of Shakin' Goin' On

When Skye arrived home, light spilled out from every window of her cottage, and vehicles crammed the driveway. Just what she needed—her family and friends waiting to pounce on her with their concern.

Their cars gave them away. The white Olds belonged to her parents, Uncle Charlie drove the Cadillac, and her brother owned the Jeep. Trixie's Mustang rounded out the group.

Skye blew out an exasperated breath and trudged up the sidewalk. What would happen if instead of going inside, she turned around and headed to Simon's? The thought of her family's reaction if she went missing kept her moving forward.

As she stepped through the front door, the sound of snoring greeted her. She crept forward and peeked into the great room. They were all asleep. Uncle Charlie had claimed the recliner, her father the sofa, and May was in the captain's chair with her feet up on the coffee table. Vince and Trixie were sprawled on the floor, Bingo curled up at Trixie's side. He opened one eye, looked at Skye, and meowed.

Bingo's greeting jerked May awake. She spotted Skye and shot out of the chair, sweeping her into a hug, crying and talking at the same time. "Are you all right? Why did they keep you so long? What's happening? Who died?"

Skye stood still and let her mother fuss. When May worked herself up to this state, she was like a Jehovah's Witness with a caffeine problem, and there was nothing you could do but let the buzz wear off.

The others gathered around them in various stages of wakefulness.

Jed awkwardly patted her shoulder. "You okay?"

"I'm fine, Dad." Skye hugged her mom, kissed her father's cheek, and then shrugged out of Charlie's hunting jacket. "Wally and the fire chief had a lot of questions. I don't think they know what happened yet. They aren't giving out the name of the victim until they notify next of kin."

There was a split second of silence while everyone absorbed the information, and then they all started talking at once. Skye sank down on the couch clutching the jacket. Her head was spinning and she couldn't focus on what anyone was saying.

Trixie put her fingers in her mouth and let out a piercing whistle. Everyone fell abruptly silent. Trixie moved in front of Skye and put a hand on her shoulder. "She needs a shower and some rest."

May and Charlie frowned, but Vince nodded and started to hand out coats. When he got to his mother, May said, "I'm staying the night. I'm not leaving her alone." Vince leaned down and whispered in her ear. She turned red, then put on her jacket. "Uh, call me the minute you wake up."

Vince was the last to leave. Just before he stepped outside Skye asked, "What did you say to Mom?"

"I reminded her that Simon would probably stop by when he was finished with the body, and if she ever wanted grandchildren it might be a good idea if you were alone when he got here."

Skye swatted Vince on the bicep. "Thanks a lot. She'll have Father Burns ready to marry us tomorrow."

"Hey, it took her mind off the fire and got her out of your hair for the night."

Skye shook her head. Vince had never been very good with the concept of future consequences, but he was excellent at living in the here and now. Grateful to be alone, she staggered to the bathroom and turned on the shower.

The hot water felt wonderful, but the stinging spray found every bruise, cut, and scrape she had sustained. And when she went to wash her hair, she discovered a lump the size of a walnut behind her ear.

Just before crawling into bed, she called the hospital. Claiming to be Frannie's aunt, she was able to get a report of her status: possible mild concussion but otherwise fine.

Although exhausted, Skye slept in fits and starts, waking every hour from bad dreams and nagging thoughts. How was Frannie? Who had died? How badly damaged was the school? What did she need to do about all of the above?

As the red digital six was replaced by the seven, she threw back the covers and got up. Bingo had been sleeping next to her and did not appreciate being disturbed. He meowed sharply and swished his tail before burrowing beneath the blanket.

Skye dragged herself into the kitchen, filled the teakettle, and put it on the stove. It was early to start making calls on a Sunday morning, but Simon rarely slept past six, no matter how late he was up the night before. She punched in his number and listened to the rings.

He picked up on the third one. "Simon Reid. May I help you?"

"It's Skye."

"Are you okay?" The concern in his voice was soothing.

"I'm fine. A little stiff and sore, but considering what could have happened, I'm okay. How about you?"

"I just got home a few minutes ago. It took a long time to process the body from the fire. But I wanted to send it to the ME as soon as possible."

"Do you know who the victim is yet?"

"No." Simon yawned. "Wally's examining the effects and will send them on to the county lab as soon as he finishes, but everything's pretty charred.

"Any news on Frannie?"

"I spoke to Xavier an hour ago. He stayed at the hospital overnight. He said she seems better. The doctor thinks most of her odd behavior was caused by shock rather than a physical injury."

"That's a relief." Skye opened two packages of Sweet'N Low and emptied the white powder into her mug. "Are they releasing her today?"

"Xavier said they have to wait for the doctor to make his rounds, but the nurses seem to think she'll be able to go home."

"Should we go over?" She placed an Earl Grey teabag in the cup and poured boiling water over it.

"No. It sounds like she and Xavier will be home before we could get to the hospital."

"Has she said anything about how she got in the locker?"

"Xavier said Quirk talked to her this morning, but she doesn't remember anything." Roy Quirk was Wally's right-hand man at the Scumble River P.D.

Skye sipped her tea, then said, "That's probably a piece of information that should hit the gossip mills sooner rather than later. We don't want whoever did that to her to think she can identify him."

"Or her." Simon paused. "Do you want to go to eight o'clock Mass? We could get Frannie's memory loss started along the grapevine there."

"You should go to bed."

"Is that a proposition?" His voice deepened.

Skye felt a ripple of response. "How about later tonight, once we've both had a little more rest?"

"If that's your best offer, when should I come over?"

"I have to go give my statement at the police station this morning, then I'm supposed to go to a brunch with my parents at two, so say six."

"What brunch?"

Skye explained the mysterious invitation from Moss Gibson and concluded with, "I'd love to skip it, but I'm almost certain Mom will still want to go, and I don't want her and Dad there alone. My instincts tell me this is some sort of con to swindle a lot of 'country folk' out of their money."

"Sounds like you better go then. See you at six."

Skye's next call was to her mother. Yes, they were still planning to go to the brunch; did Skye want to ride with them?

She declined and called Vince.

He answered after the sixth ring, his voice thick from sleep. "What?"

"Sorry for waking you. Did you get an invitation to brunch today from a guy named Moss Gibson?"

"Yeah. I threw it out. Why?"

Skye poured more water for a second cup of tea and settled back in her chair. "Mom and Dad got one too and they're going, so I figured one or both of us should be there, too."

"Do you know this Moss guy?"

"No. He's probably selling something like time-shares or some other scam and . . ."

"And Mom and Dad might be naïve enough to sign up?"

"Right." Skye put a piece of bread in the toaster.

"Okay, I'll go. You want to pick me up?"

"Sure. It's at two at the new country club between here and Laurel, so I'll be over for you about one-thirty."

"See you then."

After breakfast, Skye showered and put on a simple navy coatdress with matching hose and pumps. Simon was right. Church probably was a good idea, not only for her soul, but also to hear what the town's people were saying about the fire last night.

As always, Mass was both soothing and uplifting. Father Burns achieved a perfect balance between concern for the fire and confidence that everything would be fine. He ended the service with his usual gentle humor by saying, "Drive carefully. Remember, it's not only cars that can be recalled by their maker."

As the recessional played, Skye made her way down the aisle and joined a knot of people at the back who were exchanging opinions about the fire.

A man dressed in polyester Levis and a plaid shirt with mother-of-pearl snaps said, "Doug Jr. says it was black as the inside of a cow once the electricity blew out. Said the generators didn't work worth jack shit."

One of the women sighed. "But who would want to burn down a school with kids inside? You heard Frannie Ryan got put in a locker and near abouts burned to death?"

Skye saw her opportunity and interjected, "Too bad she didn't see who hit her and put her in that locker. But she never saw a thing."

The woman standing next to her patted her hair, which was teased and sprayed into the shape of a helmet, and added, "My Suzy said there's a gang at school that's running wild. One of them pulled the fire alarm Friday. I'll bet they were trying to get the kids used to hearing it, so they would think it was a false alarm and not get out in time."

"I think it's terrorists," the man in the plaid shirt replied. "Wally should call in the FBI."

"That's why they won't tell us the name of who was killed," stated another man with slicked-backed hair and a malicious look in his porcine eyes. "I heard it's one of them A-rabs."

Voices rose as everyone in the group offered an opinion. Skye slunk away. It was time to go see Wally. He would definitely want to know that terrorists were at work in Scumble River.

"So, the general consensus is that it's either a group of wild kids or Arab terrorists," Skye finished telling Wally, leaning back in her chair.

Wally flipped open one of the files on his desk. "We've also gotten tips that it's the Russian Mob and aliens."

"So, do the Czar and ET have alibis?"

"Very funny." Wally scowled, exhibiting no hint of his usual sense of humor. "Crap like this takes up valuable time. It's not like I have a lot of manpower."

Skye was concerned about how defeated Wally sounded. He sure wasn't his usual positive self. She thought a minute, trying to come up with a lead to cheer him up. "You know, Leroy Yoder is the person you should really check out."

"Why?"

"His son Arlen pulled the fire alarm at the high school Friday afternoon, which is a coincidence in itself, but you may remember that Mr. Yoder doesn't take it very well when his kids are punished by the school, and Homer suspended Arlen."

"And you think Yoder might have set the fire in retaliation?" Wally asked.

"It's certainly a possibility. He was really ticked that Arlen wasn't allowed to attend the dance because he was suspended."

"I'll look into it, but unless he also had a grudge against

the person who died in the fire, Yoder wouldn't be our prime suspect."

"Are you sure he doesn't?" Skye questioned. "He seems like the type who might hate a lot of people."

"Swear to keep this to yourself?"

Skye nodded and held up her fingers in the Girl Scout oath sign.

"Here's the problem." Wally got up and started to pace. "We don't *know* who died in the fire. There was no ID. No one has called to say their loved one is missing. And the face was burned beyond recognition so we can't exactly pass out pictures. All we've got is a couple of tattoos that we can hardly make out."

Skye felt bile rise in the back of her throat. Back when she was in the Peace Corps there had been a bad fire at a church where she was working. Medical personal were extremely limited, and she had been put to work tending to the victims. Burned flesh was a smell she would never forget. She usually had a strong stomach, but the mere idea of burned flesh made her gag.

Wally stopped in front of her. "You okay?"

She nodded, not trusting herself to speak.

"Anyway, we'll put out a description—height, weight, tattoos—and hope someone comes forward. But until we do, it's pretty hard to investigate the death of a John Doe."

Skye made herself detach and think clinically. This was a puzzle, just like finding out what motivated a student to misbehave. "Where were the tattoos located?"

"Upper arms and right calf. It looks like the guy was caught headfirst under some burning debris so his upper torso and head got the worst of it." Wally shook his head. "We can barely see the tattoos on the arms, but the ones on the right leg are visible."

"What are they?"

"Musical notes that form a circle around the calf."

Tattoos. Where had she recently seen someone with a lot of tattoos? Skye concentrated but couldn't bring the memory up. Instead, she said, "I guess Frannie being stuffed in that locker pretty much makes it clear the guy was murdered? If he'd had an accident, there wouldn't be any reason for someone to attack Frannie."

"True."

Abruptly she flashed to the band rehearsal Thursday night and asked, "Could you tell if the victim had any piercings?"

"Not that we noticed, but the body was in pretty poor shape. Why?"

Skye kept her face expressionless and prayed that she wouldn't throw up. She swallowed and said, "Well, Logan Wolfe, the band's vocalist, had tattoos on his upper arms, but I didn't see his legs. He also had a pierced eyebrow and a huge hole in his ear." Skye read the skepticism in Wally's eyes and persisted, "A tattoo of musical notes would make sense for him, since he's a singer."

"I'll check it out," Wally conceded, "but I doubt it'll be that easy." He sighed. "Nothing ever is anymore."

"You know, there's one odd thing, if it does turn out to be Logan."

"Only one?"

"One that seems important," Skye answered seriously. "If it is Logan, I know that he's married and lives just outside of town. Which means his wife must have heard about the fire at the school, and she has to know he was playing there last night. So why hasn't she reported him missing?"

CHAPTER 9

Beast of Burden

Skye glanced over at her brother sprawled in the Bel Air's passenger seat. His long legs were stretched out and crossed at the ankles, his right arm rested on the windowsill, and he was whistling along with the oldies station on the radio. He was the picture of ease.

Vince never seemed to worry about the past or the future, choosing to live in the here and now. Skye wondered if he would find that attitude a little hard to maintain if the body from the fire turned out to be Logan Wolfe.

If that were the case, there was no way that his recent fights and arguments with Logan would stay quiet. Someone would talk. And once the police knew about their disagreements, Vince would instantly become a suspect.

Skye chewed on her lip. Should she warn Vince that Logan might be the victim? No. It would be better if Vince didn't know. Wally might make the wrong assumption if Vince didn't act surprised enough when the body's identity was finally revealed. Which meant she really shouldn't ask him about the musical note tattoo either.

"Vince?" Skye asked.

"Mmm?" He adjusted his sunglasses and turned toward her.

"Have you talked to the other band members since the fire?"

"Rod called to ask if I knew when we could get in and salvage the equipment that got left behind."

"How much gear did the band lose?" Skye asked.

"Maybe an amp or two and some music." Vince leaned against the headrest. "I lost a couple of drums, but I think most of the other guys got their stuff out."

"Is it insured?"

"Yeah. And what we don't have covered, the school's policy will probably take care of. I'll call about the insurance tomorrow and see what we need to do."

The wind had picked up and snow was blowing across the blacktop, making the surface slick. Skye struggled to keep the big car between the lines. "Will you be able to play for Wally's 'Meet and Greet' Tuesday?"

"Sure, we all have old instruments and equipment we can drag out and use in place of anything that's missing." Vince flipped down the sunshade and peered into the mirror, smoothing a strand of hair back into place. "This will be the band's first political campaign rally. We don't want to mess that up. If we do a good job, other candidates might hire us."

"I take it you'll be playing your regular rock and roll rather than the acid rock you played last night?"Skye turned the Bel Air into the Country Club's long drive. Unblemished snow covered the course. Clearly, not even the hardiest golfer had been out to play in a while.

"We cater to the crowd, so, yes, we'll be back to the soft stuff."

As she maneuvered the huge aqua vehicle into a parking spot, she asked, "The band means a lot to you, doesn't it?"

"Sure. We could get a big break and become the next teen craze."

Her brow puckered. Vince always had such pie-in-the-sky dreams. She just hoped he wasn't headed for a big disappointment.

He bounded out of the car. "Quit worrying, Sis. Everything will turn out fine. It always does."

Together they walked through the packed lot and into the clubhouse. The building was cream-colored brick and sported huge floor-to-ceiling windows. Inside, the golf shop and offices ran the length of the right wing. The opposite side consisted of several small rooms whose dividers could be opened to form one large room.

The delicious scents of frying bacon and maple syrup wafted over Skye as she and Vince paused in the doorway of the banquet area. A salad bar, omelet station, and sweet table had been set up against one wall. Another span of starched white linen held covered pans being kept hot on small burners. Whoever Moss Gibson was, he had spared no expense for this gathering.

Long tables had been set up in a U shape, facing a small dais at the front of the room. Most people had already arrived, and many were grouped around the portable bar at the back.

Skye scanned the crowd looking for her parents. She knew they were here somewhere. She had spotted their car in the parking lot.

A cute young guy smiled at her as she and Vince stood in line for a drink. "Hi, I don't believe we've met. I'm Jess Larson."

"Nice to meet you. I'm Skye Denison, and this is my brother Vince. Do you live in town?" Skye shot Vince an enquiring look, and her brother shrugged.

"Moved in around Thanksgiving." Jess tugged at the collar of his dress shirt as if he weren't used to wearing anything that formal. "I bought the Brown Bag Liquor Store when my cousin Fayanne Emerick retired."

"Right. I did hear she sold it to a relative." Skye tilted her head in thought. Jess must be related to Fayanne through her mother, because Skye knew for a fact that Fayanne was the last of the Emericks. Her lineage had factored into a murder awhile back. "Did you buy Fayanne's other properties too?"

A strange look crossed Jess's face but was immediately replaced with a bland expression. He turned to Skye's brother without answering her question. "So you're Vince Denison. I've been wanting to talk to you. I'm adding a bar and banquet hall to the liquor store, and they should be done by the end of the month. Logan said you keep the band's calendar. Did he tell you that I'm interested in having you play when it opens?"

"No, he didn't mention it." Vince frowned. "He must've forgotten. Give me a call at the shop and we'll firm up a date." Vince fished in his pocket and handed Jess a business card.

The men shook hands and Jess walked away.

"It looks like there are place cards." Skye pointed to the tables. "Let's go see where we're sitting."

Before they could move, a voice stopped them. "Ms. Denison, nice to see you. I wanted to thank you. I understand if it weren't for you, a lot of the kids might have been trapped in the fire."

It was Quentin Kessler, Bitsy's father and owner of Kessler Dry Goods Store.

"Mr. Kessler, I'm afraid someone is exaggerating." A few months ago, Skye had accidentally witnessed a sex orgy Kessler and several other of Scumble River's most respectable citizens had been participating in, and now she had trouble picturing him any other way. She took a firm grip on her imagination and said, "I didn't do anything more than the other adults did. Is Bitsy okay?"

"She's a little shaken but physically unharmed."

"I'm so glad." Skye was never sure how parents would

take things. She was always ready for them to turn on her. "Do you know my brother, Vince?"

"Sure. He cuts my hair. Good to see you, Denison."

Vince nodded and Quentin Kessler went on, "So, how did the fire start? I've heard it was carelessness on the custodian's part, that he left oily rags lying around."

"Really?"

"Yes." He took a sip of his martini. "And if that's the truth, the school better be prepared for a huge lawsuit."

Ah, the other shoe had dropped. "I really haven't heard anything about the fire's origins," Skye said.

Mr. Kessler leaned closer. "How about the dead body?"

"Well." Skye played for time. She hated lying outright. "Of course, I've heard a lot but nothing official yet. I know all the kids have been accounted for." School personnel had called and checked on every registered student.

"Well, that's something, at least." Mr. Kessler looked around. "Guess I better find the wife."

"Yes. We need to get over to our folks, too." As Skye and Vince moved away, she asked him in a low voice, "What's your take on Kessler?"

"He's a weasel." Vince pointed. "There's Mom and Dad."

May and Jed were just taking their seats at the table. On one side of them were May's sister, Minnie; Minnie's husband, Emmett; and their twin daughters, Ginger and Gillian. Skye wasn't surprised to see that the twins' husbands weren't with them. They were nearly always working, hunting, or fishing and rarely attended social events.

Vince and Skye said hi to all their relatives and sat down.

Skye's assigned seat was next to her father. She leaned close to him and said, "It looks like a Leofanti family reunion around here."

"Yep," Jed confirmed.

May overheard her and nodded. "It sure does. My brother and his family are here, too."

Suddenly the loudspeaker squealed to life and they all looked to the front of the room. A short, rotund, older man dressed in a red suit stood behind the podium gripping the microphone with one hand and running his fingers through thick white hair with the other. He had a full beard and a sizeable belly. What was Santa Claus doing in Scumble River?

He smiled and said, "Welcome. My name is Moss Gibson, and I have a dream."

The crowd quieted. Skye narrowed her eyes. This guy didn't look like Martin Luther King, and she'd bet his dream had nothing to do with peace and brotherhood.

Moss Gibson waited a beat before continuing. "I invited you all here today because you have the power to not only make my dream come true but also to share in the reward."

Skye tensed. This was definitely some pyramid scheme. She leaned behind her parents and said to Vince in a low voice, "We need to get the family out of here ASAP."

He grinned. "Let them enjoy the show. We won't let them sign anything."

Skye wasn't as confident of their abilities to talk any one of their relatives out of something once they were mesmerized by a con man.

People were buzzing after Moss Gibson's opening statements. He allowed the excitement to build, then said, "But before I tell you all about my dream, please help yourself to brunch."

Before Gibson's last word stopped echoing, chairs were pushed back and a line began to form at the food tables.

Gibson spoke above the hubbub. "And since I want all of my new friends to have a good time, the bar will stay open."

A general cheer went up.

Owing to the clever way the buffet lines had been set up, waiting was minimal and everyone was quickly back at their tables and eating.

Emmett took a slug of his beer and said, "This guy's slick. We need to be careful."

Skye piped up, "Uncle Emmett's right. Don't sign anything today. Even if it looks good, run it by your lawyer first."

Ginger leaned past her father and a wave of gin-breath washed over Skye. "Let's keep an open mind. I don't know why everyone is always so paranoid."

"Being careful is not paranoia." Now Skye was really worried. Neither twin was the quickest horse on the racetrack.

But from the expressions on the rest of the family's faces, it was clear that they agreed with Skye and Emmett.

Ginger must have noticed, because her voice took on a cajoling tone. "Well, I don't want to ruin the surprise, but let's just say I've met Moss Gibson and what he has planned could really improve our lives." She finished her drink and looked toward the bar. "Excuse me. I'll be right back."

As soon as her cousin left, Skye caught Vince's eye. He shrugged. They would just have to wait and see what was going on.

Skye got up, saying she was getting dessert. As she walked slowly toward the serving table, she overheard snatches of conversation.

The owner of the real estate agency was saying to the people around him, "Listen, I've talked to this guy. He's going to revive Scumble River."

A little farther down, Ace Cramer said to his dining companions, "Right now the economy stinks, but Gibson's plan can bail us all out."

Skye pursed her lips. What was Gibson's plan? She put a few chocolate-dipped strawberries and some petits fours on her plate and rejoined her family.

After everyone finished eating, waiters came by with bottles of champagne and trays of glasses. While they were serving, Moss Gibson stepped back up to the dais and spoke into the mike. "Did everyone enjoy brunch?"

A polite round of applause answered him.

"Good. Now, lean back, sip your bubbly, and enjoy the show. The lights darkened and a screen descended from the ceiling. After a few seconds of blurry gray snow, an image of an amusement park appeared, and the recorded voice of a has-been movie star said, "Welcome to Spudville, located just outside the growing town of Flat Cove, Idaho. At one time, this fine community was in serious financial trouble, but now with the thousands of tourists Spudville attracts to the area, it's turned into a thriving city."

Skye watched in appalled silence. From the Mashed Potato Water Ride to the Tater Tot Train, the attractions grew tackier and in worse taste with each one shown. The pièce de résistance was something called the "French Fried Follies"—a *Hee-Haw*–type show that insulted and exploited women at every possible level.

By the time the promotional film ended, Skye wanted to scream. Not only was the whole thing hokey beyond belief, it stereotyped and insulted almost every minority on the planet.

Before she could express her exasperation, Moss Gibson began to speak. "Folks, up until now Spudville has been my pride and joy, but in less than a year, with all of your help, my new vision, Pig-In-A-Poke Land, will outshine Spudville."

As he paused for breath, Skye noted that most of the crowd looked confused, but some people were already nodding and whispering to their neighbors.

Gibson went on, "Pig-In-A-Poke Land will encompass three hundred acres, including parking and the Farmer-in-the-Dell Hotel. We'll employ over a thousand people. This doesn't count the jobs that will become available as support businesses spring up."

The audience was beginning to split into two groups—the ones sitting with frowns, shaking their heads, and the others smiling and taking notes.

Suddenly two young women in denim bikinis, straw hats, and cowboy boots appeared, pushing a wheeled table between them. A white cloth was draped over the table's contents. Voices immediately rose.

After the noise died down, Gibson said, "This is a model of Pig-In-A-Poke Land. There are also brochures." He nodded to the women, who whipped off the cover.

A collective gasp came from the spectators.

Gibson concluded his speech with, "You have probably been wondering why you were invited here today. The reason is simple. You all have an important part to play in revitalizing your town. And you all have a once-in-a-lifetime chance to make your fortune."

This was it, the pitch to invest their money.

Gibson made eye contact with everyone present before saying, "I'll be making appointments to talk to each and every one of you separately, but just so you know, I want your land, and I'm prepared to pay cash."

Skye looked at her relatives. May and Minnie were shaking their heads, her father and Uncle Emmett were scowling, but Ginger and Gillian were smiling and whispering to each other.

All around the room, voices were raised and arguments erupted. Two men were already on their feet, fists clenched.

Vince came over, squatted next to Skye's chair, and said, "Welcome to the new *Family Feud* game, the special Scumble River edition."

CHAPTER 10

Blue Monday

Shit! Skye stopped wiggling into her bathing suit and stood with the maillot around her knees. It had just dawned on her that the high school pool would be closed because of the fire. Damn! She needed the exercise, and more importantly, the stress release that swimming provided.

Great. Now she would have to face a Monday without her morning swim. And it would undoubtedly be quite a Monday. She had tried all Sunday night to reach Homer Knapik, but he didn't answer his phone. Heck, with the threat of Leroy Yoder's vengeance hanging over Homer's head and the repercussions of the fire ready to crash down on his shoulders, she'd bet big money that the principal was screening his calls, hiding under his bed, or maybe even back in St. Louis.

Skye used her foot to flip the useless swimsuit into a corner and stomped into the adjoining bath. A hot shower would have to substitute for her missed laps.

After dressing, she downed a quick cup of tea, then drove to the high school. It was still early, but she really needed to catch Homer before the day started.

Skye ambushed the principal as he walked into the school

at seven-thirty, cornering him between the teachers' mailboxes and the front counter. "Homer, I need to talk to you."

The tufts of hair sticking out from his ears twitched in annoyance. "I'm late for an administrators' meeting. Can't this wait?"

"It'll only take a second." She outlined her plan to have the homeroom teachers make a brief statement about the fire and announce Skye's availability to any student who wanted to talk. "Is that okay?"

"Yeah, sure." Homer edged away from her and slipped through the door of his office. A second later his head popped around the corner like a giant jack-in-the-box. "You better stick around here all day today. I'll let the other principals know I need you." He disappeared back into his office without waiting for her assent.

Skye had planned on staying at the high school anyway, but it would have been nice if Homer at least pretended he was asking, rather than issuing an order. She sighed and headed to the photocopy machine. Who was she kidding? Homer thought of her as his lackey, and that was pretty much the reality of her situation.

After putting information about the fire and its aftermath in all the homeroom teachers' boxes, Skye went in search of Trixie.

She found her friend standing on a stepladder stapling book jackets to the wall. "Hey, what's up?"

Trixie swung around, swayed, and then hopped off the ladder, making a perfect four-point landing. "I was just changing the display. Valentine's Day is officially over."

"Can't say I'm sorry to see it gone." Skye followed Trixie to the circulation desk and leaned a hip against the counter. "How're things with your mother-in-law's estate?"

"Owen's meeting with someone today to see if we have enough equity in the farm for a loan." Trixie changed the subject without looking up from the stack of books she was processing. "Any news on Frannie?"

"She's home from the hospital and doing fine. She'll probably be at school today."

"I take it we're canceling the school newspaper meeting after school?" Trixie asked.

"I think we should, don't you?"

"Yes. I'm busy Tuesday and Wednesday. Can we reschedule for Thursday?"

Skye flipped open her appointment book and checked. "Sure. I'm free that afternoon."

"Good. I'll let the kids know." Trixie started to reshelve books. "How about the fire? Anything on that?"

Skye followed her. "It looks like it was deliberately started." She lowered her voice. "Maybe to cover up a murder."

"Do they know who the victim is?"

"Not that I've heard. Wally seems a bit . . . distracted." Before she could say anything else, the first bell rang. "I'd better get to my office. I told the homeroom teachers they could send any kids who were upset about the fire to see me." She waved and rushed off.

As Skye hurried down the hallway, she noticed that the students appeared the same as they did most Mondays—some hyper, some sluggish, and some asleep on their feet. During the next hour, only one girl showed up at her office. For the most part, the kids seemed to think the fire had been no big deal. She was puzzled but relieved.

With the exception of gym classes being held in the band room, school went on as if nothing had happened.

At nine o'clock there was a knock on her office door, and Arlen Yoder sidled into the room. He was tall and broad and could easily find work as a body double for the Incredible Hulk. The teenager stopped a few feet past the threshold and said into his chest, "Really, Ms. Denison. It was an accident."

So much had happened over the weekend, it took her a moment to remember she had asked to see the boy about the false alarm incident last Friday. "Sit down, Arlen. You understand that whatever you say to me today is *not* confidential? I'll be sharing our conversation with school staff and your parents."

He nodded.

"Okay, then, tell me what happened."

Arlen mumbled, "Someone pushed me and I slammed against the fire alarm, and the flap on my shirt got caught, and when I tried not to fall I moved backwards and accidentally pulled the lever."

Skye talked to him for nearly half an hour and his story never changed. Finally, she let him go and started to work on a brief report of her meeting with Arlen.

The bell for first lunch had just rung when Opal Hill, the school secretary, buzzed Skye and announced, "Mr. Knapik would like to see you."

"Okay. Thanks." Skye grabbed a legal pad, pen, and her appointment book, and hurried toward the front office.

Homer's door was closed when Skye arrived, and she could hear raised voices. She hesitated.

Opal encouraged, "Go ahead in. He's expecting you."

"Who's with him?"

"Mr. and Mrs. Yoder."

Skye groaned. She knew the day had been going too well. Facing these parents was worse than being a contestant on *Fear Factor*. Heaven only knew what disgusting or dangerous stunt they'd pull.

She took a deep breath, knocked once, and eased the door open. Homer sat behind his desk. His hair was bristling and his face was the color of cayenne pepper. The Yoders were seated across from him. Mrs. Yoder was hunched in her chair as if expecting the ceiling to fall in on her. Mr. Yoder was poised at the edge of his seat, clearly ready to spring up at the least provocation.

No one acknowledged her presence. Skye dragged a chair from the back table over by Mrs. Yoder, keeping as far away from *Mr.* Yoder as she could. The man had assaulted her a couple of years ago, and at the time she had listened to Homer and not reported him to the police. This time, if he as much as touched her, she'd have Wally on the phone faster than you could say, "Arrest this man."

Homer continued to talk. "As I've said before, I'm sorry Arlen missed the dance, but I have to follow the school district handbook."

"Arlen didn't pull that goddamn alarm!" Mr. Yoder raged. "He was pushed! It was an accident!"

Homer turned to Skye. "Did you speak to Arlen this morning, Ms. Denison?"

"Yes."

"And your conclusion?"

As Skye started to speak, Mr. Yoder swung his massive head in her direction and pinned her with a simian stare. For a moment she was distracted by his resemblance to a gorilla and forgot what she was about to say.

Homer prompted her, "Ms. Denison, do you have an opinion?"

"Uh, well, I can't be absolutely certain, but I think Arlen is telling the truth. He didn't mean to pull the alarm."

Homer exhaled noisily, and a look of confusion crossed the Yoders' hostile faces.

Mr. Yoder said incredulously, "You believe him?"

"Yes," Skye declared.

"So you're saying he shouldn't be suspended?" Mr. Yoder questioned.

"Yes." Skye was getting worried. Yoder was way too calm.

Suddenly Mr. Yoder sputtered, "Then you people made him miss the dance for nothing and he—"

Without thinking, Skye cut him off. "Considering the fire, maybe missing the dance was a blessing in disguise." She tensed. Now she was in for it. This was not a man who tolerated interruptions, especially from women.

But Mr. Yoder just nodded. "Maybe." He stood up and his wife leapt to her feet. As they walked out the door, he added darkly, "And maybe there wouldn't have been no fire if Arlen was there."

Skye's stomach growled, reminding her that she had skipped breakfast and it was past lunchtime. She had forgotten to bring anything to eat, and the cafeteria was closed—darn, she had missed her opportunity to enjoy a meal of mystery meat and tater tots.

After considering her limited options, she decided to try the new sub shop that had recently opened next to Kessler Dry Goods Store. She gathered the papers spread across her desktop and locked them in the top drawer, then grabbed her purse, told Opal she'd be right back, and walked out to her car.

The sub shop was packed. Obviously the citizens of Scumble River were ready for a new culinary adventure. Skye grabbed a number from the dispenser by the door and looked at the menu written on a chalkboard mounted on the wall behind the counter. The odor of salami and pickles filled the air. She was trying to decide between the Italian and the tuna sub when she caught part of the conversation going on behind her. Two men were talking about the fire.

Before she could tune in on the men's discussion, the girl behind the counter interrupted her eavesdropping by asking for her order. Skye decided on the Italian club and then focused back on the dialogue behind her.

A male voice intoned, "It was murder."

Another questioned, "How do you know?"

"I heard it not fifteen minutes ago. I was getting my hair cut, and Wally Boyd came in and arrested Vince Denison."

Skye whirled around and grabbed the arm of the man who had been speaking. "Did you just say Vince Denison has been arrested?"

"Yes, ma'am, I did." The man tried to back away, but Skye had a good grip and didn't let go.

"Chief Boyd actually put Vince in the squad car and drove away with him?" Skye demanded. A lot of Scumble River citizens tended to exaggerate, and she wanted to be clear on what had really happened.

"Well, no. He just took him into the back of the shop and talked to him for a while and then left by himself."

Skye counted to ten, twice. As much as she wanted to, she couldn't slap this man silly, or Wally would come arrest her. Instead, she dug her nails into his arm and said in a firm voice, "If I were you, I'd be mighty careful about the rumors that I spread about Vince Denison. I hear he's dating some hot shot Chicago lawyer, and I'd hate to see a nice man like you get sued for slander . . . or is it libel? I can never remember which one it is that the judge takes away your farm for."

With that, Skye paid for her lunch, yanked the brown paper sack off the counter, and marched out of the shop.

There was a stack of pink "while you were out" slips in her box when she got back. She sorted through them as she walked to her office. Her mother had left three messages, Vince had left two, and Wally, one. Gee, all the people she wanted to talk to wanted to talk to her too. How nice.

Before she could decide whom to call first, the telephone

rang. Skye snatched up the receiver and Opal announced that Chief Boyd was waiting to see her.

Wally walked into her office and took a seat. "You were right. The fire victim is Logan Wolfe. His wife identified his tattoo yesterday, and we got word late this morning that his dental records match."

"I see." Skye played for time as she considered how to broach her questions. "Did she say why she hadn't reported him missing?"

"She thought he was spending the night with a friend. She wasn't sure who."

"Is she a suspect?"

Wally shifted uneasily, his leather utility belt creaking against the chair's armrest. "There're a lot of people we want to talk to."

"Like the friend he was supposed to stay with, I imagine," Skye prodded.

"Yes, and his other friends, too."

"I hear you've already started talking to them."

"Only a few. We just got the dental confirmation a couple of hours ago."

Skye's nostrils flared. "So, Vince was first on your list?"

Wally no longer seemed able to look her in the eye. "Not necessarily. He just happened to be the easiest to find."

"But he is a suspect?" she persisted.

"He is one of the last people who saw Logan alive."

"Besides the killer, you mean."

"Sure."

"Was Vince able to shed any light on your investigation?"

"Right now, I'm just trying to get the timeline straight." Wally fished a small pad of paper and a pen from his pocket. "That's why I wanted to talk to you. Did you see Logan once that girl starting screaming 'fire'?"

Skye took a moment to recall what had happened. "No. I couldn't see the back of the gym from where I was originally, and by the time I rounded up the kids and got them out the emergency exit, only Vince and Finn were on stage, and no one was nearby."

"That fits with what I've heard so far." Wally got up. "Do you know the name of the girl who first screamed 'fire'?"

"I never saw her. I heard a commotion by the stage while the band was still playing, started toward the noise, and then heard someone scream 'fire.' "

Wally stopped at the door. "I need to talk to Frannie Ryan. Do you know if she's at school today?"

"She's here, but wouldn't it be better if you talked to her at home?"

"I have her father's permission to interview her."

"Good. But I was thinking that maybe it would be dangerous for her if whoever killed Logan thinks she knows something and sees her talking to the police."

Wally sighed. "When does school get out?"

Skye looked at her watch. "In an hour."

"Okay. In the meantime, I'll go talk to Finn."

"I'm surprised you aren't more interested in Rod, since he was the first to leave the stage when the fire alarm started."

"I haven't been able to locate him. Unlike Vince and Finn, he doesn't have a steady job." Wally shrugged. "Besides, anyone could have snuck back in during the commotion, killed Logan, and slipped back out again.

Skye sat staring into space after the chief left. So Rod was missing. Maybe he had murdered Logan.

CHAPTER 11

Mama Said

The phone was ringing when Skye stepped through her cottage door at five o'clock. Shortly after Wally left, she had been summoned to an after-school meeting at the junior high, which had lasted until a few minutes ago. She hadn't had a chance to return her mother's calls, and her short conversation with Vince hadn't added much to what Wally had told her.

Skye scooped up the receiver and said, "Hi, Mom."

"How did you know it was me?" May demanded. "Did you get one of those caller ID thingies?"

"Nope. Just took a guess." Skye could tell from her mother's tone that May had spent the afternoon working herself into a lather. "Did you hear that the murder victim is Logan Wolfe?"

"Uh-huh. I think Wally suspects your brother of killing him."

"Why do you say that?" Skye answered cautiously, not wanting to stir May up any more than she already was.

"Because as soon as Wally found out the victim was Logan, he tore out of the station and went straight to Vince's salon."

Skye had forgotten her mother was dispatching the

seven-to-three shift today. "But he didn't arrest him. Vince said that Wally just had some questions about the timetable that night."

May exhaled so loudly it sounded like she was blowing a raspberry at Skye. "Your brother has a lot of wonderful qualities, but the ability to tell whether he's in trouble is not one of them."

Skye had to agree. "I saw Wally briefly after he talked to Vince, and he claimed he was talking to Finn and Rod, too."

"They aren't our concern. Vince is. Besides, something is going on with Wally. He's not himself lately."

So May had noticed that, too. Skye wanted to hear what her mother had observed. "How's he different?"

"It's hard to say. He seems fuzzy and not real interested in anything much."

"That's not good." Skye poured dry cat food into one of Bingo's bowls and water into the other.

"No, it isn't. Which is why I want you to help Wally find out who really killed Logan Wolfe."

"But, Mom—"

May interrupted, "Before he arrests your brother."

A sick feeling invaded Skye's stomach. She had been trying not to think about the fact that Vince had been a murder suspect once before, when an old girlfriend had returned to Scumble River and ended up being stabbed with his styling shears. After the queasiness passed, she said, "I'll keep my eyes open."

"Good." May's voice shook. "I don't want to ever have to visit my baby boy in jail again."

"Don't worry, Mom." Skye understood her mother's feelings. Visiting Vince in jail had been one of the worst experiences of her life, too. "I'll take care of it."

There was a moment's silence, then May said, "Maybe you can ask some questions at Wally's Meet and Greet tonight."

"You're still going to that? I thought you'd be mad at Wally for suspecting Vince and would boycott his campaign rally."

"Of course I'm not mad at Wally." May's tone was innocent. "I just don't want him to make a big mistake and look bad." Skye was digesting her mother's reasoning when May added, "Besides, haven't you ever heard the saying, 'Keep your friends close and your enemies closer'?"

Skye made a noncommittal sound, then said, "I thought maybe he'd cancel the rally after the murder and all."

"Why should he?" May sniffed. "People can't expect him to work as a policeman twenty-four hours. You are still going?"

"Simon's picking me up at six."

"But it starts at six. You'll be late."

Skye rolled her eyes. It didn't take more than five minutes to get anywhere in Scumble River. "Events like these never get started on time. We'll be there before anything happens."

"I'll save you some food, in case they run out early. I'm bringing a couple pans of lasagna and a batch of fried chicken."

"Sounds great." Skye's mouth watered. May's cooking was legendary. Her food alone could win the election for Wally. "See you there."

Skye took a quick shower and changed into burgundy wool slacks with a matching angora twin set. An occasion like this one was tricky. Too dressy, and people talked about you for being snooty; too casual, and people said you'd been raised in a barn.

She was trying to decide between the pearl and the gold earrings when the doorbell rang. She hurried to the foyer, looked out the window, and flung open the door.

After briefly embracing Simon, Skye said, "We'd better

get going. Mom's worried we'll be late and miss all the food."

"Let's go, then." Simon raised an eyebrow and grinned. "We can't have May in a tizzy."

May and Simon had a mutual admiration society going. May thought Simon would be the perfect husband for Skye and father for her children. And Simon thought May was the ideal mom, unlike his own mother, Bunny, who had recently reentered his life after a twenty-year absence. Skye, on the other hand, found Bunny's casual but not smothering affection refreshing.

It took them only a few minutes to drive to the VFW Hall, where the rally was being held. The veterans were backing Wally and had offered their facility for the event.

People stood three deep at the bar, creating a human wall blocking access to the rest of the building. Simon and Skye edged through the throng as they headed for the banquet hall in back. They finally made it through the doorway but could only take a few steps inside. The room was already crowded, and the people waiting in line for the buffet to open snaked twice around the perimeter.

Skye's parents waved from their spot near the front, but not wanting to start a riot, she and Simon didn't try to join them. Cutting in a buffet line in Scumble River was akin to cheating on an exam at West Point: at the least, it could get you thrown out, and at the worst, you might find yourself on the wrong end of a gun barrel some dark evening.

Simon asked, "Are you hungry?"

"Yes."

"Do you want to stand in line?"

"No."

"Then let's have a drink first." Simon tugged her toward a portable bar that had been set up at the back of the room. "My guess is that once the buffet opens up, the line will go down pretty fast."

"Okay. I'll grab a table." Skye let go of Simon's hand. "Get me a Diet Coke with lots of ice and a lime, and if they have pretzels or anything, bring some of those too, please."

Skye watched Simon disappear into the horde and then flung herself into the mass. Once she broke through the outer mob, the middle of the room was relatively deserted. Skye chose a table near the center front where they should be able to see and hear everything.

She could see instruments and amps scattered across the stage and wondered if Vince's group would still play now that they had been told their lead singer was dead. And if they didn't, who would Wally get at the last minute to fill in? She just hoped it wasn't the Maxalencovich Accordion Trio, Scumble River's only other entertainment option.

Since attendance at this event would be a declaration of support for Wally as mayor, Skye looked around to see who had come out on his side. She noticed several people she worked with, which was a bit surprising since Ace Cramer, the other candidate, was a well-liked teacher.

More expected attendees were the officers and dispatchers from the police department. Wally was popular with his employees.

Skye strained to see the rest of the room, curious as to which of the town's business owners would support the chief. A swell of voices indicated that the buffet had opened, and the mob surged forward. Simon's prediction proved right, and the line moved quickly. By the time he joined Skye at the table, nearly half the people were balancing full plates and searching for places to sit.

He put a tall glass in front of her. "Sorry, no snacks, but it looks like we'll get to eat supper soon."

"Thanks anyway." Skye smiled at Simon as he sat next to her, then pointed and asked, "Isn't that Xavier and Frannie over there?"

He looked where she had indicated and nodded. "Okay if we ask them to join us?"

"Definitely. I didn't get a chance to talk to Frannie at school today, and I want to see how she is."

Simon waved his arm at Xavier, who nodded and spoke to his daughter. The two headed toward Skye and Simon.

When they arrived, Skye said, "Hi! Mmm, the food looks wonderful."

Xavier nodded to her and Simon as he held out a chair for his daughter and then seated himself. He wore a shiny navy blue suit that Skye had seen him wearing at every wake and funeral she had ever attended. She wondered if he had several of them or if it was the same one all the time.

Frannie started talking before she was fully settled at the table. "Ms. D., I have an awesome idea for the front page of the next edition of the *Scoop*."

"Great. I'm glad to see you here. I wanted to talk to you at school today and make sure you were okay, but I never caught up with you."

"I'm fine." A shadow crossed the girl's face. "I guess you saved my life."

"No. You were all right." Skye patted Frannie's hand. "Someone would have found you sooner or later."

Frannie nodded but didn't look convinced.

Skye made a mental note to talk to the girl alone and help her process the experience, but since this wasn't the time or place, she decided to change the subject. "Nice dress."

"Thanks. Another one of my catalog purchases." Frannie retied the ribbon on the peasant neckline. "I'm finally getting some cool clothes."

Simon and Xavier had been silent while the females were talking, but now Simon spoke up. "But you always look nice, Frannie."

Frannie rolled her eyes at Skye, who shrugged. Most men

knew about as much about fashion as Skye knew about subatomic physics.

Skye turned to Xavier, who was looking at them as if they were all aliens. "I'm glad to see Frannie is feeling well enough to be out this evening," Skye said.

He dipped his head slightly. "Me too, miss." His pale blue lashless eyes were magnified behind old-fashioned horn-rimmed glasses, making them seem reptilian. "I wanted to thank you for saving her."

"Really, I didn't do anything." Skye was embarrassed by his gratitude and she tried to make light of her part in Frannie's rescue. "I couldn't have our school's star reporter get hurt."

Xavier nodded, as if understanding her discomfort. "I was happy to hear she would be spending some time with you on the newspaper. With me being older than the other fathers and her mother gone, she's needed a woman's attention."

"No problem. I like spending time with Frannie." Skye hadn't quite figured Xavier out yet. When she first met him, she had been slightly repulsed by his odd appearance, but since then, she had found a lot to admire.

The four of them were quiet until Skye said, "It was good of the veterans to donate the use of their banquet hall for Wally's campaign rally."

"We always support candidates who recognize the contribution the armed forces have made." Xavier had been a medic in Vietnam.

It was Skye's turn to nod.

Simon took her hand and said, "It looks like we can get some food now. Are you ready?"

"Yes. I'm starving." Skye got up from her chair and said to Frannie and Xavier, "Excuse us. We'll be back in a second."

As they went through the buffet line, Skye and Simon ran

into a friend from their bowling league, who said, "I hear you're reopening the bowling alley next Friday night. Does that mean we'll be able to play the Friday after that?"

"That's the plan."

"Great. I'll spread the word." He clapped Simon on the back and moved away.

Skye and Simon returned to their table in time to see Uncle Charlie mounting the steps to the stage. She had forgotten that he was Wally's campaign manager. His booming voice didn't need the microphone that he stood behind. He was dressed in his usual uniform of gray twill pants, white shirt, and suspenders. In honor of the occasion, he had added a red bow tie and polished his black work shoes.

Charlie waited for a few minutes as the crowd quieted, then he said, "Tonight it is my pleasure to introduce Scumble River police chief Walter Boyd." He paused for the applause to finish then continued, "Walter Boyd has served Scumble River well for the past eighteen years, first as a patrolman, then sergeant, and finally as the chief of police. Today he is officially announcing that he would like to continue to serve this town, but in a new capacity, as our mayor. Please welcome Walter Boyd."

The clapping rose in a crescendo and then trailed off as Wally took center stage and gestured for silence. The few silver threads in his hair emphasized its ebony color, and the faint lines that bracketed his warm brown eyes made him appear open and friendly. His muscular build and year-round tan were shown to full advantage in a well-tailored black suit and crisp white shirt.

"Uh, thank you." He cleared his throat. "Thank you. I'm deeply honored that you have all come here tonight to support my campaign. Scumble River is a special town, and I want to keep it that way, which is why I'm running for mayor."

Wally spoke for about twenty minutes and then concluded with, "Our town has had a rough couple of years. We still have not received the check Mr. Scumble promised us. The farmers have suffered from poor crops, and the recent layoffs at the power plant have put a good many of our citizens out of work. This has resulted in less money being spent, which has hurt our small business owners, who are struggling to keep their doors open."

He paused and took a drink of water. "But we don't have to roll over and take whatever someone wants to dish out to us. You've all heard about the proposed amusement park, Pig-In-A-Poke Land. So far the developer has made a lot of promises to a lot of people, but what he has not done is talk about the impact on our community. He has not discussed the increased traffic, the wear and tear on our public areas, and the danger of having so many strangers in our town. Most of all, he has not mentioned who will pay for the added police, extra repairs, and damage to our way of life."

Skye leaned over to Simon and whispered, "If Wally's elected mayor, could he stop Gibson from building that amusement park?"

"Not officially," Simon answered. "The land Gibson wants to put it on is outside the city limits. No doubt he got the county permits he'll need before anyone around here heard the first hint about the project. But as mayor, Wally will influence whether the town supports the amusement park or interferes with it."

"Oh." Skye turned her attention back to the stage.

Wally ended by saying, "We can and will recover from these setbacks without having to change the fundamental nature of the town we love."

The crowd reacted to the end of his speech with thunderous applause, stomping feet, and whistles of approval. When the noise died down, Charlie returned to the stage and said, "Chief Boyd will now answer questions." Charlie smiled genially and scanned the audience for raised hands.

Before he could acknowledge anyone, a voice from the rear of the room shouted, "If you're such a wonderful police chief, why did it take a civilian to solve the Addisons' murders? And will you need her help to find Logan Wolfe's killer?"

In the ensuing silence, Skye felt her heart sink, and she considered crawling under the table. She knew that Wally had taken a lot of flak over her involvement in some of the recent murder investigations, but up until the Addison case, she had been able to keep her part in solving the crimes fairly quiet.

Unfortunately, the local paper, which had previously only featured advertisements and sports statistics, had changed hands. The new owner, intent on turning the *Star* into a real newspaper, had run a big story about her part in solving the murders.

As Wally started to respond to the question, Skye whispered to Simon, "Who said that?" She didn't want to turn around, have the heckler spot her, and give the guy more ammunition.

Simon looked over his shoulder, then answered in a low voice, "I don't recognize him, but he looks like Santa Claus."

"Shit!" Skye dug through her purse and got her compact out. "I'll bet it's Moss Gibson." She aimed it behind her and frowned. All she could see was a man's red back as he slipped out of the room. "It had to be him, but he left before I got a good look."

Wally must have noticed the man's departure too, because he stopped what he had been saying about the police department always welcoming the assistance of anyone in the community and whispered something to Charlie before finishing his statement.

Charlie hurried away and disappeared out a side door.

CHAPTER 12

Material Girl

Wally continued to take questions until no more hands waved in the air, then said, "Thank you all for coming. Please stick around. The ladies will be putting out some delicious homemade cakes and cookies, and Pink Elephant has agreed to play while you enjoy your dessert."

So Vince's group *was* playing. Would they go on as a trio, or had they found a substitute vocalist to take Logan's place? Skye watched the stage as Wally climbed down. His ex-wife, Darleen, met him at the bottom of the stairs and took his arm. He grimaced but allowed her to hang on to him as she whispered urgently into his ear. A moment later he and Darleen, her hand still possessively clutching his arm, walked toward a nearby table and started chatting with the group seated there.

Skye frowned. Darleen had been obsessed with the idea of having a baby, and when she found out she was unable to conceive, she had divorced Wally for a man whose wife had died and left him with an infant to care for. Skye wondered what had motivated her to return.

"What's she doing with the chief?" Frannie voiced the question in Skye's mind. "I thought they had split up."

Skye kept the expression on her face neutral. "It's not uncommon for divorced couples to reconcile."

Simon looked at Skye thoughtfully before returning to his conversation with Xavier.

"Well, I don't think that's a very good idea." Frannie's face was stiff with disapproval. "You should tell Chief Boyd he can do better than her."

Darleen was the special education teacher at the junior high school. Her lack of empathy and volatile temper had made her unpopular with all the students, not just the ones she had in her class.

"I think the chief can handle his own love life without my advice." Skye's attention was drawn back to the stage when the band started to ascend the stairs.

Vince was first up. He went immediately to his drums and started checking them out. Almost on his heels was Finn, who also began adjusting his instrument. After several minutes Rod came out of the back with Heather, and they too climbed the stairs. Rod helped the girl singer with her microphone before turning to his own preparation.

Skye raised an eyebrow. So the groupie had gotten her wish; she was now singing with the band. And all it took was Logan's death. It looked like she would have to persuade Vince to talk to Wally about Heather after all.

Frannie said, "Wonder how they got a new singer so fast."

Skye blinked. Sometimes it seemed as if the girl could read her mind. "They probably have a list of subs in case of emergency." There was no way she would explain the Heather situation to the teen.

Frannie shrugged, clearly already bored with the subject, and said, "Want to go get some dessert?"

"Sure."

Frannie jumped out of her chair and took off toward the sweet table.

Skye paused before following her to ask Simon and Xavier if she could get them anything. Simon accepted, requesting chocolate cake, but Xavier declined, saying he didn't eat refined sugar.

Frannie and Skye browsed the dessert selection with the concentration of diamond experts picking the perfect stone. There was so much to choose from: slices of cake oozing with buttercream frosting, wedges of pie piled high with meringue, and brownies bursting with nuts or caramel. Best of all, whipped cream was everywhere.

Skye reached for a plate just as another hand swooped it away. She looked up into the bulging hazel eyes of Wally's ex-wife.

Darleen Boyd's penciled eyebrows rose high on her pale forehead. "Seems we both have the same taste in sweet things," she said.

Skye felt herself flush. Surely Darleen wasn't implying what Skye thought she was. Skye was pretty sure that only one or two people were aware of the chemistry between Wally and her—especially since they had never acted on their attraction.

Skye reached for another plate, her voice smooth as she said to Darleen, "There's plenty here for both of us."

"Perhaps." The other woman's glance swept Skye's ample curves from head to toe. "But while I can afford the cost of indulging, it looks like you would be better off passing this time."

Skye's mouth dropped open, and for a moment she couldn't think of a reply, but Frannie's stricken expression snapped her out of her shock, and she shrugged nonchalantly. "Guess I'm just a nutritional overachiever."

Darleen gave a brittle laugh. "I'm afraid I'm not familiar with that term."

"No, I guess you wouldn't be." Skye stared into the other

woman's eyes without blinking. "An overachiever is someone who is successful despite certain challenges."

Darleen blinked, then turned on her heel and walked away.

Skye examined the divorcée as she left. She was in her late thirties but dressed as if she were at least a decade younger. Tonight she wore a mini slip dress that emphasized her twiglike arms and legs. Her short brown hair covered her skull in feathery wisps, and her complexion was as pale as a piece of milk quartz.

Darleen joined Wally where he stood talking to a group of his supporters. As she fed him a bite of pie, her eyes bored directly into Skye's, and the message was clear: Mine. No Trespassing Allowed.

The majority of the Meet and Greet attendees left after they ate dessert, and the few who remained at the bar or on the dance floor had started to glance at their watches and say their good-byes, too. Most events that took place on weeknights in Scumble River wrapped up before ten, and it was already nine-forty-five.

Xavier and Frannie had left with the first wave, as had Skye's parents and most of her relatives. She and Simon stuck around for Vince's sake, but she was yawning, and Simon had moved into a Zen-like state. Both were worn out by the events of the last few days.

Finally, fifteen minutes later, the band finished its last song and started to pack up.

Skye and Simon climbed onto the stage. "You guys sounded great," she said to her brother.

"Yeah." Vince paused in putting a drum into a black case to wipe off his sweaty forehead with his arm. "Not bad, considering we had to substitute some equipment and were playing with a new vocalist."

"She has a nice voice," Simon commented.

"Yeah, I think she's going to work out well, if we get some other stuff straightened out." Vince shot Skye a look.

"Speaking of that," Skye leaned closer to Vince and lowered her voice, "have you mentioned her involvement with Logan to Wally?"

He shook his head and refused to meet her eyes.

"Then I'll have to."

"No!" Vince took a breath. "I mean, I don't think it's a good idea."

Simon's expression was puzzled. Skye hadn't told him about Heather. Now she filled him in, and he agreed. "Vince, it'd be a good idea for you to be the one to tell Wally about Heather's involvement with Logan and the rest of the band."

"Someone will spill the beans, and the rest of you will look really guilty." Skye took Vince's hand. "Maybe we should talk to Wally about Heather together."

He nodded reluctantly. "Okay, but she doesn't have anything to do with Logan's death."

Skye was concerned by her brother's defense of the groupie. That couldn't be a good thing. "I'll pick you up at five to seven tomorrow and we'll go to the police station. Wally works the seven-to-eleven shift, so he'll be just signing on when we get there. I'll call the school and tell them I'll be an hour or so late, due to a family emergency."

"But I have a seven-thirty appointment tomorrow."

"Cancel it." Skye took Simon's arm and started toward the stairs. "See you tomorrow."

Simon and Skye drove to her cottage in silence. As he turned into her driveway, he said, "Vince could be in a lot of trouble. The information about Heather makes him look bad."

"I know." Skye felt her chest tighten at the thought of her brother's situation. "I wish I knew what to do."

"Wally's fair. The best thing you can do is to make sure Vince tells the truth, the whole truth."

"Unfortunately, I'm pretty sure there's something he's not telling even me, and I doubt he'll tell Wally."

"You don't think he—"

"No. Of course not."

"But?"

"But I think he might have a good idea who did."

CHAPTER 13

You've Got a Friend

Tuesday morning was a typical February day in Illinois—dark, cold, and depressing. By this point in the year, eighty percent of the state's population had started to believe that winter would never end, and the other twenty percent had already absconded to Florida. Skye wished she were one of the latter. She was tired of layering sweaters, putting on boots, and fighting the wind for her hat and scarf.

At six-fifty when she pulled up to her brother's door, the headlights on her Bel Air provided the only illumination in the apartment complex's gray-shrouded parking lot. While she waited for Vince to come out, she tuned the radio to the new station that covered the Scumble River, Clay Center, and Brooklyn triangle.

The DJ was giving a weather report. "High today in the lower twenties with wind out of the north, making it feel like five below. Tonight will be in the single digits. No change predicted for the rest of the week."

Skye shivered and turned the knobs for both the heat and the fan to high.

Next up on the radio was local news. "Three area youths toppled Brooklyn's water tower in the early hours of Tuesday morning. Brooklyn's police chief said the teens used blowtorches to cut through the supports and ropes attached to pickup trucks to drag the tower down. Once on the ground, the flooded water turned to ice, which caused numerous traffic accidents as people tried to drive to work. Arrests have been made, and the offenders are in custody."

Skye wondered what in the world was going on—first Scumble River had a fire and now Brooklyn had a flood. Was Clay Center doomed to a plague of pestilence?

The squeak of the passenger door interrupted her thoughts and Vince threw himself into the front seat. He growled a hello at her.

"Good morning to you, too." Skye put the huge car in reverse and eased out of the parking spot.

Vince sat slumped on the aqua and white leather seat and complained, "I don't know why I had to cancel a paying customer to do this. The whole thing with Heather is none of Wally's business."

Skye barely stopped herself from snorting and instead said, "I know you like to pretend to be dumb, but remember, I'm your sister. I've seen the results of your IQ test, so don't try to snow me. You know very well why you have to tell Wally about the whole 'Heather and the band' affair."

"What if Mom is dispatching?"

Ah, the real reason Vince was being such a pain. "She's on the afternoon shift. Which is one of the reasons we're doing this now instead of after work."

"Oh." Vince straightened, looking marginally happier. "Well, that's one good thing."

"I always get a copy of Mom's work schedule as soon as it's posted." Skye parked the car. "Knowing where she is for eight hours every day is one of the ways I can live in Scumble River without going crazy."

She and Vince shared an understanding glance as they entered the police station.

Scumble River's police department was housed in a red

brick, two-story building bisected by a cavernous garage. The dispatcher's area and the interrogation/coffee room occupied most of the first floor. A small reception area with a counter and a bulletproof glass window took up the rest.

Skye pressed the button for admittance.

The dispatcher put down her needlepoint, buzzed them past the security door, and asked, "What brings you two out so early?"

"We have some information for the chief," Skye explained. "Is he available?"

"He's in his office. Go on up."

Vince and Skye climbed the narrow staircase to the small second floor.

Wally was sipping from a cup of coffee and reading the *Joliet Herald News* when Skye and Vince stepped into his office. He put the paper down and said, "To what do I owe this honor?"

Vince was silent, so Skye answered, "We have some information for you about Logan Wolfe."

"Have a seat. Coffee?"

Skye, having tasted the police station's bitter brew, declined, but Vince said yes.

Wally called down to the dispatcher for a cup and then said, "Who wants to go first?"

Vince stared at his loafers without speaking until Skye poked him in the side with her elbow. "Uh, I'm not sure what, I mean Skye thought we should tell you this, but it really isn't anything that important."

Wally leaned back in his chair and laced his fingers over his flat abdomen. "Just tell me everything, and I'll pick out the important parts."

"It all started when the band first began playing in public." Vince adjusted the crease on his khaki pants. "This girl, Heather Hunt, decided she was, like, our biggest fan."

"Go on," Wally encouraged.

"Well, she started showing up every place we played. She'd sit with us on our breaks, hang around after we finished, and help us pack up."

"And?" Wally's chair squeaked as he rocked forward.

"At first she was really sweet and seemed kind of innocent and trusting."

"But?"

"Then she started showing up at my shop, usually just as I was closing up for the night." Vince twisted a gold bracelet on his right wrist.

"You had an affair with her?" Wally guessed.

"Not really." Skye kicked Vince in the shins and he added, "I, uh, slept with her a couple of times, but then she wanted me to let her sing with the band, and when I wouldn't, she lost interest."

"Were the other band members jealous while you were sleeping with her?"

"No. Maybe a little, but no big deal or anything."

"What happened after she dropped you?" Wally probed.

"Almost the next day, she started in on Rod. But that didn't last more than a week or so."

"Who did she go for next, Finn or Logan?"

"Finn, and then Logan." Vince's face was red and he was sweating.

"So she did the whole band?"

Vince nodded.

"How did you guys handle that?"

"No one really cared, until . . ." Vince trailed off.

"Until?"

"Until she tried for a second round." Vince's cheeks had gone from red to crimson. "She thought we owed her a chance to sing with us, and she wouldn't take no for an answer."

Skye, who had been quiet up until this point, said, "So she went from being this sweet young thing to a she-devil?"

"Yes." Vince nodded. "She turned into Godzilla with breast implants and a real bad attitude."

There was a knock on the door and Wally got up. "So what did you boys do about her?" He took the coffee cup the dispatcher held out, thanked her, and handed it to Vince.

Vince took a sip, made a face, and put the mug on the floor. "We agreed that if we all ignored her, no more fooling around, she'd get tired of hanging around and go away."

"Did that work?"

"Not really." Vince reached for the coffee and took a big swallow.

His eyes watered and Skye wondered if it was from the scorching liquid, the bitter taste, or remorse at making a bad decision.

Wally, perched on the corner of his desk, glanced at Skye, who shrugged slightly, then asked, "What was Logan's role in all this?"

"Uh, how do you mean?"

A flicker of impatience crossed Wally's eyes, but his voice was unruffled. "How did he feel about Heather, what did he do, did he agree with the band's decision to freeze her out?"

"Logan was hard to understand." Vince slumped. Wally had asked all the right questions. "He was always looking for an angle, and he didn't treat women very nice." Vince took another slug of coffee.

"What do you mean?"

"Let me give you an example. The other night, Logan said that the only reason they call it PMS is that Mad Cow Disease was already taken."

"A lot of guys talk that way when they're with a group of other men."

"True." Vince crossed his legs. "But my take on Logan was that he treated women like he treated his TV remote control—something there to give him pleasure, and he just keep hitting buttons until he got what he wanted."

"So that's how he was with Heather?" Wally tented his fingers under his chin and spoke over the tips. "Did he agree to ignore her?"

"Yes. He agreed."

When Vince didn't go on, Skye interjected, "But he didn't keep his word. He was with her Friday."

"And since he was with her, he must have been up to something." Vince gazed at the ceiling. "Logan was a guy who always had more than a tattoo up his sleeve."

"How did the other guys feel about his reconciliation with Heather?" Wally asked.

Vince looked at Skye, and she nodded encouragement.

"They were pissed off. We were all pissed off."

After dropping Vince off at his shop and reporting to the junior high school for duty, Skye spent the rest of Tuesday worrying that she had made a mistake in insisting that Vince talk to Wally about Heather.

As she sat through the junior high's Pupil Personnel Services meeting, she pondered what Wally had said just before she and Vince left the police station that morning. When Vince went to use the men's room, Skye had asked Wally if he'd ever located and questioned Rod.

Wally's answer had been disturbing. He said that Rod had heard the police wanted to talk to him and had come to the station late Monday afternoon, but neither he nor Finn had much information to share. Both had suggested Wally talk to Vince if he wanted to know more about who might have had a motive to kill Logan. Skye figured the two musicians were just trying to get the police off their backs, but Wally didn't seem to see it that way.

That afternoon while she completed a case study evaluation at the elementary school, Skye decided she had better talk to Rod and Finn herself. If those two thought they could frame Vince, it was obvious that they needed someone to explain to them the error of their ways.

As soon as the teachers' dismissal bell rang, Skye called Vince to get the musicians' addresses. He told her Rod was out of town until tomorrow, so Finn was today's lucky winner in the "Talk to Skye" Sweepstake.

He lived in one of the new developments near the exit to I-55. Skye parked by a silver Camaro, proceeded up the sidewalk, and rang the doorbell. Finn answered immediately. Dressed in wool slacks, a button-down shirt, and tie, he looked nothing like the Pink Elephant keyboard player Skye had seen previously.

"Hi. Do you have a minute?" Skye asked. The social worker who had taught Skye to do home visits had told her it was better to get inside before explaining why you were there.

Finn nodded and stepped aside for her to enter. "You've got good timing. I just got home from work a minute ago."

"You work for Com Ed, right?"

"Uh-huh." Finn gestured to a chair and after she sat, he settled on the couch.

The electric company was one of the biggest employers in the area, but lately there had been layoffs. Skye wondered how secure Finn's job was. She looked around. He had a lot of expensive things. It would take a constant flow of money to maintain this lifestyle. "Sorry to bother you, but I wanted to talk to you about Logan."

"Oh?"

Skye leaned forward. "Do you have any idea why someone would want to kill him?"

"I didn't know him that well."

Skye raised her eyebrows.

"I mean other than the band, we weren't friends or anything."

"I see."

"Except for rehearsals and gigs, we didn't hang out together." Finn loosened his necktie. "He and I didn't really see eye to eye on much."

"Such as?"

"Morals, values, how to live your life."

Skye was silent.

He elaborated. "You know he was married?"

"Right."

"But he played around with other women."

"And you didn't approve?"

"No. I didn't."

"Especially Heather, right?"

"She was a good example." Finn swallowed. "But we all made a mistake in that case."

Skye tried another tack. "How did he make a living?"

"A little of this, a little of that." Finn relaxed against the couch's cushions. "Farming, giving singing lessons, doing odd jobs."

Finn clearly didn't mind discussing Logan's financial situation, which meant he knew nothing of interest in that area. She decided it was time to drop the bombshell. "One more question, and I'll get out of your hair."

"Sure." He grinned at her and stretched his legs out in front of him. "No problem."

"Why did you tell Chief Boyd that Vince would know who had a motive for killing Logan?"

Finn straightened, tugged at his collar, and stuttered, "I, uh, didn't, uh, exactly, uh, say that."

"Then what did you exactly say?"

"I just meant he and Logan spent more time together. Hung out more."

Skye stood up. "So you weren't trying to pin the murder on my brother?"

"No. Of course not." Finn struggled to his feet. "Vince would never do something like that."

"I know that. And I plan on convincing Chief Boyd." Skye walked to the door and put her hand on the knob. It turned easily; her escape route was clear so she said, "The question is, although Vince isn't capable of killing Logan, are you?"

CHAPTER 14

That'll Be the Day

First thing Wednesday morning, Skye sent a pass to Frannie Ryan. She wanted to see how the girl was coping, now that she'd had a few days to process last Saturday's frightening experience.

While she waited for Frannie to arrive, Skye recalled how her visit with Finn the previous day had ended. He'd denied that he had either a motive to kill Logan or the personality to do so, and she couldn't argue with him. Not that she believed him; she just didn't know enough about him to refute his claims. She had learned little from her interview with the keyboard player and hoped that her visit to Rod that afternoon would yield better results.

Frannie's entrance interrupted Skye's contemplation, and she forced herself to focus on the girl as she plopped into a seat. "Good morning, Frannie. Hope I didn't pull you out of anything important."

"Nah. Just P.E. Since we can't use the gym, Mr. Cramer has us doing papers on sports in various countries. What a yawn."

Skye silently agreed but said, "Seems like the fire has affected all of us."

"Yeah. Maybe." Frannie pulled a curtain of her hair in

front of her face and said through the shield, "It was pretty scary."

"Especially for you?"

"It was my fault for being stupid."

"Oh?"

"Yeah." Frannie sighed. "I wanted Jus—someone to see how brave I was, but he was too busy making sure that Bit—the bimbo was okay to notice me."

Skye contemplated what to say. Frannie had never really admitted her attraction to Justin, and if she didn't soon, then she would probably miss her chance with him. Skye phrased her response carefully. "Sometimes teenage boys need a hint that you like them, or they're afraid to admit that they like you."

Frannie's expression closed, and she said, "Anyway, I was dumb because I came out the emergency door, but then I thought I saw a shadow or something through the window inside near the pool, so I went back in."

That explained why Justin had seen Frannie near the pool door. She hadn't been coming out, she'd been going in. "Then what happened?" Skye asked.

"There was no one around the pool, but I heard noises in the boys' locker room, so I went to check it out."

"What kind of noises?"

"Just noises." Frannie shrugged. "As soon as I stepped through the locker room door, someone hit me on the head and that's all I remember, until seeing you when you opened the locker door."

They continued to talk throughout all of first period and most of second. When Frannie finally went back to class, Skye had only a few minutes to get to her third-period meeting. A student currently enrolled in an alternative school because of his previous violent behavior would be mainstreamed back into Scumble River High, and it had been decided that he would begin his return by taking a fine or practical arts class, rather than a core curriculum course. Skye was supposed to meet with the faculty involved and assist with his transition.

After twenty minutes of moaning, the staff decided that the returning student could do the least amount of harm in music. That music teacher was less than thrilled about the new addition to his class, but everyone else was pleased.

Since they had twenty minutes remaining in the period, they moved to the lounge, and conversation turned to a more interesting topic—the possibility of Pig-In-A-Poke Land coming to Scumble River. The news had easily overtaken the fire and the murder as the prime subject for gossip, and everyone had an opinion about it.

Trixie came in for a cup of coffee and joined the discussion. Skye watched her friend's expression as the amusement park was discussed, but she couldn't interpret it.

Finally Trixie said, "It all comes down to money. If you want or need the money, the amusement park seems like a good thing. If you don't, it doesn't."

Before anyone could respond, Trixie left the lounge. Skye hadn't thought of it before, but Trixie's farm was one of those Moss Gibson would want to buy, and the Fraynes certainly needed the money.

Although she tried for the rest of the day, Skye was never able to get Trixie alone to talk. Was her friend avoiding her? Normally, she would have hung around and nabbed her after school, but Vince's problem seemed more immediate than Trixie's, so Skye stuck to her original plan and left as soon as the teachers' dismissal bell rang.

As she drove towards Rod's apartment that afternoon, she was struck by the thought that the murder of a wannabe rock star had caused barely a scratch on the record album of Scumble River life. The kids sure didn't appear to be upset, and the adults didn't give the impression they were concerned either. Pig-In-A-Poke Land had pushed the murder to the back page of most people's interest. It certainly was odd that no one seemed to be mourning Logan.

Rod lived in an older apartment building next to the railroad tracks. Eyeing the ramshackle exterior, Skye reluctantly stepped into the entryway, found the name Yager, and pressed the bell. There was no answer. She waited and tried again. Still nothing.

She was about to give up when a teenager pushed through the inner door heading outside. He looked vaguely familiar and Skye said, "Hi. I'm looking for Rod Yager. Do you know him?"

"He's in 2C."

"Do you know if he's home?"

"Nah. He hasn't been here since Saturday. Leave him a message on his answering machine. He told me once that he checks it every couple of hours since he's a musician and doesn't want to miss a gig."

"Thanks." Skye waved good-bye as she walked back to her car. It seemed Rod was making himself rather scarce lately. Where was he hiding? And why?

Skye turned into her driveway and frowned. A red Lincoln Town Car was parked in her usual spot. Where had she seen that car before? Behind the wheel she could barely make out a tuft of white hair gleaming in the fading light. She stopped the Bel Air next to the other vehicle and got out.

The driver of the Lincoln also popped out of his car. It was Moss Gibson, AKA Mr. Pig-In-A-Poke. He sketched a slight bow and said, "Miz Denison, I presume?"

"How did you guess?" Skye made no move to go inside, even though she was freezing.

"I do believe that not too many lovely young ladies drive 1957 Bel Air convertibles."

"True." Someone had obviously described her to him. She wondered what he wanted.

He rubbed his hands together. "I'd like a moment of your time, if I could." He was wearing a red wool overcoat but no hat or gloves.

"In reference to what?"

"Could we speak inside? I'm from Mississippi and I'm not at all used to this kind of weather."

Skye thought about it and finally said, "Alright. Come in." She didn't trust him, but she wanted to hear what he had to say, and she was pretty sure she could take him on physically if push came to shove. After all, she was a good seven inches taller and thirty years younger than he was.

She unlocked the door and ushered him through, taking his coat and hanging it up along with her own. They moved into the great room and she motioned for him to sit down on the sofa.

After settling on the chair facing him she said, "So, Mr. Gibson, what did you want to talk to me about?"

He adjusted the cuffs of his red jacket and straightened the creases of the matching pants. "I hope you enjoyed that there little shindig I threw on Sunday."

"The food was delicious," Skye answered cautiously.

"Thank you. I like my friends to have the best."

Skye raised an eyebrow. "Have you made a lot of friends here in Scumble River?"

"Some." A crafty look crossed his cherublike face. "I'm fixin' to make a lot more."

"Really?" Skye fought to keep her expression from reflecting her distrust. "How are you planning to do that?"

"Easy as shoofly pie." His blue eyes twinkled below his bushy white brows. "I'm gonna put this town and its citizens in high cotton."

"By building an amusement park?"

"Pig-In-A-Poke Land is no ordinary amusement park. It's a state-of-the-art family destination, located in a natural setting representing a simpler, more God-fearin' lifestyle." He bounced off the sofa and stood with one hand holding the lapel of his jacket and the other clenched in a fist. "A family will be able to experience the rides, games, and attractions at Pig-In-A-Poke, then go into town and feel like they've never left the park—like they never left 1950."

"What if the people of Scumble River don't want to be actors in your fantasy world?" Skye let ice drip from her next words. "What if the farmers don't want to sell you the land that has been in their families for more than a hundred years?"

"Missy, you're colder than a mother-in-law's kiss."

"So I've been told." Skye leaned back in her chair. "But that doesn't answer my question. What about the residents who don't want to sell and don't want this big a change for their town?"

"Now you have me bumfuzzled." Gibson fell back on the couch as if he'd been shot. "Why would anyone not want to be rich?"

"Money can't buy happiness," Skye pointed out.

"If that don't beat all." The very idea seemed to make him dizzy and he clutched his head.

"So why did you come to see me?" Skye asked.

"I stopped by your momma and daddy's place, and they told me to talk to you first."

Skye smiled. After the brunch on Sunday, she had told her parents not to talk to this guy alone. For once, they had listened to her.

"Most of the area farmers are not in the market to sell their land, and I will certainly advise my family against selling."

"Dadgumit!" Moss Gibson straightened and said, "You'd argue with a milepost, wouldn't you?"

"Probably." Skye shrugged, thinking, *If I knew what that meant.*

The little man got back to his feet, the spring gone from

his step and the twinkle vanished from his eyes. "Listen to me, Missy." Now instead of looking like a jolly elf, he looked a lot more like a spiteful hobgoblin. "Pig-In-A-Poke Land is going up as planned and on time. I will get your family's land one way or another."

Threats didn't faze Skye. After several years of facing angry or unhappy parents, she had learned to let them slide off her back like oil off a hot griddle. "Do your best. We aren't in debt, so there's nothing you can do."

Gibson smiled meanly. His teeth suddenly looked sharp and menacing. "Gimme a holler, sweetheart, when you're ready to admit defeat."

The developer grabbed his coat and flung open the door, not bothering to close it after he marched through. Skye shivered and hurried to shut the door. She sure hoped the chill she felt was from the February wind and not from any truth in Gibson's threat.

CHAPTER 15

Stop! In the Name of Love

"February is the longest month of the year," Skye declared Thursday afternoon as she sat behind her desk at the high school with her feet resting on the half-open bottom drawer.

Simon sat in one of the visitors' chairs he'd pulled close to her. The remains of their lunch lay scattered across the blotter. He had surprised Skye by showing up with a picnic basket, whisking her into her office, and locking the door—after placing a DO NOT DISTURB sign on the handle.

"Really? I was always told it's the shortest," he said dryly.

"There are two ways to measure time." Skye stretched her arms over her head and then rested her hands on the back of her neck. "Actual time and perceived time. I was referring to perceived time."

"I see. And February has annoyed you somehow?"

She got up, grabbed the wastebasket, and started clearing away their lunch debris. "Not annoyed me exactly, but I feel like something is about to happen. Sort of like watching the pin come closer and closer to the balloon. You know you're going to be shaken up soon, and no matter how much you brace yourself, you still jump."

"Any idea of what you're afraid is about to burst?"

She shook her head. "There are so many possibilities, I'm not sure what to worry about first."

"Give me the lineup."

"First there's Trixie's financial situation."

"Her mother-in-law's debts," Simon confirmed. "Anything new since she told you about that last week?"

Skye filled him in on her theory that Trixie and Owen would have to sell their land to Moss Gibson, concluding with, "I still haven't had a chance to talk to her about it."

"I'm sure you'll catch up with her today. Didn't you say you and she have a student newspaper meeting after school?"

"True." Skye resumed her seat. "But something else Trixie mentioned last Friday is bothering me too. She said the kids have been acting funny, and I sort of blew her off, thinking that it was just the usual end-of-winter cabin fever, but now several weird incidents have occurred, and I'm concerned that something worse is going on."

"Let me see. You told me about Bitsy and Nathan's strange behavior; then there's the fire itself. Anything else?"

"Did you hear about the kids pulling down the water tower in Brooklyn?"

"Yes. But what does that have to do with Scumble River's teenagers?"

"I don't know, but I have a hunch it does. After all, it's only ten miles away." Skye rested her feet back on the drawer. "The kids *do* know each other."

"Okay. So far we have Trixie and the kids. Anything else on your anxiety agenda?"

"Moss Gibson was waiting for me at my cottage when I got home from school yesterday."

"What did he want?" Simon lifted her right foot from the

drawer, slipped off her shoe, and set her heel on his lap. He started massaging her toes, working his way down to the ball of her foot.

"He wanted me to convince my family to sell him our land." Skye closed her eyes and enjoyed the massage. "I told him to take a flying leap at a rolling donut hole, but I'm afraid that, like Trixie and Owen, other farmers in the area won't be able to resist the money. Crops have been bad the past couple of years, and people are in debt."

"I know. I've buried a lot of loved ones on the installment plan lately." Simon moved onto her arch and she sighed in pleasure.

Simon was such a good guy. Skye wondered how many other funeral home owners would allow families to pay a little at a time. She'd bet not many.

"But what's really disturbing you?"

"Logan Wolfe's death." Skye opened her eyelids a crack and asked, "Have you gotten the results of the autopsy back yet?"

"It came in this morning's mail. Blunt-trauma injury to the head. The fire damage occurred after death."

"So he was bopped on the head, and the fire was set to cover up the murder," Skye said half to herself.

"Or the assault happened during the fire, and the perpetrator merely took advantage of the situation." Simon switched feet and started rubbing her left one.

"That would make sense, too. I guess, considering Frannie's experience, Logan's death couldn't have just been an accident? Maybe he was running from the fire, tripped, hit his head, and died," Skye offered hopefully.

"No. The injury isn't consistent with a fall."

"Darn."

"Why do I think you still haven't told me your main fear?" Simon finished the massage and slipped her shoes back on her feet.

"Mom's convinced that Vince is on the top of Wally's suspect list." Skye's face took on a pinched, worried look. "And I'm afraid she might be right. Even before Tuesday, when Vince told him about Heather's involvement, it felt like Wally was concentrating on Vince."

The bell rang and Simon got up. "Then we better provide him with a better suspect."

Skye stood too, and moved around the desk. She put her hands on Simon's shoulders and pressed a soft kiss on his cheek. "Thank you." She gestured around the room. "For lunch and the foot massage, but mostly for not laughing at my worries and thinking I'm silly." Simon really had changed. Not only was he okay with Skye looking into the murder, he was offering to help. Previously he had been angry when she had become involved in this type of investigation.

"You're welcome." Simon moved toward the door and Skye followed. "Tonight I have a funeral, and tomorrow is the bowling alley's grand opening, so we won't have much private time together this weekend. Let's each make a list of people who might want to kill Logan Wolfe and then Monday we can start to look into them."

Skye felt the weight on her chest ease a little. It was so good to have someone with whom to share her anxieties. Skye and Simon parted at the school's front door.

After watching him get into his Lexus, she walked back to the main office and said to the secretary, "Opal, please call Nathan Turner out of science, and ask him to come to my office." It was time to find out why he had decided to take a shower in his clothes during a school dance.

Unfortunately Nathan was absent, and Bitsy was taking a test, so Skye's afternoon plans were thwarted, and she ended up writing psychological reports and answering phone calls instead.

The last period of the day was nearly over when Trixie

dashed into Skye's office. She plopped into a chair and blew her bangs out of her eyes. "What a day! Cramer was scheduled to bring his six classes into the library to do research—that's how they decided to handle giving a P.E. grade with the gym out of commission. But instead of staying with them, he kept disappearing. I ended up trying to supervise thirty kids and help find the materials they needed, all by myself."

Before Skye could commiserate, Trixie asked, "Do I look like I know a lacrosse stick from a cricket bat?" Skye tried once more to respond, but Trixie continued, "If Cramer is too busy for his classes now, what will he be like if he wins the mayoral race?"

This time Skye was able to slip in a question. "Will he still teach if he's elected? I sort of assumed he'd take a leave of absence."

Trixie took a Jolly Rancher from the jar on Skye's desk. "All the other mayors have kept their day jobs."

"That's true. Mayor Clapp had the used car lot, and the guy who was in office when I was in high school worked at Com Ed." Skye got up and went to her filing cabinet. "Could Wally keep on as police chief and be mayor at the same time?"

"Good question. Wasn't Andy Taylor the mayor and the sheriff of Mayberry?"

"You do realize that was a fictional town, right?" Skye was worried that Trixie had gone off the deep end. "Anyway, Andy was the justice of the peace and the sheriff. Someone else was mayor."

"Whatever." Trixie shrugged. "It never dawned on me that Wally might have to quit being police chief if he wins. Who would take over?"

"Roy Quirk is next in rank." Skye flicked through the folders, found the one marked *Scumble River High School*

Scoop, and extracted it from the row. "He's a good officer but a little young to be chief."

"Then they'd have to bring in someone new."

"Oh, my gosh." Skye sank back into her chair. "Otto McCabe has been trying to get on the force for ages. Mom says he's always picking up odd shifts." She shook her head. McCabe was a dead ringer for Barney Fife—both physically and mentally. "If he were hired, we really would be living in Mayberry, just like the Pig-In-A-Poke guy wants us to." As soon as the words left her mouth, Skye realized what she had said and looked to see Trixie's reaction.

"Speaking of that Gibson guy's plan, what do you think?" Trixie asked. She suddenly seemed to find the charms on her bracelet fascinating and didn't look up.

Skye bit her tongue. She couldn't tell Trixie the truth, but she didn't want to lie either. She answered cautiously, "I'm not thrilled with the idea of our town being turned into a tourist attraction where all the 'city folk' come to laugh and point at the local yokels."

"But the town needs money, and he's offering a lot of it." Trixie's voice lacked conviction.

Skye opened her mouth, then closed it. What could she say? "That's true. I just wish there was another way of getting it."

"Me, too."

"Why weren't you and Owen at the brunch?"

"We had no idea who Moss Gibson was until he came to see us Monday night. I had thrown away the invitation to Sunday's party, figuring it was some sort of scam."

Skye bit her tongue to stop herself from saying, *It is. He's trying to con all of us into being unpaid actors in his amusement park.* Instead she said in an offhanded tone, "Well, everyone has to make up their own mind about Pig-In-A-Poke."

"Yeah, well. Some people have no other choice."

The bitterness in Trixie's voice shocked Skye, and she resolved never to say anything negative about the amusement park in front of her friend again. She immediately changed the subject. "Are you still worried about the kids acting strange?"

Trixie straightened and appeared to shake off the other topic. "Well, the water tower incident in Brooklyn certainly qualified as outlandish. Did you hear what happened in Clay Center last night?"

"No. I turned off my radio this morning after the weather."

"Some kids broke into the grain elevator and pumped the grain out. The DJ said it looked as if it had snowed soybeans. They think they'll be able to recover some of it, but a lot will have to be trashed."

"What in God's green earth has gotten into these kids?" Skye slapped the folder she'd been holding down onto the desk. Now, to go with Scumble River's fire and Brooklyn's flood, Clay Center had gotten famine. Why were the plagues of Egypt being visited upon central Illinois?

"I don't know. But I think we'd better find out." Trixie pulled a clipboard from her tote bag and made a note. "I'll call the other school librarians and see if they've heard anything. Do you know the school psychologist at Brooklyn or Clay Center?"

"Sort of, but it's someone they share from the special ed co-op, so I'm guessing he wouldn't be around enough to be in the loop." Many of the smaller school districts obtained specialist services from a special education cooperative. These included psychologists, social workers, speech pathologists, and occupational therapists, as well as teachers for low-incident disabilities like hearing- and vision-impaired students.

Trixie looked at her watch. "Classes will be out in another minute. Maybe Frannie and Justin and their friends will have some ideas about the recent bizarre events."

The school newspaper staff was meeting in Skye's office to plan the March issue. Luckily, unlike her tiny offices at the elementary school and junior high, her high school office was roomy enough to hold ten people comfortably.

The bell rang, and seconds later kids stared pouring through Skye's door. They all grabbed a folding chair from the stack behind the file cabinets and seated themselves in a semicircle around her desk. Within a few minutes, the teens had their notebooks open and pencils ready.

Skye noticed that Justin wasn't sitting beside either Bitsy or Frannie, and both girls were seated as far from each other as possible. Too bad the road to teen romance was so full of potholes.

Currently they had three boys and five girls on staff. A lot of students had come to one meeting, found out they actually had to write, not just give ideas for others to turn into words, and never returned. Frannie and Justin were co-editors. Skye and Trixie were the faculty sponsors.

Frannie looked over at Justin, then said, "We have a question for you guys."

The "guys"—Skye and Trixie—nodded.

Frannie's smile was mischievous. "Well, if the saying 'quitters never win and winners never quit' is true, which is what Mr. Cramer always tells us, then why does Ms. Cormorant say quit while you're ahead?"

Trixie snickered and started laughing, but Skye sought a serious answer. Finally she offered, "I think it has to do with how you view the world. An optimist would agree with Mr. Cramer's view and a pessimist with Ms. Cormorant's. You can choose which type of person you want to be."

Frannie nodded, clearly surprised by Skye's thoughtful response.

Justin frowned and said, "But isn't your personality something you're born with? Can you really change it?"

"You can change your behavior, which is a big part of your personality. I won't try to con you and tell you it's easy to make that change, but everyone is capable of great good and great evil. Each of us has to decide which path we want to take in life."

Skye looked to see who had understood what she was trying to tell them and who thought she was full of beans. Most heads were nodding, but Justin still appeared skeptical. Now was a good time to segue into the topic she and Trixie had been discussing before the kids arrived. "Speaking of good and bad, Mrs. Frayne and I were wondering if any of you can explain what has been going on around here lately."

A circle of innocent faces looked back at Skye.

"I'm talking about all the trouble the teenagers in the area seem to be getting into recently." She raised an eyebrow and scanned the group, finally saying, "How about you, Bitsy? Anything you can think of that might be behind the recent rash of odd events?" Skye didn't want to be more specific, knowing that sometimes if the questions were vague enough, the person responding would fill in the blanks, and more information would be revealed.

"No, Ms. Denison." Bitsy ducked her head.

After asking a few others, Skye decided to let it go. The kids would probably be more willing to talk alone than in a group.

For the rest of the meeting, Trixie and Skye approved story ideas, helped with the newspaper's layout, and answered questions about how to word sentences. At five o'clock, Trixie announced she had to leave. Everyone gathered up his or her belongings, and Trixie and the teens filed out.

Justin brought up the rear and lingered after the others had left. "Ms. D.?"

"Yes?"

"Uh, if I tell you something, can you keep it between you and me?"

"Yes, unless you tell me something that I think will harm you or someone else," Skye answered carefully, feeling slightly alarmed.

His dark, serious eyes studied her for a long moment before he said, "I'm not sure, but I think some of the stuff that's happening is because all of a sudden there's a lot of crank floating around school."

Skye fought to keep her face expressionless. "Crank, as in methamphetamine?"

"Uh-huh." Justin nodded. "There's always been some around and a few kids using, but now there's a whole shitload."

"Do you know who's selling it?"

"Nah. Everyone knows how I feel about drugs. No one's going to tell me anything." Justin swallowed, his Adam's apple bobbing like a fishing lure. "But if you want, I'll try and ask around. You need to stop it. It's getting pretty bad out there."

"No. Don't ask around." Skye felt sweat start to form on her upper lip. She did not want the boy poking into something that could be extremely dangerous. "I'll look into it. Is it okay if I ask Chief Boyd if he's heard anything?"

Justin paused, considering, then said with reluctance in his voice, "Okay, but don't tell him you got the 411 from me."

"Sounds fair. I'll say I heard the information from a reliable source."

After Justin left, Skye sat for a while and mulled over what she had been told. A sudden rise in teenagers taking meth would certainly explain the recent weird behavior. For instance, if Bitsy had taken the drug before she came to decorate the gym, the exacerbated thought patterns that methamphetamine was known to produce might explain why a dummy lying underneath the stage might make the girl think she was seeing a dead body.

And if Nathan Turner had taken meth while at the dance, his sudden need for a shower could be explained by an increased heartbeat that would make him feel extremely overheated.

Skye shrugged into her coat and locked up. As she walked down the hallway toward the front door, it occurred to her that even the fire might be a result of the drug. Long-term users often became paranoid and had hallucinations. A person like that could easily think he *had* to burn down the school.

Skye drove home, wondering who was selling meth to the students and how she could stop them.

CHAPTER 16

Shake, Rattle, and Roll

Where in the heck was everyone? It was Friday afternoon, and during the twenty minutes Skye'd had free for lunch, she'd tried to phone both Wally and Rod again but ended up leaving them each yet another message to call her. Neither of them had returned her phone call from the night before.

Rod she understood. He probably knew she wanted to talk to him about why he'd sicced the police on Vince. But Wally's silence worried her. He needed to be told about the methamphetamine problem ASAP. Was his mayoral campaign or his ex-wife taking up all of his attention these days?

Speaking of Wally's ex, it was time to shut her up. At this moment they were attending an annual review, and Darleen had already repeated herself four times. The parents of the special ed student under discussion were starting to look annoyed.

Skye cleared her throat and said, "It sounds to me like your son has made good progress this year, but he still needs support and modification with organizational issues."

Darleen shot back, "That's not what I'm recommending. He's not disorganized. He's just lazy. If he would focus and do his homework, he'd be fine."

Skye allowed, "Yes, I understand that, but his parents have told us how difficult the homework is for him and how much time they spend helping him in the evenings, so I don't think it's quite as simple as just plain laziness." She paused, then pointed out, "And he does have auditory processing and visual-motor difficulties, so he does have to work at least twice as hard to produce what other students are able to do in half the time."

Darleen glared at Skye. She opened her mouth, but Skye said quickly, "But this is a team decision, so let's hear what everyone else thinks."

The principal, the boy's parents, and the regular education teacher agreed with Skye and felt he still needed services. As Skye finished up the paperwork, Darleen stalked out of the room without saying another word.

Skye shook her head and continued to write. It had been a busy day. She'd had eighth grade annual reviews scheduled every forty-five minutes, starting at eight-fifteen, and it was now nearly four o'clock. The law required that the school hold a meeting every year for all students receiving special education services. During this gathering, the student's progress was reviewed against the goals set in their Individual Education Plan and a new IEP was written for the next year. Eighth graders had the honor of going first in the process, in order to give the high school extra time to prepare their schedules for the next year.

After handing the parents their copy of the IEP, Skye hurried to her office, grabbed her coat and purse, and rushed to her car. She drove as fast as she could to the police station but when she arrived Wally was already gone for the day and she was forced to leave another message.

While she drove home, she wondered if she should have insisted the dispatcher call Wally back to meet with her. A glance at her watch convinced her she didn't have time for that. Simon was picking her up at five and it was already four-thirty.

A couple minutes later, she pulled into her driveway, ran inside—throwing her coat on the hall bench as she raced into her bedroom—and flung open the closet door.

"So, Bingo, what should I wear?" Skye asked the black cat who was now sitting at her feet.

The feline was staring into the closet's depths with an intensity that suggested he was about to choose an outfit for her.

But the cat didn't answer and she started to push the hangers back and forth. "What hasn't Simon already seen me wear a hundred times? That's the problem with an exclusive relationship; your clothes get old too fast."

Bingo yawned, exhibiting needlelike teeth and a pink tongue. He lifted his back leg and started washing.

"You're right. The benefits far exceed the drawbacks. But that still doesn't give me a clue as to what to put on." She pulled out a velour leopard-print shirt and a pair of black silky pants. "Is this appropriate for a bowling alley grand opening?"

Bingo didn't look up from his bath.

"A lot of help you are." Shoot! It was already quarter to five and Simon hated it when she was late.

There wasn't any more time to second-guess her choice of outfits. She tore off her school clothes and stuck her arm through the sleeve of the blouse.

The doorbell was ringing as she inserted a gold hoop into her ear. She grabbed her shoes and ran to the foyer. After a quick peek through the window, she flung open the front door.

Simon stepped in and whistled. "You look great."

"Thanks. It's really sweet the way you always notice." Skye slipped on black loafers and snatched her coat from the hall bench. "Are you nervous about tonight?"

"No. Why?"

"You're wearing one black shoe and one brown one." They both looked down at his feet.

"Damn. We'll have to stop by my place so I can change." The tips of his ears were red. "Are you ready?"

They drove over to Simon's and he ran inside. Skye waited in the car, using this bonus time to fuss with her hair and touch up her makeup. A few minutes later Simon returned wearing matching shoes and a sheepish grin.

The bowling alley was housed in a brick building close to forty years old. Simon parked his Lexus in the lot on the west side of the entrance.

As they walked to the front Simon pointed upward. "What do you think?" A new sign hung above the door. Previously called the Gold Strike, the alley was now named Bunny Lanes. "Sort of sappy, huh?"

Skye's voice caught in her throat and she couldn't respond right away. Simon's relationship with his mother had come such a long way since November when Bunny had first appeared in Scumble River. Back then he wouldn't even talk to her. But after sharing a harrowing experience where Simon was nearly killed, mother and son had at least partially cleared the air. Still, after twenty years of hurt feelings and misunderstandings, it would take more than a few months to entirely heal the breach.

Skye took Simon's arm and squeezed. "I think it's a great name. Your mom must be thrilled."

"She is happy." Simon pushed open one of the double doors and waited for Skye to enter. "I was surprised at what a hard worker she turned out to be, and she's pretty smart about running a business like this."

It was the first time Skye had seen the alley since it had been remodeled. The change was remarkable. The interior had gone from nineteen-sixties brown and orange to a sleek palette of blues with touches of silver.

"This looks wonderful." Skye turned to Simon and hugged him.

"Thanks." After returning her hug, he helped her out of her coat and hung it and his own on the shiny new coat rack. "My goal was to modernize the place enough to attract new people but not so much that I'd lose the old regulars."

Skye hoped Simon had achieved the correct balance. "It might take some people a while accept the new look." The citizens of Scumble River did not like change. "But I'm sure they'll come around."

Skye and Simon continued farther into the building. The bar area had been expanded and enclosed. Etched glass doors led into the newly created room, which now included a small stage and dance floor.

Bunny was placing bowls of snacks on small metal tables as they entered. She tottered over to them on four-inch heels and flung her arms around Simon. "Sonny. This is going to be such a wonderful night."

"Please don't call me Sonny." Simon's eyes met Skye's over his mother's head.

Skye shrugged. Some things would never change.

Bunny turned to embrace Skye. "What do you think? Son . . . Simon and I make quite a team, don't we?"

Skye was momentarily distracted by the older woman's appearance. Bunny had clearly been ordering from the Frederick's of Hollywood catalog again. Considering Bunny's past as a Las Vegas showgirl, Skye wasn't really surprised. Tonight, Bunny was decked out in a black chiffon blouse—its deep V-neck and the cuffs of the sleeves outlined in marabou—and a long black lace skirt that looked modest until she moved and the front slit opened.

"Amazing," Skye finally managed to choke out before looking at Simon.

He just shook his head.

Skye ran her finger down one of the new chairs. "I really

like these. This blue Ultrasuede fabric is beautiful." It was a big change from the old Formica tables and torn vinyl chairs.

"Look at the grill." Bunny tucked an errant red curl into the cascade of ringlets on top of her head, then took Skye and Simon by the arms and dragged them through another set of glass doors. "We're all set to go."

This area had also received a face-lift. The countertops were now blue faux marble, and the stools were upholstered in a denim fabric with silver studs.

Bunny handed Skye a pristine menu and tapped the laminated cardboard with inch-long crimson nails, saying, "We added a lot of new items."

Skye scanned the columns quickly. There was now a nice variety of food instead of just burgers and pizza. "Who's working the grill?"

"I am." A young woman stepped out from the kitchen.

Simon introduced them. "Skye, this is our grill manager, Ivy Wolfe. Ivy, this is my friend Skye Denison."

The two women exchanged greetings and Ivy said, "I know your brother, Vince. My husband used to sing in a band with him."

Skye asked, "Was your husband Logan Wolfe?"

Ivy nodded.

"I'm so sorry for your loss."

Ivy nodded again. "Thank you."

An awkward silence fell over the group. Skye searched for something more to say, but what was appropriate small talk for such a recent widow? She finally said, "I heard Logan sing on several occasions. He had a great voice."

"He had many talents." A strange look crossed Ivy's face. "Maybe that was his curse." Skye was dying to ask Ivy to explain, but the young woman turned away, saying over her shoulder, "I have to get back to the kitchen."

Skye studied the young widow as she walked away. Both

her hair and eyes were a medium brown. She had on black slacks and a cornflower blue polo shirt with "Bunny Lanes" embroidered above the breast pocket. She didn't look like the type to have been married to a rock star.

Once Ivy was out of earshot Skye said to Simon, "I'm surprised she's working tonight. He died less than a week ago."

"She said she couldn't stand to just sit around an empty house and stare at the walls."

"Where did she work before here?"

"Wal-Mart." Simon frowned. "I almost didn't hire her when she told me she'd been fired but couldn't tell me why. She said all they told her was she had behaved inappropriately and she didn't know what she had done."

"That's an odd reason to give someone for firing them."

"Yes, and they were so evasive when I called to find out why they let her go, I decided to give her a chance."

Skye squeezed his hand. "That was nice of you." Simon was getting as bad as she was about collecting strays and trying to right the wrongs of the world.

Bunny clearly felt she had been left out of the conversation long enough. She took Skye's hand and said, "You've got to see the lanes."

Skye allowed herself to be pulled to the back of the alley, marveling at how fast the redhead could walk on sandals that consisted of nothing more than thin soles and a single strap attached to stiletto heels.

Simon trailed after the two women.

When they arrived at the railing that separated the alleys from the rest of the room, Bunny swept her arm in an expansive gesture. "The lanes have all been refinished, and we have automatic score keepers and new ball returns. Isn't it wonderful?"

Skye hugged the older woman. "It's magnificent." She

turned to Simon. "I really like the new padded benches. Those molded plastic ones were so uncomfortable."

"I remember you mentioning something about that." Simon's grin was warm and sexy. "Maybe we can try them out after we close tonight."

Bunny giggled and Skye felt her face flush.

Simon glanced at his watch and his expression turned serious. "It's already a quarter to six, and we're opening the doors at seven. We'd better get to work."

"I've got to make sure the bartender has the setups ready and finish putting the snacks on the tables." Bunny winked at them. "I ordered the extra salty and spicy kinds so people would get thirsty and order more drinks. That's where the real money is in a place like this."

Simon gave her a level look. "Remember, Mother, we do not serve anyone who has had too much alcohol."

"Sure. Gotcha." Bunny walked off, not at all fazed by his admonishment.

"What do you want me to do?" Skye asked.

"There are balloons and a helium tank in the storeroom. Would you mind filling them?" Simon pointed to the door next to the grill area.

"Sounds like fun." Skye headed in the direction he had indicated.

"After you get them inflated, attach a ribbon to each one, and then tie them all around the rooms."

"Got it."

An hour later Skye had just finished attaching the last balloon to the back of one of the chairs when Bunny hurried past. Skye asked, "Do you know where Simon is?"

"He's behind the lanes showing the machinery to your dad."

"My father's here?"

"Yeah. Your mom's around somewhere, too." Bunny twisted her lips. "I offered her a drink, but she said no."

"Mmm." Skye made a noncommittal noise. May had not hit it off with Bunny when the redhead had first arrived at Scumble River, and clearly the relationship hadn't improved. "It's getting late. I'd better go find Simon and see if there's anything else we need to do."

"If you see your mom, tell her the offer for a drink is still open," Bunny called as Skye walked away. Bunny wanted to be May's pal, but the feeling was far from mutual.

Skye found Simon and her father coming out from behind the alleys. Jed had a streak of grease across his forehead and Simon's hands were black. Both men were smiling.

She hurried over to them and kissed her father's cheek. "Hi, Dad. What are you two up to?"

"Making sure it's all set." Jed was a man of few words.

"Is it?" Skye asked.

"Yep." Jed looked around. "Where's your ma?"

"I suspect she's hiding from Bunny." Skye gestured toward the entrance area. "Try by the lockers."

Jed nodded and moseyed away.

"Did the band show up yet?" Simon asked.

"Yes." Skye nodded. "I saw them come in a while ago."

"Good. Let's get everyone together for a toast before we open."

They gathered all the helpers in the bar, but as Bunny passed out glasses of champagne Skye noticed that Ivy Wolfe wasn't present. She was probably still trying to get the kitchen ready for action.

Simon raised his glass. "I want to thank everyone for their help. Jed, I appreciate all the time you spent fixing all the odds and ends. May, I'll bet that's the cleanest the windows have ever been. And, Mother, you amazed me with your organizational skills."

"Thanks." Bunny fluffed her hair. "Too bad that now I've finally gotten my head together, my body's falling apart."

"Then you must be using some terrific glue," the bartender interjected, "because it looks pretty darn good to me."

After the laughter died down, Simon continued, "Skye, well, what can I say. You kept me going when I thought the project would never get done. Here's to you all."

Everyone drank.

He added, "And to a successful grand opening."

Even though she realized this wasn't *Fantasy Island*, Skye was a little disappointed that Simon didn't say, "Places, everyone."

Bunny led the way to the front doors and Simon and Skye followed. Bunny looked at Simon, who nodded, then reached over and turned the key. She flung the doors wide, and people started streaming in.

Two hours later, Skye looked around smiling. There were at least three hundred people crowded into the various areas of the bowling alley. All twenty-five lanes were occupied, the stools in the grill were full, as were the tables in the bar, and small groups stood everywhere. The only noticeable absentees were Trixie and her husband. Skye was sad to see them missing out on this good time, but she understood they probably weren't in the mood to socialize.

Simon and Bunny had hardly been able to move all evening as wave after wave of people surrounded them, asking questions and offering congratulations. Bunny glowed under all the attention, but Simon looked like he could use a break. Skye had just started over to him when a commotion by the bar entrance drew her attention. She quickly changed course and hurried over there instead. What was going on?

As she neared the bar, she could see half a dozen teenagers squared off against several adult men in front of the glass doors. Skye groaned. This couldn't be good.

She groaned again when she spotted Arlen Yoder. First

the false fire alarm, now this. What had gotten into that young man? She sure hoped it wasn't methamphetamine.

Skye knew all the kids present from previous dealings with them at school and in the community. They weren't bad, just impulsive, and not too bright, or as her grandmother used to say, "all wax and no wick." Unfortunately, the combination of recklessness and foolishness made it easy to steer them astray.

At the end of September, their leader had been removed from the high school, and Skye had thought she had gotten the rest of the group on the straight and narrow, but it looked as if they had drifted from the path once again.

Skye watched in alarm as the smallest of the teens drew himself into a boxing position and hollered, "Get your dukes up. I can whup all of you."

The men looked bewildered, glancing at each other to see if anyone else would make a move, clearly not knowing what to do. The boy wasn't even five feet tall and didn't weigh a hundred pounds. Thank goodness no one seemed willing to be the first to beat up a munchkin.

Skye pushed her way to the front of the crowd and yelled, "Elvis Doozier, you stop that right now and get over here." She had dealt with most of the Doozier clan in the years she had been the Scumble River school psychologist, and poor Elvis wasn't even the sharpest thorn on a family tree full of stunted branches. Although he was nearly sixteen, physically he resembled a twelve-year-old and mentally he functioned a year or so below that.

Elvis's quick glance at Skye indicated no recognition, which was strange, and he continued to try to punch the man blocking the door to the bar. "Get outta the way. Me and my buddies come to hear the music, and nobody's gonna stop us."

Usually he responded to Skye's directions, and she was

concerned by how overly agitated he appeared to be. She tried to step closer but several hands held her back.

"What's the matter with you?" One of the men Elvis was confronting thumped a sign to the right of the entrance with the back of his hand. "It says no one under eighteen admitted. Can't you read? Are you some kind of dummy?"

Elvis took a wild swing and missed. His face was red and his eyes were glassy. "Who you callin' a dummy? I ain't no retard."

Skye frantically searched for something to say or do before one of the kids got hurt or hurt someone else. Maybe one of the other teens would listen to reason. She raised her voice above the noise and shouted, "Arlen Yoder, make Elvis stop." Arlen still owed her for getting him off the hook for pulling the fire alarm.

Arlen was another kid who wasn't the sharpest pencil in the cup, but generally he respected adults and did as he was told. Tonight he wasn't listening either.

What was up with these kids? Were they high on meth? Skye had no idea what to do next. Although she knew the other teens, they were even less likely than Elvis and Arlen to do as she asked. Things were turning ugly fast. She had no choice. She had to call the police.

The kids were crowding the bar door, and several more men had joined those defending the entrance. Both groups were shoving and pushing. In a few seconds a punch would connect or a knife would appear in someone's hand, and that would be it. Once violence erupted there would be no going back.

Skye had turned to go for a telephone when without warning all the lights went out. The music died, the mechanical sounds of the lanes ceased, and there was a moment of complete silence before everyone started talking at once. Just as abruptly a dazzling beam of light appeared between the teens and the men.

Skye took advantage of the situation by moving through the crowd, hauling Elvis to her side, and whispering furiously into his ear, "Do you want me to call your brother Earl and have him come down here, or will you leave on your own?"

He tried to wiggle out of her grasp, but she had several inches and more than a few pounds on him. He wasn't getting away that easily.

Finally, he focused on her face. "Aw, Miz D., we were just havin' some fun. No need to go ape-shit."

Skye tightened her grip, prepared to drag him out of the building if she had to, when a voice behind the high-powered flashlight spoke. It was Bunny, and she sounded seriously ticked off. "What's the problem here?"

One man managed to be heard through the babble. "These kids were trying to go into the bar, and we pointed out they weren't allowed."

Bunny aimed the beam of light at the teens. "Is that what happened?"

One of them whined, "That's bogus. We just wanted to hear the band."

"Sorry, boys. We can't take a chance with our liquor license."

Angry teen voices rose in protest and Bunny directed the light into their eyes. They squinted and put up their arms up against the glare.

Bunny moved past the teenagers, leaned casually against the bar door, and said, "Here are your choices. Come with me, sit at the grill where you can hear the music and I'll treat you to free sodas and French fries, or continue to try and push your way past all these men." She paused dramatically before continuing. "Of course, I should probably mention that I called the police just before the lights went out. They'll be arriving any second."

The sound of sirens getting closer bore out her statement.

"What's it going to be, boys? Me or the cops?" The kids muttered but followed Bunny to the grill.

Unwilling to let Elvis go, Skye trailed the older woman and the rest of the teenagers.

Bunny turned to Skye. "Keep an eye on our guests while I turn the lights back on and talk to the police."

Skye nodded mutely. She had never seen Bunny so together and in charge. The redhead must have learned crowd control when she worked the Las Vegas casinos.

The lights went on within moments of Bunny's departure. Next the music started back up and within seconds, it was as if there had never been a problem.

After supplying the kids with sodas and asking Ivy to give them each a basket of fries, Skye went down the line trying to find out what had stirred the teens up, but no one was keen on chatting.

When Simon finally arrived in the grill area, Skye pulled him to the side and demanded, "Where were you?"

His hair stood on end, his shirttail was hanging out of his pants, and he was sweating. "I was in the bathroom."

"Did you get locked in or something?"

"Something. Nate Turner was in there too, and when the lights went out he completely lost control."

"How?" Skye knew Nate Turner, an obnoxious, pushy, Neanderthal whose son Nathan was the boy who had decided to take a shower during the dance. She couldn't imagine Nate being afraid of the dark. "What do you mean?"

"Turns out he has a phobia about the dark."

"You're kidding." Skye was amazed. Who would have thought that someone as pugnacious as Nate Turner would be afraid of anything, let alone something as harmless as the dark?

"I wish I were." Simon smoothed down his hair. "As soon as the lights went out he grabbed me and said he couldn't breathe and was having a heart attack."

"What did you do?"

"Well, he's too big for me to carry so I had him lie down on the floor. I kept trying to go for help, but every time I'd go to stand up, he'd grab my arm."

"So what happened?"

"I had just found my cell phone and was getting ready to call 911 when the lights came back on." Simon retucked his shirt. "Turner jumped up as if the floor was electrified, pushed me out of the way, and raced out the door."

"He is certainly an odd duck." Skye gestured with her thumb at the kids sitting at the counter. "Then you missed the whole hullabaloo with the teenagers?"

"Right. I ran into Bunny as I was coming out of the bathroom and she told me about the problem." Simon frowned. "I didn't think of it before, but I guess I should hire someone to work security."

"Might be a good idea." Skye took his arm and squeezed. "But Bunny was amazing."

"She has a lot of hidden talents." Simon's expression was inscrutable.

Skye tipped her head. "I just noticed. The music's stopped again. They're probably just taking a break, but maybe we should check and make sure everything's okay."

"I suppose we'd better." Simon put his hand on the small of her back and guided her toward the door to the basement. They climbed down the concrete steps. "I told Vince and his group that they could use one of the rooms in the basement. If they're on break, they're most likely down here."

Simon and Skye found the band members sprawled on chairs guzzling the beverages of their choice from a cooler of beer and sodas.

"Everything okay?" Simon asked.

Two voices answered variations of yes, but Rod said, "Any chance of some food?"

"There was supposed to be a tray of sandwiches and

chips down here." Simon turned to Skye. "Ivy must have forgotten with all the commotion. I'll be right back."

After Simon left, Skye sat next to her brother. "How's it going?"

"Good." Vince stretched and yawned.

"Heather's really a good vocalist." Skye shot a glance at the girl singer, who sat a little apart, filing her nails. "How's that arrangement working out?"

"Okay." Vince scratched his head. "It's funny, but now that she's singing with us she's stopped trying to get us all to . . . uh, you know, uh . . ."

"Sleep with her?"

"Yeah."

"So, did you ever think maybe she only wanted to boink you guys so you'd let her in the band?" Skye rolled her eyes. Men could be so dense.

"Yeah, but . . ."

"But what?"

Vince smiled. "But Macho Law prohibits me from admitting I might have been used."

Skye socked him in the shoulder and then looked up when she heard a voice saying, "Hi, guys. Sorry I forgot your snacks."

Ivy Logan was picking her way carefully down the stairs, carrying a huge serving dish of sandwiches and chips. As she reached the bottom, she glanced up and caught sight of Heather. Brown eyes locked with blue, and everyone held their breath.

Ivy broke off the stare-down, turned to the men, and her voice dripping acid, asked, "What is she doing here?"

Clearly, she had not been at Wally's campaign rally, and no one had told her that Heather had joined Pink Elephant.

When they didn't answer her, she repeated her question.

Vince, his face a dull red, mumbled, "Singing with the band."

Ivy flung the tray at Vince's head and lunged at the younger woman, screaming, "You bitch! You killed my husband!"

Heather tried to evade the enraged woman, but Ivy landed squarely on Heather. For a second it looked as if Ivy was giving Heather a lap dance, but then the chair toppled backward and both women landed on the floor.

Ivy grabbed Heather's ears and started banging the singer's head against the concrete. Skye glanced at the men, who weren't moving. She blew out an exasperated breath and waded into the fray. She was getting really tired of breaking up fights.

Skye wrapped her arms around Ivy's waist and tugged. At first it didn't seem as if Skye could peel Ivy off Heather, but suddenly the two combatants popped apart, sending Skye and Ivy into an ungraceful heap.

Heather scuttled up the stairs. They heard voices, and a moment later May appeared at the bottom of the steps. She took one look at Skye sprawled on the floor beneath Ivy, and Vince still wearing the contents of the sandwich tray and screamed.

CHAPTER 17

Beat It

"Vince is fine, Mom." Skye wedged the receiver between her shoulder and ear and continued to sort laundry into piles.

"He needs to go to the doctor." May was warming up to the subject like a batter taking a practice swing. "This is the second time he got hit on the head in a week."

Actually it was the third, but Skye had no intention of correcting her mother, who didn't know about the incident at the school dance. "You saw him playing drums last night *after* it happened. He was fine. The tray only glanced off his forehead."

Skye smothered a giggle. Not that she didn't feel sorry for Vince, but he had looked so funny covered in ham and cheese, with a ring of raw onion hanging from his ear and a tomato slice pasted to his cheek. All he needed was a pineapple hat and he could have doubled for the Chiquita banana lady on the old TV commercial.

"He'd play even if he had a concussion. I went through two handkerchiefs and half a box of Kleenex before that cut on his temple stopped bleeding."

"Vince is fine," Skye repeated. "Even superficial head wounds bleed a lot."

"My hankies are ruined."

Skye saw a chance to divert her mother, especially since they had been over this ground at least five times already—three times at the bowling alley last night and twice this morning. This was May's second call. "Maybe not. I found this new detergent that works really well on blood."

"How do you know it works so good on blood?"

Skye opened her mouth to remind her mother that she had a chance every month to test it out but decided she didn't want to go down that road. Knowing May, they'd somehow end up talking about when Skye would get married and start having children. Instead, she said, "I saw it on TV. Want me to drop some off at your house when I run my errands this afternoon?"

"Don't bother. I'll use good old Clorox. I don't need any of that fancy stuff. What else are you doing today?" May liked to know where her baby chicks were at all times.

"Laundry and housecleaning this morning, then the bank, and groceries after that."

"Are you seeing Simon tonight?"

"He's helping Bunny at the bowling alley this weekend. I might stop by and say hi if I get bored." Skye added a pair of gray slacks to the dark pile.

"You know there'll be a lot of women hanging around that bowling alley. You'd better be there, too. You've got to protect your property."

"Sure, Mom. Good idea." May's 1950s way of looking at male-female relationships continued to amaze Skye, but she had figured out it was best to agree with her mother and then quietly do what she wanted. "Hey, the dryer just stopped. I've got to go before those clothes get wrinkled." Another lesson Skye had learned was that a foolproof way to get off the phone with her mother was to have a domestic emergency. May would never stand in the way of good housekeeping.

It was past one-forty-five by the time Skye finished cleaning and looked at the clock. Shoot! She was down to her last couple of dollars and needed to get some cash. Thank goodness the bank had extended their Saturday hours and was open until two, but she'd have to hurry. Too bad the only ATM machine in town was still out of order.

She washed her face and brushed her hair back into a ponytail but didn't have time to shower or change from her jeans and orange University of Illinois sweatshirt. Maybe she'd get lucky and be able to run in and out without seeing anyone she knew—except, of course, there was no avoiding her cousins, who worked as tellers.

Fifteen minutes later, Skye walked out of the bank tucking her wallet back into her purse. Her plan was to go home, clean up, and then come back uptown to do the grocery shopping. But as she opened her car door, she realized that she still hadn't talked to Wally about the possible drug problem in Scumble River.

How could she have forgotten, especially after the altercation with those kids last night? And then there was Ivy Wolfe's declaration that Heather had killed Logan. Wally needed to know about that, too. She had called him first thing that morning and left another message, but after that May had distracted her, and he had never called back.

Skye told herself another hour wouldn't make any difference, and she really needed a shower before she was fit for polite company, but as she turned the key in the Bel Air she caught sight of the time—two-fifteen. Wally only worked until three, and lately he wasn't hanging around even a minute after his shift ended. She would miss him again if she didn't go over there right now. She really hated appearing in public like a slob, but there seemed to be no choice.

The police station parking lot held three cars—the dispatcher's dented Chevy Cavalier, the librarian's Gremlin, and a brand-new, shiny red, two-seater BMW. Skye parked her Bel Air as far from the expensive car as possible. The last thing she wanted was to accidentally ding it with her door or scrape it when she backed up. Her insurance was high enough already. As she walked into the building, she wondered who owned the forty-thousand-dollar vehicle.

After being buzzed in and exchanging greetings with the dispatcher, Skye asked, "Is Wally here? I've been trying to get a hold of him since Thursday night, and I really need to talk to him."

Before the woman could answer, the inner door banged open and Darleen burst through, yelling, "Why did you let her in? I told you she was not to be allowed back here anymore."

Skye gaped at her, speechless.

"Get out," Darleen sputtered. "Haven't you done enough harm? Get out and don't come back."

The dispatcher scuttled from the room, throwing an apologetic look at Skye before slipping out the door.

"What are you talking about? Have you gone crazy?" Skye had finally recovered from her shock. "I have official business to discuss with Chief Boyd."

"I don't know what he sees in you." Darleen scanned Skye up and down, then rejected her with the flick of an artificial eyelash. "You're a fat slob and you don't even bother to fix yourself up and try to look attractive."

"My appearance isn't any of your business," Skye snapped. "In fact, my presence here is none of your business either." She tried to push past Darleen, but the other woman planted herself squarely in the doorway.

"I told Walter when he decided to run for mayor that you were a liability he couldn't afford, and I've tried to protect him from your interference with his cases, but this is the last straw." Without taking her eyes from Skye, she fumbled in the pocket of her dress, pulled out a crumpled newspaper page, and thrust it into Skye's hand. "Read it."

Skye scanned the sheet as quickly as she could. It was a page from the *Star*, Scumble River's weekly newspaper, which came out on Saturday. It had a story hyping Skye's involvement in solving local murders the last few years and recapping the article it had run when she solved the Addison case last fall.

For a minute, Skye wondered why she hadn't received any calls about the article, but then realized most Scumble Riverites bought the paper when they did their Saturday grocery shopping and didn't read it until they sat down to relax after supper.

One mystery solved, Skye asked about the other. "Why is this so awful? I would rather have kept out of the spotlight, but it's not as if everyone in town didn't already know."

"Are you dense?" Darleen's bulging eyes nearly popped from their sockets. "Ace Cramer is going to use this to smear Wally and ruin his chance of being elected mayor."

Skye felt a twinge of guilt but wasn't going to let Darleen see it. "Then why didn't Wally call me and talk to me about it?"

Clearly, Darleen didn't have a ready answer for that question, but with a quick, dismissive emphasis she finally said, "He's having a *tiny* crisis of faith—doesn't know if he really wants to be the mayor or not, but he'll come around. I'll see to it that he does."

"Maybe you will, or maybe he's figured out that the trouble with being in the rat race is that even if you win, you're still a rat." Skye narrowed her eyes. "Anyway, why do you care so much whether Wally is elected mayor or not?"

"Because I was born to be Mrs. Mayor. The power behind the throne." Darleen's smile was like a straight razor. "I have plans for this town. Did you see my new car? That's the life I deserve."

So that's who the Beamer belonged to. "But you divorced him," Skye reminded her. "You won't be Mrs. Mayor."

"You interfering, home-wrecking, arrogant bitch!" Darleen exploded. "Don't think for a minute that you're going to stand in the way of anything that's mine."

Skye was shocked by Darleen's venom. The woman had left Wally to search for motherhood and greener pastures. Darleen had no right to be bitter about the divorce.

The next thing that popped out of Skye's mouth was beyond her control or common sense, maybe both. "But that's the point. He isn't yours, and even if he is elected mayor, the power of that position wouldn't be yours either."

Darleen leaned close to Skye, spittle flying, and let loose with a string of curses that would make a rap singer blush. Abruptly the older woman sputtered to a stop.

Skye had immediately jumped backward when the saliva had started to spray; now she grabbed a tissue from the desk and wiped her face. She'd had enough. Time to stop being Miss Nice Guy. "Anything else you want to get off your little itty bitty chest, Darleen?"

The other woman's mouth opened and closed, but nothing came out.

"Darleen." Skye patted her on the arm. "Try not to let your mind wander. It's too small and fragile to be out by itself."

Darleen's mouth snapped shut so fast Skye was sure she heard a filling crack. The other woman's face was an unhealthy scarlet and her hands were curled into claws.

Skye knew when to hold 'em and when to fold 'em, and this was the latter. She looked at her watch and said, "Oops. Got to run. Time flies when you're driving someone crazy. See you at school Monday."

Darleen must have finally regained the power of speech because her voice floated after Skye as she hurried out of the station. "Maybe Wally hasn't been returning your phone calls because your brother is one of his main suspects in Logan Wolfe's murder, and it's a conflict of interest."

It wasn't until Skye tried to put the key into the Bel Air's ignition that she noticed how badly her hands were shaking and that her breathing was out of control. So it was true; Wally did suspect Vince. May was right. Which meant Skye had better get busy and find out who had really killed Logan Wolfe.

She was nearly home when she realized that once again, she had not talked to Wally. This was getting ridiculous. Should she go back to the P.D. and try again? No, with Darleen skulking around, that probably wasn't a good idea. Well, she couldn't let a jealous, power-hungry, ex-wife get in her way. There was too much at stake between the alleged drugs floating around Scumble River and Vince's neck on the line for Logan's murder.

She'd keep trying to get through to Wally by phone and maybe her mother could slip him a message, although May rarely saw him as he worked days and she usually worked afternoons. In the meantime, Skye knew just what she had to do.

Ivy had accused Heather of killing Logan. If she had any proof to back up her allegation, Skye wanted to know what it was.

On the one hand, Skye knew she should tell Wally about Ivy's accusation and let him question her first. On the other hand, she had left him a phone message and tried to report to him in person; there wasn't much else she could do. Besides, she had to act in Vince's best interest, not Wally's.

Bunny had mentioned that Ivy would be working the evening shift at the bowling alley—six-thirty to two-thirty—which meant she would probably be home and getting ready for work about an hour or so before then.

With that in mind, Skye took the time to return to her cottage, shower, and change her clothes before setting out to talk to the widow. At four-thirty she pulled out of her driveway and headed toward her parents' road.

According to Charlie, Logan lived on forty acres located between her family's property and Trixie's. If the Wolfes had their name on their mailbox, their house should be relatively easy to find—and if worst came to worst, she could stop and ask Trixie for directions or call her mother at the P.D.

Skye passed her folks' house, then her Uncle Dante's on the right. A quarter mile farther on stood a dark, deserted farmhouse. Skye felt the same catch in her throat she experienced every time she saw it. It had belonged to her Aunt Mona and Uncle Neal, but after her aunt's death, her uncle had shut down the house, moved out of state, and sold the land back to the family trust.

A lot had changed the past few years. Her grandmother's old house, which should be next on the road, had been torn down after her death. The land was worth more than the building, and there was no trace of the farmhouse now. All that was left was a field covered in snow, with an occasional cornstalk sticking up like a headstone in a graveyard.

Skye took a deep breath and concentrated on the present. She had come up on Hines Road, and if Charlie was correct, she needed to go north. The Wolfes' driveway should be on her left as soon as she passed the turn for Scumble River Road, and there it was, a dented mailbox with WOLFE painted in white. The house itself was invisible from the road, but a rutted lane disappeared into the trees.

Skye maneuvered the Bel Air down the long driveway. Her headlights were the only illumination in the darkness created by the canopy of evergreen trees that lined the path. Suddenly the road ended and a house appeared out of nowhere, almost as if she had opened a children's pop-up book.

Tarpaper patches punctuated the brown asphalt siding,

and the porch was propped up by two-by-fours cemented into rusty coffee cans. An equally decrepit garage stood off to the side. In contrast, a brand-new machine shed sat slightly behind the house, its bright silver paint shiny and unblemished.

Skye parked to the side and got out. At the sound of the car door, a large gray dog raced around the side of the house, baring its teeth and growling.

She froze. It was too late to attempt to get back into the Bel Air, and the dog stood between her and the house. The animal stopped a few feet from Skye but kept barking and growling.

Skye tried frantically to come up with a plan, but her brain seemed to have turned off. The dog edged closer. A scream halted in her throat when she heard the squeak of hinges and the house's front door swung open. Thank God, someone had come to help her.

She turned her head slightly and opened her mouth to thank her rescuer, but the words froze in her throat when she saw that the figure on the porch was holding a shotgun, and it wasn't pointed at the dog.

CHAPTER 18

Superstar

The person on the porch moved out of the shadows and Skye recognized Rod Yager. So this was where he had been hiding out. What was he doing at Ivy's, and more importantly, why was he pointing a gun at Skye?

Skye ran her tongue over her lips, already chapping from the cold and the wind. She tried to swallow, but her mouth was too dry. Her voice cracked like a dead tree branch, and her words came out all in a rush. "Rod. It's me. Skye Denison. Vince's sister."

He eyed the length of the lane behind her. "What do you want?"

The dog had continued to creep closer and now was within a few inches of her. She was aware of its hot breath on her ankles through her socks. Skye sidled back until she could feel the car's door handle pressed into her hip. "The dog, could you please call him off?"

Rod ordered, "Fluffy, down."

The canine immediately went into a half-sitting, half-crouching position.

She eyed the snarling dog. *Fluffy? Talk about false advertising.*

"Come up on the porch, but move forward slowly," Rod directed her. "He won't hurt you unless he's told to."

Skye obeyed. "I came to talk to Ivy. Is she around?"

"Inside."

She hesitated, not sure if Rod was giving her another command or answering her question, and since he still hadn't lowered his gun, she was loath to make a mistake. "Uh, you want me to go inside, or Ivy is inside?"

"Both."

It appeared that Rod was not much of a conversationalist.

"Could you put down the gun?" Skye pleaded as she entered the house. "It makes me really nervous." The front door opened directly into the living room.

For a long moment he studied her, then lowered the weapon and yelled, "Ivy, company." Turning back to Skye, he motioned her to sit on the sofa. He slotted the gun into a rack by the door and said, "Ivy's had some problems with those survivalists from that camp a couple miles over."

With his explanation, Skye's heart finally started to beat in its natural rhythm again. "We've had trouble with them, too. They don't seem to think anything about trespassing and poaching on other people's property. They used to drive my grandma nuts." The survivalists' camp shared a property line with her family's back forty.

Rod nodded.

"It about drove Logan crazy, too," Ivy said. She had entered while Skye and Rod were talking. She was tucking her Bunny Lanes polo shirt into black jeans. "But you didn't come out here to talk about that, did you?"

"Not exactly." Skye tried to gather her thoughts by glancing around the room. The furniture all looked new. So new that she spotted a tag still attached to the leather easy chair Ivy sank into. It made an odd contrast to the thirty-year-old rust and brown shag carpeting on the floor and the peeling paint on the wall.

Ivy shifted impatiently, making Skye aware that she needed to say something soon. "Actually, I was just wondering when the services for Logan would be."

"As soon as the police let me, I'm having him cremated." Ivy scowled. "He didn't have many friends in this town. People around here didn't like how he lived his life and were jealous of his talent. No use having a big wake or funeral. Not many would show up, and the ones who did would be hypocrites."

Skye had noticed the lack of grief among the Scumble Riverites but figured there would be someone mourning Logan. "How about his family and the band?"

Ivy shrugged. "Maybe I'll have a memorial service in the spring." Her voice thickened. "He hated the cold." She stared into space for a minute, then pinned Skye with an angry glare. "Anyway, I don't believe for a minute that's why you came out here. What do you really want?"

Skye decided to go with the truth. "You're right. I came to see if you really meant what you said last night." She'd already had a dog at her throat and a gun held to her head; how much worse could it get? "Do you really think Heather killed Logan?"

"She killed him, all right." Ivy shot up from her seat and waved her finger at Skye. "That bitch knew the only way she could sing with the band was to get rid of him."

"It seems a little unbelievable that someone would kill to join a small-time rock band," Skye said.

"But Pink Elephant was close to getting their big break." Ivy's eyes shone with the thought. "Real, real close."

Skye fought to hide her skepticism. "Something like that is pretty hard to predict, isn't it?"

Ivy hurried over to an old, battered desk that was tucked into the corner of the living room. She moved a vinyl and chrome kitchen chair from in front of it, pulled open the middle drawer, and stuck her hand inside. Snatching a couple of envelopes, she rushed back to Skye and thrust them at her. "Look at these. One is from a record producer and the other is from that new TV talent show *American Star*. Both of them want Pink Elephant to audition."

Skye opened the first one and started to read. She became instantly wary and hurriedly scanned the other letter. It was the same. They wanted Logan alone. In order to make the deal, Logan would have to dump Pink Elephant. Which meant, if the group knew about these offers, the other three musicians, including Vince, had a reason to hate Logan. She turned to Rod and asked, "Have you read these?"

He shrugged. "No, I'm not much of a reader, but Logan told me about them. He told all of us about a month ago. We've been getting ready for the auditions ever since—extra rehearsals, Vince and Finn writing new songs, the whole nine yards."

It was clear why Logan hadn't told the band the auditions were for him as a solo act. If he had, he wouldn't have had anyone to help him get ready for his big break. He needed the other band members to help him rehearse and write new material.

Skye wondered if Ivy was in on the scam, but no, she wouldn't have shown the letters to Skye if she had been. "Did you read these, Ivy?"

"Not word for word." She flipped her hand back and forth in a sort of gesture. "But Logan read them to me when he first got them. Why?"

Skye hedged. "Just wondering if you, uh, had, uh, talked about the details." If Ivy didn't know, Skye wasn't about to reveal the real contents of the letters to her. No reason to let her in on the fact that the other members of Pink Elephant had a motive to kill her husband—especially when one of those people was Skye's brother.

"Not much." Ivy took the envelopes from Skye and stuffed them back in the desk drawer. "All Logan could talk about was that this could be his big break. His chance to be a star."

Skye thought quickly. She wanted to get Ivy and Rod's minds off those letters. What could she say? When in doubt, attack. "So, you're trying to tell me the only reason you accused Heather was because you think she wanted Logan's place in the band?"

"I'm not *trying* to tell you anything." Ivy flopped back down in the recliner. "That is the reason she killed him."

"Maybe, or maybe you accused her because she was sleeping with Logan, and you want her punished."

There was dead silence for close to sixty seconds, then Ivy brayed with laughter. "Honey, if it weren't for the fact that Logan was my only chance to get rich, I would've divorced that no good son of a tomcat years ago. But he was finally about to hit the big time and make some real money. He could screw the entire female population of Illinois. Heck, he could sleep with the guys, too, for all I cared. There was no way I was getting off the gravy train. At least not until I had a real good ride."

Skye felt her mouth drop open.

"Logan was a child cleverly disguised as a responsible adult," Ivy said, continuing to laugh. "Heather wasn't the first slut he slept with, and she wouldn't have been the last."

"So, your marriage wasn't a good one?"

"You aren't too swift on the uptake, are you?" Ivy snorted in exasperation. "Guys are all the same. Do you know what you call a handcuffed man?"

Skye shook her head, feeling like she had been swept up in a tornado and was being whipped across the fields with no way to get her bearings.

"Trustworthy." Ivy laughed at her own joke.

Skye looked at Rod, who didn't seem all that amused. She asked him, "Do you think Heather killed Logan for a place with the band?"

"Nah." His jaw jutted out belligerently. "She's barking up the wrong bimbo." He jerked his head in Ivy's direction. "It was one of those Pig-In-A-Poke people."

"Why?"

"They've been out here on and off the past month, trying to get Logan and Ivy to sell their land to them."

"Before last Sunday?" Skye asked. Why had they approached the Wolfes before the rest of the landowners?

Rod looked over at Ivy, who nodded and said, "Yeah, they first came by right after Martin Luther King's Birthday."

"And you and Logan weren't interested in selling?"

"No way!" Ivy wore an expression of righteous indignation. "We got to protect our farmland. What's everybody going to eat if we cement over all the fields?"

Skye tried to make sense out of what she was hearing. Ivy wanted money bad enough to stay with a philandering husband but not bad enough to sell her farmland. What was wrong with this picture?

She turned back to Rod, who still stood by the gun rack. "So you think Moss Gibson killed Logan?"

"Maybe. Or it could be one of the pro–Pig-In-A-Poke people from town."

"Like who?" Skye wondered if he was just trying to distract her from looking at Ivy, or even him, as possible murderers.

"There's quite a few people who stand to gain a lot financially if that amusement park gets built, not to mention those who want to sell their land and won't be able to if everyone else doesn't go along."

"Name names." Skye frowned, tired of Rod's innuendos. "Who in town gains, money-wise?"

Rod hesitated, then blurted out, "Nate Turner, for one. I heard that Gibson promised him the landscaping contract for Pig-In-A-Poke."

"If that's true, something like that would be worth hundreds of thousands of dollars," Skye murmured half to herself. "Who else?"

"The guy who bought the Brown Bag Liquor Store. What's his name? Jess Larson," Rod declared. "Gibson has said that Pig-In-A-Poke won't sell booze, but that doesn't mean people either going into the park or coming out won't want a drink."

"Even if they did sell alcohol at the amusement park or at least in the restaurant and hotel, Larson would stand to make a lot of money from people who would stop at his place, thinking that the alcohol would be cheaper there."

Rod had named only two of the town's businessmen who would gain from Gibson's plan. If she thought about it for a while, Skye was sure she could add to the list. Then there were the people who owned the land Gibson wanted to buy. There might be a few pros in that group, too.

"I see what you mean." Skye had found herself nodding, going along with Rod's logic until it suddenly hit her that if Logan was killed because he was standing in the way of Pig-In-A-Poke, her family would have to be next on the list because they weren't selling either. She shook her head. "Sorry, Rod, your theory doesn't really work. Why kill Logan? It's not as if he were the last one standing in the way of the amusement park."

Rod shrugged. "Maybe he is, and we just don't know that everyone else has agreed."

Skye started to say her family wasn't selling but then thought better of it. Why put them in danger if there was even a tiny chance someone had gone crazy and was killing off anti–Pig-In-A-Poke people? "I suppose anything is possible."

"Hey, I got to finish getting ready for work." Ivy walked over to the door and stood there, her hand on the knob, making it obvious that Skye's visit was over.

"Well, thanks." Skye stuck out her hand, which Ivy ignored. "It was nice of you to talk to me."

"Your boyfriend's my boss, and I want to keep my job. Did I have a choice?"

As Skye stepped outside, she remembered about the dog, but Ivy and Rod had already closed the door behind her. She looked from side to side. No sign of the animal. She should get straight into her car and drive away, but she wanted a peek in the machine shed. Its newness bothered her.

Skye cautiously climbed down the steps, glancing back at the house. The shades on the windows were down and no one seemed to be looking out. What could she say if they caught her snooping? 'Hi, I was looking for a place to pee' just didn't seem sincere.

She backed toward the shed, keeping an eye out for the dog. As she neared the building, she saw that there were no windows. She went around the corner and tried the door. It was locked. She bent over and yanked on the handle of the big garage-type door, but it wouldn't budge either. Shoot!

As she made her way back to her car, she thought that it was odd that the shed's doors didn't face the driveway.

Skye paused as she passed the garage. *It* had windows. On impulse she looked inside. A sleek, black Jaguar was parked beside a rundown white Dodge Dynasty. A bumper sticker on the Jag read: JESUS MAY LOVE YOU, BUT EVERYONE ELSE THINKS YOU'RE AN ASSHOLE.

Funny, Skye couldn't recall ever seeing that car around town, and with that horrible saying on its rear end, she would have remembered it. How could the Wolfes afford a car like that? Or was it Rod Yager's? Wally had said Rod didn't have a job. So, how *did* he support himself?

CHAPTER 19

Who's Sorry Now?

Skye shot up into a sitting position, shoved the hair out of her eyes, and looked around wildly. What was that noise? Who had turned on the television? Her heart raced. Had someone broken into her cottage? But why would they turn the TV on? Her glance fell on the coffee table, and she sagged back on the sofa.

Bingo was crouched on the tabletop playing with the remote control. He must have pressed the power button when he was batting it around. Either that or the feline was a secret Home Shopping Network fan. Come to think of it, that would explain why her Visa bill was always so high, and he did seem to be watching the hostess demonstrate the newest in kitchenware with an acquisitive interest.

She extracted the remote from between his paws and said, "We've got enough pans, especially since neither of us does much cooking."

What time was it? She squinted at her watch. Five a.m. Her late night Friday and all of the excitement on Saturday had caught up with her. She must have fallen asleep the minute she got home from talking to Ivy and slept on the couch all night—nearly eleven hours.

She stretched and yawned. Might as well shower and go

to early Mass. Afterward, she really did have to talk to Wally, Darleen or no Darleen. Vince and Heather were also on her to-talk-to list.

When Skye walked into church, she was surprised to see Simon there. The bowling alley was open until two a.m., so he couldn't have gotten to bed much before three.

She slid in next to him and whispered, "Good morning. How did things go last night?"

"Good." He gave her a quick hug and a kiss on the cheek. "Nice crowd and no one got rowdy."

"How's your mom managing?"

"Like she was born to run a bowling alley." Simon rubbed his hand across his eyes. "Which is a good thing, because the hours are too much for me. After today, she's on her own."

"Did you find someone to work security?" Skye didn't like the idea of Bunny not having any backup.

"He starts Tuesday." The bowling alley was closed on Mondays.

The beginning of the processional stopped their conversation, and it wasn't until after the service when they were walking out to the parking lot that Simon asked, "What are your plans for today?"

Skye filled him in on her strange encounters of the weird kind the day before, then explained, "So, I want to tell Wally about the increased drug use and make sure he got my message that Ivy is accusing Heather of killing Logan. Then I'll probably talk to Vince, and maybe Heather, if I can find her."

"You're hoping to substitute Heather for Vince as Wally's prime suspect?"

She couldn't fault the guy's observational skills. "Yes, I am."

"I wish I could go with you when you talk to Wally and Heather, but I really want to stay with my mother one more day." Simon rested his hip against his Lexus. "But I did make a list of the business people in town, and Monday I'll start calling around to find out who is pro and who is con on the amusement park issue."

"Great." Skye leaned next to him and put her arm around his waist. "Bunny needs you today and I'll be fine. After all, I'll either be with the chief of police or my own brother."

"How about Heather?"

"If push comes to shove, I think I could take her two falls out of three."

Simon straightened, bringing her more fully into his embrace. "Stop by the alley afterwards, and tell me all about your adventures." Then to her surprise, since he usually wasn't demonstrative in public, he kissed her deeply, his tongue hard and sweet and promising.

Skye adjusted her sunglasses and pulled the knit hat covering her hair farther down. She felt like a stalker. After borrowing Vince's Jeep, with the promise of a full explanation when she returned it, Skye had spent the last two hours sitting across from Wally's house waiting for Darleen to leave.

A call to the police station had confirmed that the chief was off duty all of Sunday. Unfortunately, Darleen had answered when Skye phoned Wally at home and hung up on her when she heard Skye's voice. So now she was forced to spy on him as if they were a part of some preposterous James Bond movie.

Skye took a sip of her Diet Coke and slouched back in her seat. Her reasoning was that unless Darleen had moved back in, and surely Skye would have heard that gossip, she would have to leave at some point, if only to get a change of clothes. Skye just prayed that Wally wouldn't go with her.

Finally at eleven o'clock, the door to Wally's house

opened, and he and his ex-wife emerged. They stood on the porch arguing until Wally turned on his heel and went back inside, slamming the door behind him.

Darleen hesitated, then trudged down the steps, got into her BMW, and squealed out of the driveway.

As soon as the red car disappeared around the corner, Skye was out of the Jeep, across the road, and ringing Wally's bell. She waited several minutes, but no one came. Why wasn't he answering?

Just as she pushed the button again, the door was flung open, and Wally bellowed, "Give it a rest, Darleen."

"It's Skye." She jumped back. "But I can see this is a bad time. I'll talk to you later."

The look on his face could have melted wax, but after a moment his features smoothed out, and he said, "Sorry. No. Now's fine. Come on in."

Skye eased past him and stood in the entryway. "I'm the one who's sorry to be bothering you on a Sunday, but I haven't been able to get a hold of you. Have you gotten my messages?"

"No." Wally gestured for Skye to go into the living room and take a seat. "I haven't had any messages from you."

She had never been in Wally's house before and wasn't sure where to sit. She chose the sofa, not wanting to take whichever he considered *his* chair, but Wally sat next to her and said, "How many times did you call?"

Skye counted out loud, "Thursday night, Friday during school, and Saturday morning."

He frowned. "I didn't get any of them. I'll have to have a talk with the dispatchers about the importance of giving me my messages."

"Uh, I hate to accuse someone without proof," Skye began—she couldn't let Wally yell at the dispatchers when she was fairly sure it wasn't their fault, "but from what

Darleen said yesterday afternoon when I tried to see you at the station, I think she may be intercepting your messages."

"That's ridiculous." His expression was critical. "I know you don't get along—Darleen's told me about some of the problems you two have had at school—but suggesting she's interfering with official police business is serious. Do you really want to make that accusation?"

His words hit Skye like an ax blow, but she refused to let him see how he had hurt her. In an offhanded tone she said, "Darleen and I do have issues at school, but that has nothing to do with this. I'll let you handle the missing messages. I suggest we move on to the information I was trying to give you."

"Fine." His voice was flat. "Go on."

Skye took a moment to collect her thoughts. She wanted to present a concise list of what she knew and get out of there before she either smacked him or started crying or both. "Thursday after school, a student mentioned to me that he or she had observed an increase in the availability and use of methamphetamine in the Scumble River area. This observation is consistent with some of the unusual teenage behavior that has been recently reported."

"Explain."

Skye matched his clipped tone. "Exacerbated thought patterns, increased heartbeat causing one to feel overheated, and paranoia and hallucinations in long-term users."

"What are exacerbated thought patterns?" Wally asked.

"All your thoughts are exaggerated." Skye struggled to put the psychological concept into simple terms. "It's sort of like you see a pretty flower, but you think it's not just a pretty flower, to you it's the most beautiful flower that ever bloomed. The flower is so gorgeous it makes you cry."

Wally's expression was still puzzled, but he shrugged and asked another question. "You mentioned hallucinations. Would that be like a voice telling them to burn down the school?"

"Exactly."

He got up, went into another room, and returned with a legal pad. He jotted something down, then asked, "Who told you about the increased availability?"

"I can't say—confidentiality."

"That didn't stop you with Grady Nelson."

His comment, light as the flick of a whip, had hit its target. Guilt was a sharp knife plunging into her stomach. Wally knew how difficult it had been for her to break confidentiality. Even when doing so seemed justified, it was always a judgment call and one she continued to question.

What had gotten into Wally? Why was he being so awful to her? Instead of asking, she defended herself. "As I explained at the time, I told you about Grady because there was an immediate potential that he might hurt himself or someone else. In this case, there is no such impending danger. The student has told me all he or she knows and is not a possible instrument of harm."

"Fine." Wally blew out an exasperated breath. "Is there anything else you *can* tell me?"

"In a separate, but perhaps related issue, Ivy Wolfe accused Heather Hunt of killing her husband."

"When did this happen?"

"At the bowling alley Friday night. Ivy didn't know that Heather had started singing with the band, and when she found out, she screamed that Heather had murdered Logan."

Wally made another note. "Any idea why Ivy thinks Heather is the killer?"

"Maybe . . ." Skye trailed off. She had planned to tell Wally about yesterday's visit to the Wolfe farm, but he had been so mean and so unreasonable she was afraid of his reaction. Still, she'd better tell him everything now. He'd just be more upset if he found out later.

"Maybe what?"

Defiantly she looked him in the eye and said, "When I talked to Ivy yesterday, her explanation was that Heather wanted to be a part of the band so badly, she was willing to kill to take Logan's place as the singer."

"You talked to Ivy Wolfe yesterday?"

"Yes."

"Why did you do a stupid thing like that?" His voice rose in anger.

Skye had had enough. "Because when Darleen refused to let me talk to you at the police station yesterday afternoon, she said Vince was one of your main suspects in the Logan Wolfe murder case, which is something I had already figured out." She'd come to Wally in good faith to share information with him and he was treating her like dirt. She didn't know what line of bull Darleen had been feeding him about her, but if he was fool enough to believe his ex-wife, so be it. The gloves were coming off.

"And that gave you the right to tamper with a possible witness?"

"Yes." Skye leaped to her feet. "You tried to railroad Vince once before. I'm not letting you do it again."

"If you think I would do something like that, I don't know why you even bothered to come over today to share your information with me."

"And if you think I would accuse anyone, even Darleen, of something without a mighty good reason, you obviously don't know me very well." Skye stalked into the entryway and flung open the door. As she marched out, she said over her shoulder, "And you obviously don't trust me like you claim to."

Skye ran across the road to the Jeep and jumped inside. She jammed the gearshift into drive and roared away. A few miles down the road she pulled to the side and let the tears flow. What in the world had just happened? What had gotten into Wally? And what had gotten into her?

After a few minutes, she fumbled in her pocket for a tissue, wiped her eyes, and blew her nose. She needed to talk to someone about this—not Simon or May, and Trixie had enough troubles of her own right now. Uncle Charlie would probably punch Wally in the nose for upsetting her, so Vince would have to do. Anyway, she had to return his Jeep, and she wanted to hear what he had to say about the big break Logan had promised the band.

Vince was watching an old Three Stooges movie on TV when Skye entered his apartment. She collapsed on the sofa beside him and put her head on his shoulder.

When the commercial came on, he switched off the set, and asked, "What's wrong?"

"I just had the strangest encounter with Wally." She briefly described what had happened. "So, has he gone crazy or have I?"

"Well . . ." Vince teased.

Skye straightened and hit his arm with the back of her hand. "Well?"

"Well, look at it this way. The man is being besieged by his ex-wife, is in the middle of a mayoral campaign he may or may not want to win, and has just had a murder case land in his lap." Vince grabbed Skye's hands and held them so she couldn't hit him again. "And then the newspaper runs an article on the Scumble River Nancy Drew. Do you really think he can be held responsible for anything he says right now?"

Skye gave her brother a speculative look. "You're pretty generous toward a guy who has your name high up on his list of prime suspects."

"I didn't do it, and it'll all work out in the end." Vince

let go of her hands and reached for the remote. "You worry too much, Sis. You're getting as bad as Mom."

"Thanks a lot." Was she really as much of a worrywart as May? Nah. It was just in comparison to Vince that she looked like a fussbudget. Her brother wouldn't be concerned even if the IRS called him for a surprise audit. "Before you return to your movie, I have a couple of questions."

"Shoot."

"Did Logan tell the band that they were about to get their big break? That he had letters asking Pink Elephant to audition for a record producer and *American Star*?"

"Yes."

"Why didn't you say anything about it to me?"

"Logan always thought everything was going to be our big break. We just went along with him. No one else thought it would amount to anything."

"If you felt that way, why did you agree to all the extra rehearsals and start to write new songs?"

Vince shrugged. "The band needed all the rehearsals it could get, and I'm always writing new songs."

Skye found her brother's explanation hard to believe. Maybe Vince felt that way, but did the other two musicians? "Did Logan ever show you or the other guys the letters?"

"I didn't see them, and I don't think the others did either. Why?"

"Ivy let me read them today."

"So?"

"The auditions were for Logan as a solo act. They didn't include Pink Elephant."

Vince frowned. "Are you sure?"

She nodded.

"So Logan was just using us?"

"Seems that way."

Vince threw the remote he had been holding across the

room, where it crashed into the wall and exploded in little plastic pieces. "That son of a b—"

Skye cut him off. "Do you think maybe either Rod or Finn found out what Logan was up to and killed him because of it?"

"If Finn found out, he would have told me and Rod. He likes to stir things up."

"And if Rod was the one to find out?"

"He's usually pretty quiet, likes to let things go with the flow, but I have seen him blow up once before. And when he does, he loses all control."

"Interesting." Skye contemplated that piece of information for a moment, then asked, "So if you guys weren't mad at Logan about him going solo, why were you all so ticked off the night I attended your rehearsal?"

"Well, part of it was the whole Heather issue."

"But there was more?"

"Logan had turned into a real pain in the ass. Everything had to be his way. We could only do songs he approved of and only take gigs he thought were worthy." Vince wrinkled his forehead, thinking. "He was always late, so we had to wait for him. Then he'd hang out with the teenyboppers, which made Finn uncomfortable. He and Rod wanted to replace him with another vocalist."

"*You* didn't?"

"I didn't want to confront him. I thought he'd straighten out. You know how I hate conflict."

Vince had given Heather's phone number to Skye but claimed not to know where she lived. Skye tried calling her from his apartment but got an answering machine. It featured Heather singing something about living forever and everyone remembering her name.

There was only one option left. If Skye really wanted to find Heather, she would need to ask May. Her mother either knew where everyone lived in Scumble River or knew someone who did. Since Skye was already in the car, she headed to her parents' house.

White pea gravel crunched under the Bel Air's tires as Skye turned into their driveway. It had finally stopped snowing, but the temperature still hovered around the freezing mark.

Skye crossed the patio to the back door, glancing at the concrete goose at the foot of the steps. She had finally given up trying to stop her mother from dressing the lawn ornaments and now found it interesting to see what outfit May had chosen for it this week. A little like a Rorschach test for farmwives.

Today the statue wore a tiny white powdered wig and black suit. An ax was strapped to its wing. It took Skye a minute, but the set of false teeth positioned over its beak was the giveaway. Today was George Washington's Birthday.

As she entered the utility room Skye called, "Mom, it's me. Are you home?"

She had crossed through the kitchen and stepped into the living room before she heard a voice answer. "I'll be out in a sec."

Her father was asleep on the big leather recliner in the corner. A nature program was playing on the TV, its soundtrack of roaring animals punctuated by Jed's snores. It was amazing; he was louder than the lions and more annoying than the hyenas.

Skye took a seat on the sofa and picked up the book section from the *Kankakee Journal*. She wanted to see what was being reviewed this week. Skye's tastes and the columnist's were usually similar.

Several minutes later, May emerged from the bathroom. Her hair was newly combed, and she had on fresh lipstick.

She asked, "Have you eaten? We had roast and mashed potatoes. I can fix you a plate."

Skye debated with herself. She hadn't eaten and in fact couldn't remember the last time she'd had a real meal, as opposed to a sandwich or a salad from a plastic bag, but she had vowed to be more independent and not let her mother baby her so much. Her stomach won. "If it's not too much trouble, that'd be wonderful."

"Trouble? Don't be silly. You know your father and I would like you to eat all your meals here."

In the past, May had tried to get Skye to move back home, but when she got Bingo, her mother stopped issuing that invitation. May couldn't abide animals in the house.

As May bustled around the kitchen heating leftovers, Skye sat at the counter and asked, "Do you know the new girl with Vince's band?"

"I saw her at the bowling alley Friday. I don't really know her, but I've heard about her."

"I don't recall the name Hunt. Is her family from around here?"

May slid a heaping plate in front of Skye and handed her a fork. "They're part of the Doozier clan."

Skye took a bite of mashed potatoes. These creamy spuds hadn't come from any box. She savored the buttery taste before saying, "I thought I knew all the Dooziers. How are the Hunts connected?" In a funny way, Skye counted the Dooziers as friends. Maybe not pals you'd go to the movies with but allies she could count on.

May scrunched up her face in thought. "MeMa Doozier was a Hunt, so Heather would be some sort of cousin to the family."

As close as anyone could judge, MeMa, the matriarch of the clan, was well over a hundred years old. The next oldest in the line was her great-grandson Earl, the current patriarch of the family. The middle generations had been wiped out in an accident involving a rickety porch, an out-of-control pickup, and several kegs of beer.

"Then Heather isn't a close relation?"

May shrugged. "You know the Dooziers. They're a very tight-knit family." She put a piece of chocolate cream pie in front of Skye and asked, "Why are you so interested in Heather?"

Skye paused, a bite of pie halfway to her mouth, trying to decide how much to tell her mother. May already knew that Vince was a suspect, but she didn't know the whole sordid Heather story, and Skye saw no good reason to tell her. Still, she needed an explanation for her curiosity. She decided to try the casual approach. "Just wondering, since she's joined Vince's band and all."

May shot Skye a sharp look and went right to the heart of the matter. "Is Vince involved with that girl?"

"I don't think so," Skye answered honestly. Thank goodness her mother hadn't asked if he *had* been involved with her.

"We need to make sure he doesn't start." May wiped the counter in vicious circles. "From what I hear, she's been hit on more than Vince's drums."

Skye choked. Her mother didn't often talk about someone that way. After taking a sip of water, she said, "I think Vince is safe from her charms."

"You need to warn him about her."

"I'll do that. And I'll warn her to keep away from him." Skye kept her face expressionless. "You wouldn't happen to know where she lives, would you?"

"Sure. She shares an apartment with the girl who runs my exercise class. It's in the building right behind the high school."

Skye rang the bell next to the card marked Hunt/Price. It was a little after three on Sunday afternoon and should be a good time to catch someone like Heather at home—late enough to be out of bed but too early to go out. A voice came from the intercom, "Yes?"

"I'm looking for Heather. Is she home?"

"Sure. When you hear the buzz, turn the knob right away, then go up the stairs and to the left."

Skye smiled to herself, glad she didn't have to explain who she was and what she wanted while standing in the lobby and shouting into a little metal box.

Heather was standing in an open doorway. She seemed confused to see Skye. "Do I know you?"

"I'm Vince's sister. We met the other night. Could I talk to you for a minute?"

The singer shrugged and backed into the apartment. "I guess so. Do you want to sit down?"

Skye nodded and looked around. The room was filled with typical grandma's attic castoffs. A hideous purple plaid couch upholstered in a material that no one had been able to wear out in the past forty years took up most of the space. A couple of easy chairs with chenille bedspreads thrown over them occupied the rest of the floor plan. Brightly colored plastic milk crates served as occasional tables and the walls were papered with posters of Britney Spears, J.Lo, and other female rock stars.

"Heather," Skye said after they both were seated, "I was at the bowling alley Friday when Ivy Wolfe attacked you. Could I ask you a couple questions about that?"

A tiny line formed between Heather's perfect eyebrows. "She was really, really mean to me."

"Yes, accusing you of killing Logan was pretty nasty." Skye sat on the edge of the couch, leaned forward, and assumed her best counselor position, hands lying palm up on her knees. "Do you know why she would say something like that?"

Heather's lower lip thrust out. "She was jealous of me."

"Because of Logan?"

A look of confusion settled on Heather's face. "Maybe that too, but mostly 'cause I have star quality and she doesn't. She can sing okay, but she doesn't have the looks or the stage presence you need to be a superstar."

Skye was having trouble following the girl's reasoning. "But why would Ivy's lack of charisma cause her to accuse you of murdering Logan?"

"Silly! Logan and I were just about to get our big break." Heather's cornflower-blue eyes sparkled. "He and I had auditions set up to do a duet for a big record producer and for that TV show, *American Star*."

"I'm still not following how that would give you a motive to kill Logan."

Heather shook her head, clearly unable to believe Skye's stupidity. "Just before the fire, Logan told me that Ivy wanted to sing the duet with him instead of me. And that meant he'd have to sing the song me and him had written together with Ivy instead."

Because she was thinking what a rat Logan had been—stringing along this poor girl *and* the members of Pink Elephant to further his own ambitions—it took a moment for Skye to realize what Heather had said. Even then, she wasn't sure she had interpreted it correctly. "Do you mean you talked to Logan at the high school the night of the dance, after he and Vince had their fight in the break room?"

"Yeah."

"Right before the fire started?"

"Yes. I was standing in the wings and there's a spot where there's a long instrumental part, so Logan stepped off stage and that's when he told me." Heather's little girl voice became even more breathless and high pitched. "We were arguing, but when the alarm went off I just ran out of the building and came home."

"What about Logan? Did he run out too?"

Heather shrugged. "He probably went back for his guitar."

Skye sucked in a breath. Heather clearly didn't realize she had admitted to being the last person to see Logan alive. Except for his murderer. Unless they were one and the same.

CHAPTER 20

Stairway to Heaven

Monday morning was never one of Skye's favorite times of the week, and this one was turning out to be worse than most. After stopping and saying hi to Simon and Bunny at the bowling alley Sunday night, she'd spent the rest of the evening at home fretting about how to tell Wally about Heather's presence in the gym at the time of the fire. She did not want to speak to him again after their nasty conversation that morning.

Finally she had compromised and written him a note detailing her chat with Heather. She disguised her handwriting on the front of the envelope, in case Darleen saw it before Wally did, and dropped it at the police station on her way into work.

Skye was scheduled to be at the elementary school that morning to teach social skills in the kindergarten classrooms. She had just finished explaining about listening and had started the kids role-playing what they had learned when the PA announced, "Miss Denison, please report to the office."

As she hurried to the front of the building, she wondered what more could go wrong. She'd already had a student wet his pants during the session on sharing, and during the lesson on taking turns another kid had tugged on the skirt of her dress so hard that it had ripped at the waist. Currently two safety pins were all that was holding Skye together.

She rounded the corner into the office and stopped dead in her tracks. The school nurse was standing in the doorway to the health room wearing rubber gloves and holding a comb. That could only mean one thing—and it wasn't that Scumble River Elementary School was opening up a beauty salon. The school had an outbreak of lice!

Skye tried to back out of the office, but the principal had snuck up behind her and blocked her escape. "Oh, no, you don't. We're all in this together."

Three hours later, the nurse, the principal, the school secretary, and Skye had examined over six hundred heads—including each other's. Sixteen students had been sent home, three mothers were hysterical, and a first year teacher was threatening to quit.

At one o'clock, the principal finally agreed that Skye could leave, and she headed over to the junior high.

Neva Llewellyn, the principal there, was pacing in front of the door when Skye came up the sidewalk. "What took you so long? You left the elementary fifteen minutes ago."

"I went through the McDonald's drive-thru and picked up something to eat." Skye held up the familiar brown bag.

"We don't have time for that now." Neva grabbed the sack and tossed it into a garbage can, then seized Skye's arm and pulled her inside. "Cletus Doozier is on the roof claiming he can fly."

"Yikes!" Skye trotted beside Neva, who had made a sharp left and then headed up the stairs. "Who's with him?"

"Ursula, and counseling is not her strong suit, so hurry." Ursula was the school secretary, and her idea of empathy was to tell a depressed child to snap out of it.

"Have you called 911?" Skye shook off Neva's hand and

paused to catch her breath—she really had to get back to swimming soon.

"The fire department is on its way, but I doubt any of the volunteers are trained for this. The dispatcher is tracking down Chief Boyd."

Skye caught up as the older woman pushed open the door to the boys' room.

"Why are we going in here?" Skye asked, panting.

"There's a ladder up to the roof out this window."

"Why?"

"I have no idea, but I noticed it when I took over as principal." Neva gestured to a milk crate pushed against the wall under the open window. "Never had to use it before though."

Scumble River Junior High was the oldest of the three school buildings—it had originally been the high school—and the architecture was by far the oddest.

"Isn't there another way up there?" Skye cringed as she pictured herself scaling the outside of the school in a dress.

"There are stairs, but he's blocked the door somehow. I've got the custodian working on it." Neva pointed. "Just swing your foot a little to the side when you climb out and the ladder is right there."

Skye hesitated. "Is this how Ursula got up there?"

"Yes." Neva pushed her forward. "Hurry, before he jumps."

Skye kicked off her pumps and stepped up on the crate, then put a knee on the windowsill. "You're positive this is the only way up there?"

"I'm sure," Neva insisted.

Skye groaned and hoisted herself to a sitting position in the opening. The metal ladder attached to the side of the building was where Neva had promised it would be. Skye scooted as close to it as she could, grabbed it with her left hand, and swung out on to it.

For a long moment she swayed, not fully on the rung. Finally she steadied herself and started to climb. As soon as she could see over the top she stopped. Cletus was facing the opposite side flapping his arms. Like his Uncle Elvis, he was small for his age and could easily pass for several years younger than his true thirteen. He'd had a rough life. His mother was dead and his father was in jail. He lived with his Uncle Earl.

Ursula stood to his right, her arms crossed, shivering. She was dressed only in a knit pantsuit.

Skye crawled over the parapet. The gravelly texture of the flat roof dug into her stocking feet, which were already freezing. The wind blew in gusts, and she was thankful she had never had a chance to take off her coat.

She didn't want to scare the boy, so she called in a low, steady voice, "Cletus, it's Ms. Denison. Are you all right?"

He looked her way with an unfocused gaze. "I'm Superman. I'm a bird; I'm a plane." He ran in a tight circle and flapped his arms. He had a gym towel tied around his neck like a cape.

Skye edged up to Ursula, who looked blue from the cold, and whispered in her ear, "Why don't you go inside and warm up? I'll take over."

Ursula frowned and shook her head. "I think I should stay."

"What we really need is for you to try to unblock the door. I think I hear the fire engines." When Ursula nodded and turned to leave, Skye added, "And make sure someone has called Earl."

Cletus seemed unaware of the adults, almost as if he were watching a movie playing in his head.

Skye had no idea what to do. Should she talk to him? Try to grab him? They hadn't covered this situation in her school psychology training and she doubted it was in the *Best Practices* manual.

Cletus had stopped circling and was examining the ledge

that went around the roof. It was about three feet high and twelve inches wide.

Skye felt her throat close. She had to do something before he crawled on top and jumped off. Her mind raced and she snatched the first idea that came to her.

She stepped closer and said, "Superman, it's me, Lois Lane. You can't fly from this roof. Lex Luther planted Kryptonite up here."

Cletus looked at her. "You sure?"

"Yes."

"Good work, Lois." He nodded and moved back from the edge. "We gotta go find another roof."

Skye took his hand and subtly directed him toward the door. Ursula was just removing the last of several pennies Cletus had stuffed around the lock and between the door and the frame.

The door immediately swung open and the fire chief burst through, followed closely by Wally.

Before the men could speak, Skye said, "Superman has agreed to find another roof since this one is contaminated with Kryptonite. Please step aside and let him through. He's in a hurry to save the world."

The men silently made a path, and Skye and Cletus walked out.

As they went down the stairs, Cletus said, "No offense, Lois, but ain't you put on a little weight?"

Skye, Neva, Wally, and Charlie had gathered in Neva's office. Earl had shown up in time to accompany Cletus to the hospital in an ambulance. They were waiting to hear word of his condition. In the meantime Charlie was sharing his frustration.

"What in blue blazes is going on around here?" he thundered. "I was watching my afternoon programs when I heard the emergency call to the junior high on the police scanner."

He wiped his face with a large white handkerchief. "First the fire, now this. What's next? A riot at the grade school?"

Skye figured this was not the time to mention the lice outbreak at the elementary school, and no one else said anything either.

Finally, Wally glanced at Skye, then cleared his throat. "This is not to leave the room."

They all nodded.

"Sunday I received some information about possible increased availability of methamphetamine in the area. Officer Quirk and I have been following up on that lead ever since and have confirmed that report. We've talked to several neighboring police departments and the county sheriff. They too are experiencing an increase in the use of this drug."

Charlie asked, "So, you think it's all connected—the murder, the fire, and the sudden crazy behavior among the students?"

"That's our working theory."

Neva spoke thoughtfully from her seat behind her desk. "Judging from today's incident, it seems as if the drug has infiltrated the junior high as well as the high school."

"Except for Cletus, have you had any other bizarre incidents?" Skye asked.

"No. None of which I'm aware."

"Then maybe Cletus is the first." Skye ran through the last week's events in her head. "His uncle, Elvis, was part of the teenage group that caused a problem at the bowling alley Friday night, and I'd bet my next season's clothes budget that he was high on something. So, if that's true, it would be reasonable to assume that Cletus got the meth from Elvis, so he might be the conduit into the junior high."

"I've sent Quirk to the hospital to talk to Cletus." Wally headed for the door. "I'll radio for him to question Earl, too, and I'll talk to the rest of the family myself."

Neva, Skye, and Charlie watched the chief leave, sinking

into a brooding silence until the hospital called at four-fifteen and confirmed that Cletus had indeed taken methamphetamine but would be fine once the effects of the drug wore off.

There was a familiar looking pickup in Skye's driveway when she got home. Sighing, she parked the Bel Air and cut the engine. She really didn't feel like dealing with anyone else today. She wanted supper—having lost her lunch to the trash can—a bath, and a good book. But most of all she wanted to be alone.

But what she wanted and what she was actually going to get were two different things. As soon as she got out of the car, Justin and Frannie emerged from the truck and met her at her front steps.

Justin spoke first. "Ms. D., do you have a minute?"

There was no way she could turn away the teens so she said, "Sure. Come on in." Skye ushered the kids inside and hung their coats on the hall bench.

Bingo took one look at the teens and disappeared into the bedroom. He had met Justin and Frannie before, but who could tell with cats?

"Have a seat." Skye gestured toward the great room. "Would you like a pop?"

They nodded and she detoured to the kitchen. As she poured glasses of soda and emptied a bag of potato chips into a bowl, she noticed the message light on her answering machine was blinking. Wearily she shook her head. Whoever it was would have to wait.

Skye put the tray on the coffee table and once everyone was served, Justin said, "I think we've got a lead on where the meth is coming from."

"I thought we agreed you weren't going to investigate that," Skye protested.

His shoulders twitched in what might have been a shrug.

"We didn't really investigate." He shot a fleeting look at Frannie. "At least not at first."

Skye took a handful of chips—she was starving—and before stuffing them into her mouth said, "So what happened?"

"Well, at first, I just wanted to know more about meth, so I went online."

Skye nodded, her mouth full.

"There was all kinds of info on meth. Everything from how users behave to how to manufacture it."

She swallowed. "Really?" Skye could use a computer's word-processing programs, but since she didn't have access to the Web on a regular basis, she had never learned how to use it to get information. The few computers that were available at the schools were old and not hooked up to go online. "You mean anyone could find out how to make an illegal substance just by looking on the computer?"

"Yeah." Justin took a gulp of soda. "But the best Web site was the one that told what to look for if you suspected someone was making meth."

"What did it say?"

"I think it was meant for someone who thought their neighbor had a meth lab, because it talked about checking their garbage for empty boxes of cold medicine and discarded watch batteries. Also, for used cans of automotive starter fluid with holes punched in the sides."

"Interesting, but there's not much you could do with that info unless you had a suspect." Skye hoped Justin hadn't been poking around Scumble River's trash.

"That's what I thought, too. But then it dawned on me. Not only would they have to throw the used-up packages away, they'd have to buy it to begin with. And where would you get that kind of stuff?"

"A drug store," Skye speculated.

"Buzz. You couldn't buy enough without people wondering what you were up to."

"True." The owner of the local pharmacy employed his mother as a clerk, and anything one bought there immediately became the cause of much speculation among the rest of the little old ladies in town. Needless to say the store did not do a big business in condoms or home pregnancy tests.

"So, where would you go?" Justin took another swig of soda, then answered his own question. "A big store a few towns over where people didn't know you and you didn't have to check out with the same clerk every time."

"Wal-Mart in Laurel," Skye deduced.

"That was my guess." Justin beamed. "My next question was who from here worked there and would be willing to talk to me?"

"How did you find someone?" Skye asked.

"Well, I knew the high school had a vocational program and that some of the juniors and seniors worked part of the day instead of going to school, so I asked the teacher if any of them worked at Wal-Mart." Justin was clearly enjoying himself.

"And . . ." Skye wished Justin would get to the point, but she couldn't deny the boy his pleasure. He had been extremely clever.

"And a couple did, but they were girls, so I asked Frannie to talk to them." Justin blushed. "I didn't know if they'd tell me anything or just think I was hitting on them."

"So Frannie approached them, and they told you what?" Skye turned to the girl.

"I asked them if they remembered anyone buying a lot of cold medicine, batteries, and/or starter fluid. They hadn't, but one said she'd ask the other clerks—the ones who aren't students and work there full-time." Frannie paused to eat some chips.

"And?" Skye's patience was wearing thin.

"And the girl who works there told me this morning that another clerk said one guy used to come in all the time for the entire shopping list, and he always made a point to check out at his wife's register, even if she had a long line."

"Who was it?"

"The dead guy," Frannie answered. "Logan Wolfe. His wife was fired about a month ago, and everyone thought she must have been letting him get by without paying."

"No one knew for sure?"

"No," Frannie answered. "But the clerk said she hadn't seen him at the store since his wife was sacked."

"Was there ever anyone with him?"

Frannie nodded. "The clerk said a couple of times his brother came along."

Skye frowned. She was pretty sure Logan was an only child. "How did she know it was his brother?"

"She said they looked alike, except his brother had real short hair."

Skye tucked that piece of information away and asked, "I know it's only been a little over a week, but have you noticed any less availability of the meth since Logan was killed?"

Justin shook his head. "Not that I noticed." He looked at Frannie. "How about you?"

"I don't hang out with the kids who use, so it's hard to say."

"I see." Skye quickly considered the situation. She had to tell Wally what the teens had found. "What's the name of the clerk who recognized Logan?"

"The girl wouldn't tell me. She had promised to keep her out of it," Frannie answered. "And I promised not to tell her name."

"Great," Skye muttered. Wally was going to have a cow when she couldn't give him names. "You know Logan's dead. He can't hurt the clerk or your friend."

"It's the druggies at school she's scared of." Frannie looked at Skye as if she had grown another head. "And do you really believe a meth lab is run by only one person?"

Skye had no idea. She clearly had to do some research before she went any further. Almost to herself, she said, "I wish I knew how much meth was made in a batch and how long that supply might last."

Justin answered her, "It varies, depending on the lab." He reached in his jeans pocket and pulled out a bunch of crumpled papers. "Here. I printed out the stuff I found on the Web. I figured you'd want to read it."

"Thanks." Skye smoothed the sheets.

Frannie stood up. "I gotta get the truck back to my dad. He needs it to go to work in a little while."

"Okay." Justin got to his feet.

Skye followed them to the foyer. "I really appreciate the information you found out, but don't do any more digging, okay? It's just too dangerous. I'll let Chief Boyd know what you discovered, and he'll take it from there."

Justin and Frannie nodded, and Skye hoped they had really heard what she said.

After the kids left, Skye called the police station and left a detailed message for Wally. She hoped he would get it.

Having done her civic duty, she went into the bathroom, turned on the bathtub faucet, and poured in some vanilla-scented oil. While the tub filled, she ate a sandwich. As soon as the bath was ready, she turned out all the lights, put on a Patsy Cline tape, and slid into the hot, foamy water. She knew she'd never be able to put the day's events out of her thoughts so instead she allowed her mind to free associate. So much had happened in the past week and a half. Was it all somehow connected?

What was the first incident? Skye closed her eyes and ran the days backward through her mind until she came to the band rehearsal a week ago last Thursday. Vince had said everyone was mad at Logan because of his behavior, but maybe he didn't know the real reason. Maybe one of the other band members had found out that Logan had a meth lab and was selling drugs to teenagers.

Skye put Rod and Finn on her "to-talk-to-again" list and asked herself: *What happened next?* The false fire alarm, Bitsy's melt down while they were decorating the gym, Nathan's impromptu shower at the dance, and, of course, the fire itself. As she had pointed out to Wally, those kids were probably all high at the time of their misbehavior.

And then there was Heather's presence at the fire. Was she really there to talk to Logan about singing, or was she in on the meth sales too?

Skye nearly drifted off to sleep, but the image of a pig kept wafting through her mind. She sat up abruptly, splashing water over the side of the tub and on to Bingo, who had been stretched out asleep on the bath mat. He yowled and ran away.

The Pig-in-A-Poke Land amusement park was also a recently added element to the local mix. Could Moss Gibson or his grand plans for Scumble River's future have anything to do with the current goings-on? Logan's land was a part of the parcel Gibson wanted to acquire, but Ivy had claimed to be antidevelopment. The prodevelopment people Ivy and Rod had mentioned went to the top of Skye's "to-talk-to-immediately" list.

As Skye was thinking about the rest of the week the phone started ringing. Darn. She should have listened to her answering machine before getting into the bathtub. Oh, well, she decided, whoever it was would just have to leave a message.

Still, she got out of the tub and was drying off when the doorbell buzzed. She hurriedly slipped on her robe and ran for the foyer. After peeking out the window, she flung open the door, grabbed Simon's necktie, and hauled him inside, saying, "You won't believe the day I've had."

"Well, let's see if I can do anything to make it better," he murmured, kissing her neck.

After Simon shrugged out of his overcoat, Skye took his hand and tugged him toward the bathroom. While she ran more hot water into the oversized tub, she filled him in on her activities. She concluded with, "And then Justin and Frannie left."

He ran down the roll of Scumble River business people he had spoken to that day, indicating who was for the amusement park and who was against it. Happily, the end of his list coincided with the last of Simon's clothes hitting the floor.

Hours later, after Simon had left and just before she fell asleep, Skye realized that the one variable she had left out of her equation was the mayoral election. Could Wally's candidacy have anything to do with what was going on? And come to think of it, where had Darleen gotten the cash for her fancy new car? There was a lot of money in selling drugs, and who had a better excuse for talking to teens than a teacher?

CHAPTER 21

Slippin' and Slidin'

Skye was kept busy Tuesday morning dealing with the aftermath of Cletus's actions from the day before. He had been sent home from the hospital and was none the worse for wear, but both teachers and parents were in an uproar over what had happened. Neva and Skye took turns handling the calls and visits.

Earl Doozier had arrived about an hour after school opened. He entered the building shouting, "This really sticks in my craw. What in the hell is going on around here?" He had dressed for the occasion in orange sweat pants and a yellow and black striped sweater. With his short stature and small beer belly, he looked like an angry bumblebee. Twin tufts of hair sticking straight up from the crown of his head quivered like antennas.

Skye spotted him first and steered him into the principal's office. Once he was seated, she and Neva murmured soothingly until he had calmed down.

Finally, Skye was able to ask, "Earl, do you have any idea where Cletus got the drugs?"

He took out a big blue hanky, blew his nose, and after examining the contents, put it back in the pocket of his sweatpants. "I'm not for sure of that, Miz D. But he says he got it from Elvis, and Elvis ain't sayin' where he got it."

Darn! Between the lice and Superman, Skye had forgotten she wanted to speak to Elvis on Monday about what had happened at the bowling alley Friday night. She'd have to try to have a word with him that afternoon. If they could get the kids to say where the meth was coming from, they could put a stop to it. But odds were, no one would tell.

They talked for a while longer, until Earl eventually stood and said, "I know you folks are tryin' real hard to make sure the kids get smartened up, but right now, it might be more better if you turned your attention to findin' out who's dealin' dope to them."

Neva and Skye agreed that Earl's assessment of the situation was correct, even if his grammar wasn't. Unfortunately, Neva had no idea how to solve that particular mystery, and the only thing Skye could think to do involved a return trip to the Wolfe farm. She hoped it wouldn't come to that. If the police would look into Logan's possible meth involvement she wouldn't have to.

Skye had been unable to get to the high school that afternoon, so she called Trixie and asked her to have a chat with Elvis. Trixie called her back about an hour after the last bell to report that her interview had been less than fruitful. Elvis had declared that he wouldn't "rat on his friends." Trixie said she didn't think they'd get anyone to tell, and Skye had to agree.

While she gathered her things and walked out to the car, she considered her alternatives. It seemed that the murder investigation had hit a dead end. She needed to approach it from a new angle. Maybe Rod had been on to something when he suggested Logan's murder was tied to Pig-In-A-Poke Land. She was convinced there was some connection between the development and the problems Scumble River was suddenly having. It was time to look into the amusement park issue.

Having made that decision, the next logical move was to talk to some of the business people who were in favor of the park. According to Simon's list, Nate Turner was the most vocal supporter, but Simon had been unable to get a hold of Jess Larson, the liquor store owner, and Skye was curious about the newcomer's position.

So, whom should she talk to first? Turner, who resembled Jabba the Hut and had the disposition of a grizzly bear with a toothache, or Jess, who was sort of cute and had flirted with her at the Pig-In-A-Poke brunch? Hard choice.

Skye turned toward the Brown Bag Liquor Store, located across Maryland Street from the motor court owned by Uncle Charlie. Both establishments appeared to be enjoying a brisk business, if their full parking lots were any indication.

Previously the Brown Bag had hunkered on the riverbank like a malevolent toadstool, but with the construction of the bar and banquet hall additions, the original building had lost its funguslike air.

Jess was checking people out at the cash register and didn't look up as Skye entered and joined the line.

She was relieved when no one got in back of her. When it was her turn she said, "Hi. You probably don't remember me. We met at the Pig-In-A-Poke brunch. I'm Skye Denison."

Jess's smile was slow and sexy. "Sure, I remember you. Your brother's band is going to play for my grand opening."

"Right." Skye leaned a hip on the edge of the counter. "Looks like I just missed rush hour."

"Yeah. The aerosol plant's day shift gets out at four-thirty and some of the guys stop here on the way home for their nightly six-pack."

"Why don't they just buy a case? They'd save money."

"My guess is that if they had twenty-four cans of beer at home, they'd drink that many."

"Oh." Skye's stock of small talk was exhausted. She'd have to broach the actual subject she was interested in or take the chance that another rush of customers would come in and steal Jess's attention. "So, how's business?" Fayanne had always moaned she wasn't making any money, but she seemed to do pretty well when all was said and done.

"Not bad." Jess hitched up his belt. "Could be better."

"A lot of people stock up at the Wal-Mart in Laurel."

"So I noticed." He gave Skye a crooked grin. "What I want to know is if Wal-Mart is lowering prices everyday, how come nothing is free yet?"

Skye laughed politely. She'd heard that joke before. "Where are you from?"

"Los Angeles."

"What made you decide to move to small-town Illinois?"

"My father was military and we moved around a lot. No place was really home." Jess's expression was hard to read. "Cousin Fayanne's letters made Scumble River seem like a cross between *Mayberry RFD* and *Leave it to Beaver*. It sounded . . ." He hesitated, obviously searching for the right word. "Friendly."

"Is it living up to your expectations?"

"So far."

"I was sure surprised at that brunch when Moss Gibson unveiled his Pig-In-A-Poke idea," Skye said, edging her way to the heart of the matter. "Was it a surprise to you too, or were you already aware of it?"

"Moss Gibson had talked to me earlier." Jess leaned back against the wall and rested the heel of one sneaker on the plaster. "He figured since I was new in town, I'd have less attachment to the land."

"Oh. You own some of the land he wants to buy?"

"A few acres between Scumble River and County Line Roads."

Skye wasn't very good with directions, so it took her a minute to realize where he meant. "I think you share your eastern boundary with some of my family's acres."

He tipped his head in agreement.

"I imagine it's crossed your mind that if the Pig-In-A-Poke amusement park goes in, it would be good for your business."

Another small nod.

"So, I suppose you've agreed to sell your land to Moss Gibson?"

"Nope."

"No? Why not?"

"I don't need the money."

"And?" Skye felt there was something she wasn't getting.

He shoved off from the back wall and came out from around the counter. Skye hadn't realized that he was only a couple of inches taller than she. It was nice to look a man in the eye without cricking her neck. Simon, Vince, Wally—all the men in her life were so tall.

Jess's brown eyes stared into hers.

Skye felt her heart do the rumba and scolded herself. Not only was Jess a good five years younger than she was, she already had a boyfriend.

"And I moved to Scumble River, in part, because it wasn't Generica."

"Generica?"

"Generica is the interchangeable landscape of most American cities." Skye's expression must have broadcast her confusion, because he continued, "You know: strip malls, housing developments, and fast food restaurant chains, all in a row with no character and no imagination."

"Ah. I see." Skye finally figured out where Jess was coming from. "Even though you're new to Scumble River you don't want it to change."

"Exactly. Growth is not always progress."

Skye nodded. At one time she would have disagreed with him, but her opinion had changed in the last couple of years. There was a lot to be said for not trying to improve on a good thing.

It seemed to Skye that she could cross Jess Larson off as a suspect. He was on the same side of the amusement park issue as the late Logan Wolfe and didn't seem to have any other connection to what was going on.

Which meant there was no getting out of it—she'd have to talk to Nate Turner. Since he seemed to be the most vocal supporter of the amusement park, there was a good chance he would know if someone on his side was gunning for Logan. There was also the strong possibility that Turner himself might have wanted Logan dead for standing in the way of Pig-In-A-Poke Land and the money it would bring to Turner's company.

No matter how much she dreaded the thought, she had no choice. May trusted her to clear Vince, and Justin and the rest of the kids depended on her to stop the meth production, and there was a good chance the recent events were all connected in a way she just hadn't figured out yet.

Skye turned west on Maryland, then took a right on Veterans' Parkway, the first road after the bridge. Turner's business was located on the northwest corner of Scumble River.

It was close to six o'clock when she turned into the gravel drive and drove under a wooden arch painted with the words: TURNER LANDSCAPING AND SNOW REMOVAL. She pulled up behind a bright green "dually" truck with four rear tires instead of two, which gave it the appearance of a squatting frog.

A neon orange bumper sticker read MY KID CAN BEAT UP YOUR HONOR STUDENT. Trust Nate Turner to embrace a grotesque parody of the original that proud parents used to tell the world that their child was an academic achiever. She had seen that truck several times since returning to Scumble River and always wondered who drove the butt-ugly vehicle.

The landscaping company headquarters was housed in a small trailer. Skye picked her way up the slippery metal steps—it had started sleeting in the short time it had taken her to drive over from the Brown Bag—and knocked on the door.

Turner's rough voice called out for her to come in. He was seated at a battered desk and using two fingers to type on an old manual typewriter. He looked up as she entered and growled, "What do you want?"

"How do you know I didn't come to hire you?"

"Because your family does all its own landscaping and snow removal. You have a goddam cousin for any job that comes up."

"True." Uninvited, Skye took a seat on a folding metal chair. "Do you have a minute?"

"Why not?" Turner yanked out a piece of paper from the typewriter's platen, wadded it up, and tossed it in the general direction of the wastebasket. He missed, and it joined several other crumpled sheets on the floor. "What do you want?" As if it suddenly dawned on him, he demanded, "Is my boy okay?"

"Well." Skye wasn't sure how to answer that question. "As far as I know, he's fine right now, but I am concerned about him and some other students."

"Oh?" Turner's wooden chair creaked as he pushed back from the desk. "Why?"

Skye held her breath. Would this sumo wrestler come after her if she suggested his son was taking drugs? She exhaled and went for it. "Nathan's actions the night of the dance were so unlike him that I'm concerned he's fallen into bad company and might be taking methamphetamine." She braced herself for a blow and was surprised when the big man sagged back in his seat.

He mumbled, "Me too."

"You've noticed a change in his behavior?"

Turner nodded. "He's always been a good kid. Captain of the basketball and baseball teams, popular with the girls, straight Cs. But lately he doesn't sleep—I got up the other night and he was pacing around the downstairs like a cat looking for a mouse. And he's real emotional—he cried when we ran out of chocolate ice cream. His grades have slipped and I'm surprised he hasn't gotten kicked off the basketball team. Coach Cramer has been real tolerant and concerned. He calls all the time to talk to Nathan."

Skye ran through the list of behavior Turner had described. Taking into account her previous knowledge of meth's short-term effects and what she had read last night in the papers Justin had printed for her off the Internet, Nathan's use of the drug appeared to be a slam-dunk certainty.

Despite the fact that Turner was a jerk in most aspects of his life, in this instance Skye felt sorry for him. He seemed to genuinely love his son and want to do what was best for him. What she was about to say would be very painful. Many parents would ignore her advice, but regardless of the obnoxious persona Turner usually showed the world, Skye thought he might listen to her and get his son the help he needed.

"Mr. Turner, it sounds to me from the behavior you've described, and what I've observed, that Nathan is probably taking meth. It's come to my attention that there's recently been an increased availability and use of the drug in this area. Chief Boyd is aware of the situation and is looking into it. Which means it's important for you to get Nathan into a treatment program ASAP—both for his health and for his future, so he doesn't end up with a police record."

Skye waited for the man's reaction—gauging the distance between her and the door. She no longer believed Turner was a bodily threat to her, but better safe than sorry.

Turner moaned, his head sinking into his chest. He reminded Skye of a silverback gorilla who had been shot and couldn't understand what was causing his pain.

"How? I mean where?" Turner stood up and moved toward Skye. "What do I do?"

Skye stood, too. She took a notepad from the desk, wrote a few lines, and handed the paper to him. "This is the name of a hospital in Chicago that specializes in this problem. Ask for the drug treatment unit and make an appointment. They'll probably agree to see you immediately. Put Nathan in the car and drive him there. Don't let his pleading and promises sway you. Check him in and do what the doctors tell you."

Turner took a deep breath and clutched the sheet of paper to his chest. "I really appreciate your helping Nathan like this. If there's anything I can ever do for you, you let me know."

Skye hated to bother him at a time like this, but she needed answers. "Could I ask you a couple of questions that may help me figure out who is supplying the kids with meth?"

"Believe me, if I knew the answer to that, I wouldn't be standing here, and they wouldn't be breathing."

"Well, I have no proof. It's purely a guess on my part, but I think there may be some connection between the increased meth availability, and the fire, the murder, and the proposed Pig-In-A-Poke development."

Turner narrowed his eyes. "I know your family is against the amusement park, but it would really help this town. You sure you aren't trying to connect it to the drugs just because you want it to be dirty?"

Skye paused and thought about his question. Was that the reason? Could it be a coincidence that Pig-In-A-Poke came along at the same time she became aware of the increased drug use?

"Well?" he growled, fingering the telephone, obviously anxious to make the call to the hospital.

"You might be right. But I feel I need to check everything out, no matter how far-fetched." Skye moved to the door. "I can't risk overlooking something and have a kid die because of my carelessness."

The big man tightened his lips. "Okay. This is all I know about Pig-In-A-Poke. Moss Gibson told me that he could build either north or south of Scumble River Road. But if he can't get all the land he needs on one side of the road, he'll have to take the amusement park to another town."

"So even if he can't buy the Leofanti farm, which is currently a part of his southern border, he could go north, but he would need the Frayne acreage and the Wolfe property."

"Yeah. There's also a little piece on the corner, but the owner inherited the land, lives in the city, and has already signed an option to sell."

"So it's all up to the Fraynes and the Wolfes?"

"Right. Gibson has to have land along either County Line or Scumble River Roads. He explained to me that because of land formations, government leases, and other factors, no other acreage in the area meets his needs."

"Thanks." Skye climbed down the stairs and yelled up to where Nate Turner was still standing. "Good luck with the hospital, and call me if I can be of any help."

He nodded, waved, and disappeared inside the trailer. The metal door made a hollow sound as it thumped shut. Skye maneuvered the Bel Air back out onto the road. She only hoped that Turner would follow through on her suggestion and that they had caught Nathan's problem in time.

She had been with Turner for an hour. Her stomach was growling, and her neck was throbbing from the day's frustrations. She was trying to figure out what she should do next when an approaching vehicle's headlights blinded her.

Skye checked to see of she had accidentally put on her brights. No. She flicked them on and off to indicate to the other driver to turn off his high beams. They didn't dim.

She clutched the steering wheel. It looked as if the lights were coming straight at her! She slowed down to twenty miles an hour. Shit! Were a bunch of teens playing chicken? She had always hated that game when she was in high school. Two drivers would aim at each other and the first to pull over was the "chicken."

Honking her horn, she slowed even more and moved as far to the right as she could. The asphalt was slick with sleet and she could feel the Bel Air's rear end slide as she tried to edge even closer to the shoulder.

The headlights coming toward her shifted in her direction, then sped up. There was no doubt. They were aimed straight at her. Skye wrenched the steering wheel to the right, trying to escape the steel monster bearing down on her.

She heard a scrape; the car fishtailed and then slid over the edge—rear end first—into the eight-foot deep drainage ditch running along the road. Although it felt like she was moving in slow motion, there was only a couple feet of water in the ditch, and the Bel Air hit bottom almost immediately. The car settled on its rear bumper, wedged in the icy mud at a seventy-degree angle.

For a moment she sat without moving or thinking, dazed by the impact and the events leading up to it. Finally, she looked around. Her seatbelt held her in place and except for the weird position, the car didn't appear to be damaged. Of course, she couldn't see the exterior.

Skye struggled to unhook her seat belt, but the buckle was stuck and refused to open. She rolled down the window and started shouting for help. Thank goodness the Bel Air was an old car with crank-style window handles versus an electric button, because the engine had died on impact.

She continued to yell for assistance as she put all her weight behind trying to free herself from the seatbelt. She was already beginning to feel the cold, and she had to struggle to keep her teeth from chattering.

Several minutes went by and she was resting her voice when a light appeared at the top of the ditch. From the way it moved, Skye guessed it was a flashlight. She opened her mouth to call for help but closed it without making a sound. She had just realized that there had been no one on the road except for the vehicle that had run her off it. And once she had gone into the deep ditch no one could see her car. Which meant the person wielding the flashlight was probably the same person who had run her off the road.

Had it been a bunch of teenagers out for a joyride, after too much liquid refreshment, or was it someone who knew she was investigating Logan Wolfe's death and/or the meth business and wanted to stop her—maybe for good?

CHAPTER 22

Tuesday Is Gone

Skye was furious with Wally. It had been a long time since he had forced her to sit in the back of the squad car instead of in the passenger seat, and that was only one source of her resentment. This time it was Wally who had gone too far. She had been careful to provide him with all the information she had discovered—and it hadn't been easy, considering the barrier his ex-wife had put up around him—and how had he repaid her? He'd assigned one of his officers to follow her around like she was some sort of criminal.

Granted, Officer Quirk's presence had come in handy in extricating her from the ditch. But what was the use of having a police escort if he wasn't even able to catch the bad guys who had tried to hurt her? Quirk's lame explanation was that his orders were to make sure she was all right before apprehending the wrongdoer. He had screwed up and just didn't want to admit it.

Skye blew out an exasperated sigh. She was thoroughly sick of sitting in Wally's cruiser. She had already examined every inch of the floor, seat, and ceiling, and nothing had changed from her previous occupancies.

At least she was warm; Wally had left the engine running

and the heater on. Another plus, the squad car was parked on the opposite side of Veterans' Parkway from the ditch Skye had been forced into, so she had a fairly good view of her car being hauled from the ditch by the tow truck and the activities surrounding the extraction.

Skye thought back to her rescue. As Officer Quirk had cut her loose from the seatbelt and helped her up the slippery slope of the ditch, he had explained that he'd been following her since she left school. Chief Boyd had ordered him to keep an eye on her, but because of the deserted road, he'd had to keep back in order to remain out of sight. The car that had forced her off the road had been long gone by the time Quirk discovered Skye in the ditch.

Paramedics had arrived within minutes and after examining Skye had said that although she appeared to be okay, she should go to the Laurel hospital to be checked out. She had refused. Except for the bruise forming across her chest where the seatbelt had restrained her, she wasn't hurt.

Her throbbing head wasn't the result of an injury. Its cause was a mixture of hunger, frustration, and the fact that she wanted to smack Wally upside the head. Thinking about whacking Wally reminded her that she also wanted her purse, which as far as she knew was still in the Bel Air.

She had just decided to get out of the cruiser and go find her handbag, thus disobeying Wally's orders to stay put, when he opened the front door and slid in, shaking his head. "Good thing Quirk found you. It's colder than a witch's ti— nose out there tonight, and your car is invisible from the road."

Skye bristled but held her temper. "I would have figured out a way to get out myself. I have a Swiss Army Knife in my purse. As soon as I remembered that, I could have cut the belt."

"Maybe. But we found your purse wedged into the back window shelf. It would have taken some amazing contortions for you to reach it." He tossed the object in question at her without looking behind him.

"Thanks." Skye's gratitude was grudging.

Wally continued to stare out the windshield. "Why were you talking to Jess Larson and Nate Turner?"

Skye opened her mouth to make a smart reply but caught herself. She had planned to tell Wally everything anyway, so why rile him up before she really had to? "I was wondering about which side of the Pig-In-A-Poke issue they were on."

Abruptly he turned sideways on the seat and scrutinized her. "Why? What does the amusement park have to do with the murder?"

She met his gaze without flinching. "I'm not sure. Rod Yager said Moss Gibson had been hassling Logan to sell, and when I thought about it, it seemed that all of Scumble River's current troubles started when the developer came to town."

"Interesting point but flawed logic." Wally managed a smile, although Skye could tell it required effort on his part.

"I know." She rummaged in her purse for her pillbox, popped the lid, and dry swallowed an Aleve. "But I really have a feeling that the fire, the drugs, and Pig-In-A-Poke are connected. Did you get my message about Logan Wolfe buying huge numbers of items associated with meth production from the Laurel Wal-Mart and his wife being fired from her job there?"

"Yes. Who told you that?"

"A couple of the kids came to me with the information, but they wouldn't say who told them," Skye answered. "Anyway, it doesn't matter who told me. You can look into Logan's involvement without that information."

"But Logan's dead, so that isn't a great lead, is it?"

Skye clenched her fists. What had gotten into Wally lately? Was it politics or Darleen? "Logan may be dead, but I doubt he was running the business on his own. You need to investigate his known associates to see who else was in on it."

"Let's see, his known associates—who would those be? I know. How about your brother?"

Skye sagged back in the seat. Great! Had she really just aimed the police at Vince again? She straightened and tried again. "Forget Vince. He wouldn't do that. But how about Rod? After all, he was with Ivy when I went by to talk to her, and he doesn't seem to have any visible means of support. Or how about Ivy? Clearly she must have been involved."

"We've interviewed them both. Neither admitted anything." Frustration was evident in Wally's voice. "Even if your 'source' came forward, with Logan dead we don't have enough to get a warrant to search the Wolfe place."

"So you're not making *any* progress?"

"We're working on other leads," Wally claimed. "You still haven't said anything that makes me think there's a connection between the murder or the drugs and the amusement park."

There was something. It had come to her just before she had been forced off the road. What was it? Suddenly she remembered and blurted out, "The car."

"The car that hit you?"

"No. The night of the dance, there was no one around when I arrived, but there was a car parked in the handicapped space." Skye closed her eyes and visualized the vehicle. "It was a red Lincoln Town Car, which is what Moss Gibson drives."

"You think Gibson started the fire?"

"Maybe. Logan *was* standing in the way of his development."

Wally's expression was skeptical. "I'll check it out." He turned and put the cruiser in drive.

"Wait." Skye sat forward. "What about my car? Where

are you taking me?" Her questions became more panicky as he pulled onto the road before answering.

He looked at her in the rearview mirror. "The tow truck will bring it to the garage the police use. I want to have it examined for paint scrapes from the vehicle that hit you. And to answer your last question, to your mom at the police station."

"This is kidnapping," Skye grumbled. The last person she wanted to face was her mother.

May was waiting for them in the doorway of the reception area. Seeing Skye's bedraggled appearance, she turned on Wally. "Walter Boyd, why isn't this girl in the hospital?"

He raised his hands in mock surrender. "She refused to go, and you ordered me to bring her here."

"I'm okay, Mom. I just need a shower and I'll be fine."

May ran her fingers over Skye. "Well, you don't seem to be bleeding anywhere."

"Can I go home now?" Skye asked tiredly.

Wally shook his head. "Wait for me in my office. I want to talk to the tow truck driver before I let you go. Quirk tells me you didn't see who hit you."

"I couldn't see anything because of the headlights."

Skye detoured to the women's room. After using the facilities—now she knew what people meant when they said something scared the pee right out of them—she washed her face and smoothed her hair back into a barrette. The bottoms of her slacks were heavy with mud and her shoes were ruined, but otherwise her clothes had survived remarkably well.

When she finished, Skye went to Wally's office. It was empty and dark. Flipping on the light, she looked around. His padded chair beckoned, and she sank wearily into its cushioned depths. She noticed an envelope on his desk. Its typed label showed it had been sent to Mrs. Darleen Boyd at an address in Clay City. The return address was Gibson Enterprises.

Skye chewed her lip. Should she or shouldn't she? Tempted, she ran her fingertip along the edge. No, she wouldn't. Wally could handle whatever mischief his ex-wife was up to. She had her hands full with more important matters.

Hearing footsteps in the corridor, Skye hastily moved to a chair on the other side of the desk. Moments later Wally walked around her and dropped into his chair. Skye forced her glance away from the desktop.

Wally's gaze went from Skye to the envelope and his voice became dangerously quiet. "Were you snooping?"

"No, I was not." Her face mirrored her indignation. "Why? Is there something you don't want me to see?"

Wally swept the envelope into his middle drawer and closed it with a thump. "Something that's none of your business."

"Fine." She stood and said, "In that case, I'll be going."

"Quirk will drive you home." Wally turned and stared at the wall, dismissing her, but as she reached the door, he said, "Let it go this time. You can't stop the amusement park from going up, you can't figure out who killed Logan Wolfe, and you can't single-handedly end drug use in Scumble River."

It sounded like Wally was talking about himself. Skye squared her shoulders, ignoring her aching head and neck, and said quietly, "Maybe not single-handedly, but with help from my friends I will."

Wally snorted. "People say they want the police to lower crime rates and win the war on drugs, but talk is cheap. Supply exceeds demand." He tore his gaze from the wall and focused on her, a defeated expression settling on his features. "I'll be forty years old next month. I've been a cop for eighteen of those years, and I've finally figured it out. The public doesn't want to pay the cost of what it would take for us to succeed."

Skye left without replying. Forty. Maybe that was what was getting Wally down. Was he experiencing a midlife crisis?

When Skye got home, she called Simon and filled him in on her latest adventures. He wanted to come over, but she convinced him she would rather be alone.

Too many images were crowding her thoughts. There was Wally when he first came to Scumble River as a twenty-two year old fresh out of the police academy. That Wally, the one she'd had a crush on as a teenager, would never have done or said the things the current Wally was doing and saying. Then there were all the kids and families who had already been harmed by meth use. Lastly, there was Logan Wolfe: was he the villain or the dupe? Either way, no one had a right to kill him.

Now she just had to figure out what to do about it all. After being run off the road tonight, she didn't fool herself. Whatever she did, she would be exposing herself to danger. But with Wally in his current funk, she didn't seem to have much choice. Someone needed to clean house around Scumble River, and Skye was determined to find just the bottle of 409 to do it with.

CHAPTER 23

Fire and Rain

The next morning, Skye called Trixie for a ride to work. After explaining about the accident, Skye waited for her friend's usual interest and concern, but except for a few perfunctory questions, Trixie was strangely silent.

Finally as they were walking into the school building Trixie asked, "Do you really believe that the amusement park development has something to do with the drugs and murder?"

"I can't figure out exactly how,"—Skye shrugged—"but yes, I do think there's some connection."

"Last night, Owen and I signed the papers giving Moss Gibson an option to buy our farm." Trixie twisted the strap of her purse. "If you're right, I'll feel as if we're somehow supporting a drug dealer."

Skye hugged her friend. "You did what you had to do. Besides, I'm sure Moss Gibson isn't the one making or selling the drugs. There's got to be some other link."

After parting with Trixie, Skye went to her office and made a list of kids she wanted to talk to. Then she got out her appointment book and figured out where she could fit them into her already overbooked schedule. She knew she was probably wasting her time by questioning them, but she had to give it a try.

The first one she shoehorned in was Elvis, grabbing him in the lobby before school officially began. He refused to tell her anything about who had supplied him with meth, although he did say he had "protection" from a big shot at school. Could Nathan Turner have been the dealer? With him gone now, what would happen?

The other teenagers were even less communicative. Those who knew weren't talking, and those who didn't know wanted to keep it that way. Skye could empathize. There was a sense of dread hanging over the school—almost as if the jury was out and everyone was waiting for a verdict.

When she walked outside after school that afternoon, her father was sitting at the curb in his old blue pickup, his brown lab, Chocolate, riding shotgun.

"Hi," Skye said as she hopped into the cab, nudging the dog toward the center of the seat. Chocolate woofed but allowed himself to be moved. She scratched behind his ears, and with an elaborate doggy yawn, he stretched out between her and Jed.

"Your ma and I picked up the Bel Air from the garage and brought it to your place," Jed said, putting the truck in gear and driving toward the exit. "Needs a new seatbelt; otherwise it's fine."

"Thanks. How long will it take to get the new belt?"

"Couple weeks."

"I probably shouldn't drive it without one, right?"

Jed shrugged.

Skye thought about that and told herself she'd only drive it around town, not on the highway. Besides, she rarely got above thirty-five miles an hour in Scumble River.

Jed turned into her driveway and stopped at the front door.

Skye gave Chocolate one last pat and jumped out of the cab. "Thanks, Dad. Let me know how much I owe you for the new seatbelt." AAA had covered the towing charge. "See you tomorrow for Grandma's birthday party." Jed's mother, Cora Denison, was turning eighty-four the next day, and the family was getting together for cake and ice cream after the mayoral debate.

Jed nodded, waved, and drove away.

Bingo greeted Skye as she walked into her cottage. She fed him, gave him fresh water, and cleaned his litter box, then went to change her clothes. She'd had all day to figure out what she would do next, and the only thing she had come up with was to go and see Ivy Wolfe again. Clearly, Wally didn't intend to do anything more about the information regarding the Wolfes' possible drug connection. Skye was pretty sure that the answers to at least some of her questions were out at the Wolfe farm.

Earlier that afternoon, Skye had checked with Bunny and found out Ivy was off work on Tuesdays. Then she had phoned Vince and asked him to call an emergency Pink Elephant meeting for six o'clock so that Rod would be occupied. If things went as planned, Ivy would be home and alone.

The minutes ticked by slowly. Skye ate supper and tried to watch TV. Impatiently, she flicked off the set and glanced at her watch—another half an hour before she could leave for Ivy's.

She paced. Who had killed Logan and why? Was it a band member who was jealous of Logan's opportunity for stardom? Was it Heather or Logan's wife, upset over his straying affections? Or was it something to do with selling methamphetamine? If it were the meth, was he killed because he was cheating his partners or because he had sold drugs to the wrong parent's child?

At precisely six o'clock, Skye turned into the Wolfes'

driveway. She had forgotten how dark and unnerving the canopy of trees made the lane leading up to the house. It seemed to go on forever.

As she parked the Bel Air, Skye looked around for the dog. She had come prepared this time, having picked up a box of dog biscuits at the grocery store on the way over. She grabbed a handful, ready to use them to barter her safe passage from the car to the porch.

Skye got out and made her way to the front door. She knocked, waited a few minutes, and knocked again. The lights were on and a radio blared rock and roll, giving every indication that someone was home. Was Ivy just not answering her door?

After a moment Skye thought she heard footsteps behind her. She whirled around but saw nothing. Could it be the dog or were other animals roaming around?

A minute or so later the door was opened, and Ivy stood with a bath towel wrapped around her head, panting. "Sorry, I was washing my hair."

Skye made an apologetic face. "Oh, I'm sorry for disturbing you. Do you have a second?"

"Just. I'm getting ready to go out."

"It won't take long."

Ivy gestured Skye inside. "What do you want?"

Skye sat on the edge of a chair. "Uh, well, I talked to the people you and Rod suggested." It was hard to start by asking if the woman's dead husband had made dope for a living.

"And?" Ivy sprawled on the couch, looking totally apathetic.

"Seems that your property and the Fraynes' farm are the key pieces in Moss Gibson's development."

"Then he's not going to be able to build. I told you, I'm against that stupid amusement park."

"The Fraynes have agreed to sell, so that would mean you're the only one in his way."

"And you think he killed Logan?"

"Could be." Skye saw an opening. "Unless Logan was involved in something else dangerous. Something that someone might want to kill him over."

Ivy's eyes flickered, then she jumped to her feet and moved toward the door. "Nothing I know of. Look, sorry to throw you out, but I have to leave in a few minutes and I need to finish getting dressed."

Skye couldn't come up with any way to get Ivy to admit Logan was a meth "cooker" so she allowed herself to be ushered out of the house.

Back in the Bel Air, she thought hard. If Ivy were leaving soon, that would be the perfect time to look around. Skye put the car in gear and drove back down the lane. She had noticed a small turnout about a quarter mile down the road. She parked there, snatched the box of dog biscuits, and headed back to the Wolfe farm on foot.

She stuck to the side of the road, and planned to duck behind the trees if she met Ivy's car coming down the lane. It was even creepier walking down the shrouded path and she was relieved to arrive back at the clearing.

The lights in the house were off and it looked unoccupied. Ivy must have already left. This was Skye's chance to take a good look at the shed and garage. She had her Swiss Army Knife in the pocket of her jeans and thought she could probably pick the cheap button lock on the shed's small door.

Skye approached the shed cautiously, keeping an eye out for the dog. As she neared the building, she paused and sniffed. What was that sickeningly sweet smell? She edged around the corner. The overhead door was up and Ivy was standing behind a table loaded with a mixture of kitchen utensils and science lab equipment.

The scene was exactly as the Internet article had described it. This was a meth lab, and Ivy was the "cooker." Had she always been, or had she taken over when her husband died? Did she kill Logan to get the business? There was no time to figure that out. Skye needed to get back to her car and go for the police.

She flattened herself against the side of the building and poked her head around, prepared to pull back at any indication that she'd been seen. As soon as Ivy seemed distracted, Skye would make her getaway.

She watched as Ivy picked up a heavy glass beaker and placed it on a hot plate, then paused and consulted a well-thumbed spiral-bound notebook. Muttering to herself, she reached for a stack of coffee filters, "Logan, why'd you go and get yourself killed? I can't run this lab on my own." Empty blister packs of cold medicines were scattered along the table's surface.

Skye started to inch away from the shed, hoping Ivy was too busy to notice any noise she might make during her retreat. A sound behind her made her freeze. She scanned the area but saw nothing. Had it been the dog? After waiting a few seconds, she continued to ease away from the building and toward the lane.

She was nearly all the way to the driveway when she heard a shot. Immediately, she dropped to the ground, rolled under some bushes, and covered her head with her arms. She waited, tensed for the next shot. Nothing happened. She had finally convinced herself that she hadn't really heard anything and had just lifted her head to look around, when blue jean–clad legs ran past her heading for the road.

Ivy had been wearing black jeans. Someone else was running around the Wolfe farm. Should she go see if Ivy was okay, should she run like heck back to her car, or should she try to get in the house and call the police?

Before she could decide, she heard a *whoosh*, saw a blinding flash, and felt a wave of heat roll over her. She curled into a ball and started to pray, but the next explosion was even more powerful. Pieces of burning material began to rain down on her, something hit her head, and everything went black.

CHAPTER 24

Born to Run

Skye spent all night Wednesday and most of Thursday at the Laurel Hospital. She kept telling everyone she was fine, but no one believed her. Granted, when she had first opened her eyes and seen the firefighter she hadn't been able to tell him her name or where she was or what day it was. But that information had all come back to her in a minute or two, or at least most of it had.

The scariest part had been seeing everyone dressed in hazardous material suits and wearing respirators. The EMTs had put her in an ambulance and brought her to the hospital despite her protests. They kept talking about head injuries—the blood flowing down the right side of her face was a bit disturbing—and chemically-induced pneumonia from the contaminated air.

It must have been a slow night at the emergency room because the doctors and nurses had swarmed over her as if she were the last ticket to a sold-out rock concert. After what seemed like forever, they finally put her in a room and told her to rest. Which she would have been perfectly willing to do, if they'd just stopped waking her up every hour to check on her.

Early Thursday morning, when the doctor lifted his ban

on visitors, Wally was the first through her door. Marching in, he stood to one side, towering over her, his eyes raking her from head to toe. Suddenly Skye was aware that she had not been allowed to shower, wash her hair, or put on makeup. She didn't so much look like something the cat had dragged in, but more like something the cat had barfed up.

There was a fleeting expression of concern when Wally's gaze reached the huge bandage taped to her forehead, but his frown quickly returned, and he snarled, "What in the hell were you doing at the Wolfes'? And how did you get there? I thought your car was in the garage."

That explained why Quirk hadn't been tailing her. "Dad got it out for me." She'd have to ask Jed to pick the Bel Air up before the police discovered its present location. It would be hard to explain why she had parked there.

"Driving without seatbelts. I'll add that to your list of violations."

"Fine." Skye refused to be bullied. "I told you I thought Logan was running a meth lab, and you said that you couldn't get a search warrant, so I went out to see if Ivy would tell me anything."

"And did she?"

"No."

"So why didn't you leave?"

"I did." Skye hedged. "But I came back."

"Why?"

Skye debated with herself, then prevaricated. "I forgot to ask something, but Ivy wasn't in the house so I looked around. I thought maybe she was in one of the outbuildings. And she was, in the machine shed, cooking up a batch of methamphetamine. I was sure that shed was the meth lab, and I was right."

"So, we can add interfering with a police investigation and trespassing to your record? What other crimes have you committed? Picked any locks, broken into any buildings?"

"No and no. I wasn't trespassing either. Ivy never said I wasn't welcome on her property." Skye had had enough of Wally's rotten attitude. She was the one who had been right. "And tell me exactly how I was interfering with a police investigation. It's not like I locked Quirk up somewhere or raced by him as he was approaching the Wolfe property. You told me yourself you couldn't get a search warrant."

"Damn!" Wally thundered. "You're poking your nose into meth labs and drug dealers. Do you have any idea how dangerous these people are?"

"Of course I do. I watch the news and read the papers. But *these people* have come into the schools and abused my hometown. This is no longer some story on a TV screen. The kids who are being harmed are the ones who trust you and me to protect them, to keep them safe until they're old enough to make good choices."

"Did it ever occur to you that the police might be dealing with this matter?" It was clear that Wally's temper was dangerously close to igniting like a bottle rocket.

Skye didn't care. She'd had enough of him and his feelings. So he was turning forty; it was time for him to get over it. "I gave you every bit of information I had, and I didn't see you making any progress with traditional police methods. Either there's a lack of ingenuity on your part, or you didn't think that what I was telling you was important enough to investigate. This is my fault in what way?"

"Just because you didn't see any progress doesn't mean none was being made." Wally scowled. "We do work on cases without telling you our every move."

"Glad to hear it." Skye was beyond displeased with Wally. Either running for mayor or his ex-wife's return to his life had changed him and not for the better. He seemed to be becoming more rigid and narrow-minded every time she spoke to him. "Have you made any progress?"

"What have *you* accomplished?"

"How am I supposed to know? No one will tell me anything," Skye fumed. "What exactly happened? Is Ivy okay? What blew up? The meth lab?"

"I'm not at liberty to discuss that right now." Wally's voice was as chilly as his eyes.

The nurse chose that moment to chase Wally out of Skye's room and insist that she rest. After that Skye was only allowed one visitor an hour and then only for fifteen minutes.

May claimed the next visit; it took the full quarter hour to calm her down. She was frantic with worry, but after seeing and talking to Skye, she seemed to feel a little better. Jed was mutely concerned, and Uncle Charlie was frenzied. He spent his time ranting about the drug users in Scumble River and vowing to stop them. None of them would tell her anything specific about what had happened at the Wolfe farm. Either they didn't know or Wally had sworn them to secrecy.

Simon finally got in to see her at eleven. He brought a bouquet of yellow roses, a box of chocolates, and the newest mystery by Carolyn G. Hart.

After a sweet kiss, he sat by Skye's bedside and took her hand. "Bunny sends her love, but I talked her out of coming over."

"Thanks. With all these people waiting to see me, I feel like I'm terminal and no one will tell me."

"Everyone's just concerned." Simon squeezed her fingers. "How *do* you feel?"

"A little sore, but otherwise fine." Skye braced herself for the lecture she expected from Simon.

But he only said, "I guess I'd better buy you a helmet and a Kevlar vest for your birthday this year. It seems you're destined to be at the wrong place at the wrong time."

"Maybe full body armor would be better." Skye snickered. "Do you know what hit me?"

"A piece of the machine shed sliced into your forehead.

You'll probably have a scar, but it's right at the hairline so it shouldn't show."

Skye fingered the bandage. "Why was the doctor so worried?"

"There were dangerous chemicals in the air and head injuries are tricky. Since you lost both memory and consciousness, they had to be careful." Simon squeezed her hand. "Do you have any residual memory loss?"

"No. I was just dazed at first. I remembered everything after a couple of minutes. I remember seeing Ivy in the meth lab, the explosion, and getting hit in the head."

"That's a good sign."

"The meth lab blew up, right? Did Ivy get hurt?" She'd been asking this question since she'd come to back on the farm, but no one had answered her.

Simon pursed his lips, a debate obviously going on in his mind. After a minute, he said, "Ivy's dead. She was caught in the heart of the explosion."

Skye swallowed the sudden lump in her throat. There would be no second chance for Ivy. "What a horrible accident," Skye murmured, then paused. Or was it? Another thought was teasing Skye. There was something else she remembered, but just as it was about to surface, the nurse stepped in and told Simon his time was up.

Next on the visiting list were Vince, Trixie, Frannie, and Justin. The teens were planning on writing a story for the newspaper. Skye only hoped that Trixie would edit it carefully.

At four, the doctor appeared and told Skye she could go home. All the test results indicated that she was okay. He wanted to see her in a week to remove the stitches. She was to come back immediately if she experienced any blurred vision or memory loss.

Simon was waiting to drive her. "Did Dad get my car?" Skye asked.

"Yes. He and your mom dropped it back at your cottage."

"I'm surprised they weren't here to pick me up."

Simon reached over and caressed her cheek with the back of his hand. "I won the coin toss."

"Really?"

"No. But May seemed to understand I needed to be the one to get you. However, she is waiting at your cottage."

"Great. She'll probably want me to move back home so she can take care of me." Skye leaned her back against the headrest. The pain pills made her sleepy.

The next thing she knew, they were pulling into her driveway. Simon took her elbow and guided her up the front steps and inside.

May was dozing in the recliner, but her eyes flew open when Skye stepped into the great room, and she shot out of the chair. "How are you feeling?"

"A little groggy, but okay."

"I made you some homemade chicken noodle soup and chocolate cupcakes."

Skye smiled. "Sounds great. I'm starved. Hospital food is awful." Whenever she had been sick as a child, May had always made her soup and cupcakes.

While Skye ate, the three of them talked about Scumble River's reaction to the meth lab explosion.

When Skye finished, May looked at her watch and said, "The mayoral debate is in half an hour. Are you going?"

The thought of the noise and the smoke and facing Wally and Darleen again were too much. "No."

May nodded. "Good. You need to rest."

"But I am coming to Grandma's birthday party afterwards. What time do you think it will be?"

"The debate is supposed to last an hour, and then there'll be questions, so we're all meeting at the house at eight."

"That's pretty late," Skye teased.

"Well, a lot of the family wanted to attend the debate and

the others wanted to have Grandma's birthday party on her actual birth date, so this was the compromise."

"Okay. I'll be at your house at eight."

"Then I'll get going, if you're sure you're all right?"

"Go." Skye looked at Simon. "You, too. I want to know how the debate goes."

Simon stood and kissed her cheek. "I'll pick you up and drive you to your parents' for the party."

"Thanks. See you then."

Once they were all gone, Skye sank back on the couch. Bingo had been hiding while May was there, but he came out and stretched beside her. It was a relief to be alone for a while. Now she could think.

One mystery was solved. Logan had been the one "cooking" the meth, and his lab was no doubt responsible for the increased use of the drug in and around Scumble River. Now she just had to figure out who had killed him. Who had the most to gain from his death? Not the band members. Without Logan, they were no closer to their big break than if he were alive and auditioning as a solo act, so what would be the point of murdering him?

How about Heather or Ivy? Neither woman seemed that broken up over the singer's death. Granted, with Logan gone, Heather got to sing with the band, but was that really enough to kill for? Small-town garage bands were a dime a dozen.

And Ivy had cleared herself with her last words. She wanted Logan there to run the meth lab and to get his big break and share the success with her.

Who did that leave? Skye thought over what she had learned. Nate Turner had told her that Moss Gibson needed the Wolfe land in order to build Pig-In-A-Poke. Trixie had confirmed that she and Owen would sell to Gibson, and he already had the third piece, which meant only the Wolfes stood in his way.

But then why didn't he kill Ivy too? He couldn't have counted on her having a fatal accident. Wait a minute—the gunshot just before the explosion. Skye sat up abruptly, making her head spin, but she kept a firm grasp on what she had been thinking. Maybe Moss Gibson hadn't relied on an accident. Maybe he had just tried to make it look like one. The killer had to be Moss Gibson. None of the other suspects wanted both Logan *and* Ivy dead.

Wally needed to know about the gunshot, but since at this moment he was tied up with the mayoral debate, she'd wait and call him in the morning. Informing Wally could wait twelve hours, but making sure Simon ordered an autopsy on Ivy Wolfe couldn't. Skye would talk to him as soon as he picked her up for the birthday party.

At seven Skye started to get ready. Her movements were stiff and her head ached. She had decided to take the pain medication only at bedtime because it made her too groggy otherwise. It took her several minutes to find a shower cap—the doctor had told her she couldn't get the wound wet—but she persisted, and was rewarded with a refreshing shower.

Makeup and an attractive outfit did wonders for both Skye's appearance and her morale. She was waiting in the foyer when Simon rang her doorbell, and they were at her parents' house in less than five minutes. On the way over she had told him about the need for Ivy to be autopsied and he'd called the medical examiner on his cell phone.

She and Simon were among the last to arrive, everyone having come directly from the mayoral debate. As they walked in the back door, they greeted the women in the kitchen, and then Simon went to sit with Jed and the other males in the living room. These parties were strictly segregated by sex. The only ones allowed to intermingle were the children or the women serving the food.

After Simon was gone, Skye asked, "Is there anything I can help with?"

May looked around. The birthday cake was on the counter surrounded by piles of dessert plates, napkins, and forks. The coffee urn was percolating and cups, spoons, creamer, and sugar were set out near it. "No, I think we're all ready."

"Did Maggie make the cake, Mom?" May's friend and exercise buddy was well known in the area for making all the special occasion cakes. Her creations were both beautiful and delicious.

May nodded.

There was a brief flourish as Cora Denison arrived and everyone wished her a happy birthday. She was a big woman, five foot ten and solidly built. At eighty-four, she had buried a husband, two children, and a grandson but was not ready to lie down and die herself. She was famous for her dinner rolls and her dry sense of humor.

As she enfolded Skye in a hug she said, "I hear you've been getting into some serious scrapes the past couple of days."

Skye shrugged, not knowing exactly what her grandmother was getting at.

"Your mom tells me it's because you're trying to figure out who killed that Wolfe boy and why there are so many drugs around lately."

"Lots of kids have gotten hurt and the police don't seem able to do anything."

Cora nodded. "I can see you've got Grandpa Denison's strong streak of justice running through you. It obliges you to get involved, even when you could be harmed yourself."

"I guess that's true. I tell myself that this time I'm not going to get mixed up in the situation, but I always end up in the middle of things." Skye was surprised to hear her grandmother refer to her grandfather. No one talked about him or how he had died. In fact, Skye knew nothing about his death except that he had died young.

Cora touched Skye's bandaged forehead lightly. "Just remember: eagles may soar, but weasels don't get sucked into jet engines." Cora turned to talk to another well-wisher.

Skye stood there trying to puzzle out her grandmother's message. Cora's bits of advice were often cryptic.

After "Happy Birthday" was sung, the candles blown out, pictures taken, and the cake served, Skye sat by her mother and asked, "So, how did the mayoral debate go?"

"It was disgraceful. Ace Cramer played dirty pool." May tsked.

"What did he do?"

"He made poor Wally look like a fool."

"Really?" Skye took a sip of coffee. "How?"

"Well, for the most part they talked about the normal issues like replacing the water treatment plant, building new sidewalks, and improving parking downtown."

"Those sound like fair issues for a debate." Skye savored a bite of frosting.

"They were, but then someone from the audience brought up how *you* keep solving Wally's major crimes for him and asked if he were elected mayor, would you be running the town for him, too?"

"Shit!"

"Watch your tongue." May did not abide cursing. "Anyway, Cramer went after Wally on that issue like a squirrel with a new ear of corn."

"How do you think it ended?"

May shook her head. "Cramer would win if the election were tonight."

"Sh—" Skye glanced at her mother's censorious expression and ended, "—oot."

Skye got up and put her dish, cup, and silverware by the sink, then went and sat near her grandmother.

They talked about what had been going on the past couple of weeks; then Cora said, "The Wolfe family never had any luck."

"How's that?" Skye loved hearing the old stories. Maybe she'd write a history of Scumble River someday.

"Logan's grandfather was a rich man. Back in the forties, he owned the big dance hall and a factory that manufactured wooden window shades. But during the war, rumor got around town that he was a German collaborator, and the dance hall burnt to the ground. Due to the mysterious circumstances, his insurance company refused to pay."

"But he still had the factory?" Skye asked.

"Orders dried up, and he couldn't get material or labor. His product wasn't essential to the war effort, so eventually he had to shut it down."

"Was he a collaborator?"

"I doubt it." Cora shook her head. "He went from being one of the wealthiest men in Scumble River to barely eking out a living on forty acres of farmland."

"That had to be rough."

"It was harder on his wife. She committed suicide shortly afterwards." Cora took a sip of her coffee. "But much later on he did remarry."

"That's good."

"Not so's you'd notice." Cora put her cup down. "His new wife was more than twenty years younger and she immediately had two babies—a boy and then a girl. She died giving birth to the girl."

"Oh, my. Poor Mr. Wolfe."

"Poor babies," Cora corrected.

"The boy, who was Logan's father, made out all right. But Wolfe couldn't bear to see the girl, so he sent her over to Clay City to his wife's sister to raise."

Skye was fascinated by this modern-day tale of Job. "What happened to that generation?"

"Wolfe left everything to Logan's father, not that there was much, just the land mostly. But Logan's dad was killed in a farming accident when Logan was five or six."

"Jiminy Cricket." Skye couldn't believe how cursed this family was. "What happened then?"

"Logan's mother ran off—she couldn't face trying to farm and raise the boy on her own—so he was sent to live with his aunt and her family."

"The aunt who was disinherited?" Skye asked. "That must have been fun."

"I think she treated him okay, and he and his cousin seemed to be pretty close. Logan and Ivy socialized with him and his wife quite a bit." Cora got up. "In fact, I was surprised to hear that Ace went through with the mayoral debate today. I would think he'd be too upset after what happened to Ivy last night."

It took Skye a moment, but she finally processed what her grandmother had said. "Do you mean Ace Cramer was Logan Wolfe's cousin?"

"Yep. And since they were both only children, a few years apart in age and raised together, they were really more like brothers. Before Logan grew his hair so long and Ace got a buzz cut, you could really see the family resemblance." Cora moved toward the sink. "I even heard a while back that Logan had signed over half the farm to Ace."

CHAPTER 25

Black Friday

Ace Cramer was Logan's cousin and owned half the Wolfe farm. Skye paced back and forth in her bedroom going over the facts. Could she be right? Could Ace be the killer?

He certainly had opportunity. Ace had been at the dance, and Skye couldn't remember seeing him for quite a while after the fire alarm had sounded. He hadn't been in the parking lot, and he turned up at the junior high at the same time Skye arrived, which was odd since she had been among the last to get there because of her search for Frannie.

As to means, Ace knew his way around the school, especially the gym, and he could have stored the cans of starter fluid in his office until he needed them. In fact, come to think of it, Skye remembered that he had remained in his office watching the whole time the boys were going in and out to get the punch ingredients prior to the dance. He had never allowed the students to be in his office alone.

Now that Grandma Denison had supplied the motive, it all fell into place. Ace was rabidly in favor of the amusement park development. Finally Skye knew why. He owned the vital piece of land Moss Gibson needed. Gibson had probably offered him a huge sum to sell, maybe even a percentage of the amusement park's profits—and the only people standing in Ace's way were his own cousin and that cousin's wife.

The single piece that she wasn't sure of was the meth lab. Was Ace a part of that, too? As a teacher, he was in a perfect position to sell the stuff to students. But if they sold the farm to Gibson for Pig-In-A-Poke Land, they'd have to discontinue making the drug. Is that what Ace wanted—to go legit?

Skye stopped pacing and made a decision. Even if she was wrong, she had to tell Wally her theory. Thank goodness she hadn't called him earlier and accused Moss Gibson. She snatched up the receiver and dialed before she could change her mind.

Both the dispatcher and the officer on duty were part-timers, not exactly the ideal people to share her ideas with. She left Wally a message but was afraid the story was so convoluted he might not understand. Next, she tried his home phone—but no luck there either. When the answering machine picked up, she left an urgent message for him to call her as she had important information regarding Ace Cramer, the murder, and the amusement park development.

Should she drive over to Wally's house? Maybe he was home but just not answering the phone. It was after midnight. Wally would think she had flipped out if she showed up on his doorstep now and tried to explain her concern.

She took a deep breath and considered her options. She could try to track Wally down, or she could talk to him in the morning. Did the situation warrant a midnight pursuit of the police chief, especially considering the very real possibility that she would find him in bed with Darleen? Skye shuddered at the picture and decided to wait until morning. After all, it wasn't as if Ace were about to kill again.

Tomorrow would be soon enough. She would phone Wally from school and ask him to come over and talk to her.

If he refused, she'd go to the police station on her lunch break. There really was no need to run around like a chicken with its head cut off. Wally would be much more likely to listen to her if she presented her case coolly and calmly. Besides, she'd left several messages; maybe he'd return her calls and the issue would be resolved.

Skye slept badly and was up early. Wally had not returned her calls. On the bright side, except for a few bruises and a headache, she felt fine. She had been extremely lucky to survive both the auto accident and the explosion with such minor injuries.

There were a couple of cars in the school parking lot when Skye arrived at seven, but most teachers wouldn't appear for another half hour. Her plan was to give Wally time to get to the police station—he was on the seven-to-three shift—have a cup of coffee, and listen to his messages. At which point, he should call her. If he didn't get in touch by seven-thirty, she'd phone him.

This time she wouldn't rush in and do something foolish. Once she convinced Wally of Ace's guilt, she'd sit back and let the police handle the matter. No way would Wally, the newspaper, or even Darleen be able to blame her for how this situation turned out.

Skye signed in at the counter, grabbed the messages from her box, and headed down the hall. It would be a busy day. After she solved the murder for Wally, she had three meetings to attend and a psychological evaluation to complete.

Her phone was ringing as she let herself into her office. Thinking it might be Wally, she snatched up the receiver. A vaguely familiar voice said, "This is Cal. Mr. Knapik wants you to meet him in the gym immediately," then hung up.

Why was the custodian calling with a message from Homer? And why did the principal want her to meet him in the gym, which was supposed to be off-limits while the construction crew was working there? Skye shrugged. This wasn't the goofiest order he had ever given her. Not by far. She dropped her purse and tote bag on her desk and went to meet her boss.

It was creepy entering the darkened gymnasium with its smoky odor and singed walls. Scaffolding and other building materials were jumbled in with the abandoned dance decorations. In the dim light the combination looked surreal.

Skye was glad she hadn't taken off her coat. There was no heat or electricity in this area while construction was underway.

She called out, "Homer, where are you?"

"Over here." A male voice echoed through the cavernous room.

"Where?" Skye walked toward the sound.

Suddenly, Ace Cramer stepped in front of her, grabbed her by the arm, and dragged her across the gym and into his office. Skye screamed and struggled to break his hold.

He flung her into a chair and said, "No one can hear you."

He was right. Since the fire, no one had any reason to be in this wing of the building. She eyed him. He obviously knew that she knew he was the killer, but how had he found out?

As if reading her mind Ace said, "Darleen intercepted your message to the chief and called me. No one will be coming to your rescue."

"Darleen was in on the murders with you?" Skye didn't like the woman, but . . .

"No, you silly cow. She thinks your theory that I'm the killer is stupid, but she was afraid you'd screw up the Pig-In-A-Poke deal, so she called to let me know what you were up to." Ace leaned against the desk and folded his arms. "Darleen has an agreement with Moss Gibson. In exchange for keeping him informed about what Wally and the other antidevelopment people are up to, he pays the lease on her new car."

"Oh." Skye measured the distance between the door and Ace. Could she make it out before he grabbed her? "But wouldn't helping you throw the election for Wally? I thought she wanted to be Mrs. Mayor."

"She realized a while ago that I was going to win and decided to give up gambling on being Mrs. Mayor and go with the sure thing, Pig-In-A-Poke. Gibson promised her one of the concessions in exchange for sabotaging Wally's campaign and going in with us."

"So, Gibson had it all figured out." Skye tensed to make a run for it.

"All except for you." Ace paced in front of her, his face growing redder by the second. "I thought for sure you'd back off after I ran you off the road, but you just couldn't leave it alone, could you?"

Skye shrugged, not sure if he meant her activities surrounding the murder or against the amusement park development.

"Gibson said that if one more thing got in his way, he'd move the park to another town." Ace ran his fingers through his hair. "I had to make sure that didn't happen."

"So you killed your cousin?"

"It wasn't my fault." Ace bounded off the desk, grabbed Skye by the arms, and dragged her up from the chair and through the office door. "Logan wouldn't listen to reason."

Shit! She had miscalculated his reaction. She thought fast and said, "I've heard that about Logan. That it was impossible to change his mind or make him see that he was wrong."

"That's right." Ace stopped in the middle of the gym and his grip loosened marginally. "I was only trying to protect the children."

"Of course." She eased a half step back from him, looking for an escape route. "Otherwise you would have killed

Frannie, too, instead of just shoving her into the locker." Skye paused. Had she gone too far? No, he was nodding.

"Frannie walked into the locker room while I was holding the empty cans of starter fluid. I couldn't let her see me, so I snuck up behind her and pulled a pair of gym shorts over her head." Ace wiped his forehead with his arm. He was sweating profusely despite the cold. "I thought she'd be safe in a locker. I thought they were fireproof."

Skye kept her expression neutral. "That was a reasonable assumption."

"I never meant to kill Logan. I just wanted him to get rid of the meth lab." Ace shook his head. "I asked him how it would look if people found out I was part of something like that—I'd never get elected mayor. He just laughed at me. He forced me to continue to sell meth at school."

"He really was irrational." Skye angled herself toward the exit. So Ace had been Logan's partner, as she had thought. "I'm sure you tried to talk him out of making that horrible drug and selling it to our kids. Any judge and jury would take that into account."

"They would, wouldn't they?" A furtive expression crossed Ace's face. "They'd understand why I had to get rid of Ivy, too. I was shocked that she was continuing the meth lab even though Logan was dead. I pleaded with her to stop, but she wouldn't. I had no choice but to shoot her and blow up the lab."

"The courts hate drug pushers. You'd probably get a medal for killing Logan and Ivy rather than go to jail." It almost gagged Skye to have to say these things.

"Logan said that cooking meth was a lot better than raping the land, which is what I would be doing if I sold the farm to Moss Gibson." Ace looked at Skye beseechingly. "How could he think like that?"

"His brain was probably damaged by the drug fumes." Skye was willing to say anything at that moment. She stole a peek at her watch. The teachers' bell would be ringing in less than a minute. That would be the time to make a run for it.

"So, I started a little fire in the storage area under the stage, waited for him to run by, and grabbed him. Once I had him out of sight, I hit him on the head with a piece of lumber, shoved him into the fire, and left."

"Completely understandable," she soothed. If she could just keep him distracted for a little longer . . .

"Then you understand why I have to get rid of you, too?" Ace tightened his grip and started dragging her toward the stage. "Good thing they didn't get too far in repairing the gym since there's going to be another little fire."

Skye screamed and he yanked her to his chest, putting one hand over her mouth and twisting her arm behind her back. It hurt, but she forced herself to calm down. There had to be a way out of this mess.

Ace was a lot stronger than he looked, but he was still a relatively small man and Skye was not a petite woman. It was time to use her God-given bulk to her advantage. She pretended to faint. He grunted as her full weight slammed against his body. He let go of her arm and mouth, trying to push her off, and in that instance she shot away from him and ran for the nearest exit.

As she pushed the door open, a cold wind whipped around her, and she plunged outside. She headed for the corner, aiming for the front of the building, but suddenly found herself flat on her chest, the breath knocked out of her. Ace had taken a flying leap and tackled her like she was a football dummy. His muscular body had her pinned to the ground.

Gasping, she tried to get her breath.

She could hear him cursing her. "Bitch, fat cow, nosy whore."

Skye pulled in a long breath of air and bucked like an untamed bronco in a rodeo. Ace tightened his hands around her throat and pushed her face into the snowy slush covering the ground. It froze her cheeks and she tried to squirm away.

Her heart roared in her ears, sounding as loud as the six o'clock coal train. Sometime during the struggle her stitches must have been ripped out because blood was dripping into her right eye. She could feel her head start to swim from lack of oxygen, but just before she passed out, he took his fingers from her throat. She managed to take small mouthfuls of cool air.

Now he grabbed her by the shoulders, trying to yank her to her feet. She clung to the dead grass, digging her fingernails into the frozen roots. A pathetic whimper emerged from her injured throat when she tried to scream.

She couldn't let him take her back inside. Once she was in the gym, there would be no one to find her. She had to think. She'd had classes in both self-defense and takedowns for out-of-control students. Surely she could apply something from that training to this situation. But her facedown position made her helpless. She'd have to let Ace pull her erect.

She waited for him to put all his strength into heaving her upright and then used his own momentum and his lack of balance to push him backward. He fell with a thump, and she heard his head bounce off the frozen ground as she started to run.

She rounded the corner; the parking lot was only a few feet away. Relief flooded through her. She would make it. She'd opened her mouth to call for help when a hand clamped over her lips and an arm grabbed her around the waist from behind.

Acting on instinct, she reached across her body and pinched the inside of his armpit, digging her nails in as deeply as she could, thankful he was wearing a short-sleeve shirt that offered no protection. He jumped back, cursing, and she swung her fist in a low backward arc, slamming it into his groin.

Not bothering to check the damage she had inflicted, she started screaming for help and sprinted the last few feet to the parking lot.

Homer was just getting out of his car. Skye flung herself at the surprised man and started babbling her story. To his credit, the principal immediately grasped what she was saying, shouted for the teachers and students just arriving to get inside, and hustled Skye through the school's front door.

He yelled directions as they ran. Skye reminded him of the gate between the gym and the rest of the school, and he sent several of the larger male teachers to close and guard it. Everyone else huddled in the front offices.

Skye dove for the phone on the secretary's desk as soon as they had cleared the front counter. In less than five minutes a procession of official vehicles led by a Scumble River police cruiser and a white Lexus roared into the parking lot.

Wally leapt out of the cruiser and Simon out of the Lexus. Both raced up the steps and toward where Skye stood just inside the school's front door.

In unison, Simon and Wally asked, "Are you all right?"

She nodded wearily and hastily told them what had happened. Wally ran off toward the gym, shouting into his walkie-talkie for backup as he ran.

Simon put his arm around her, then questioned her more closely. "Are you sure you're okay?"

"Yes." Her throat hurt and her head wound had reopened, but other than some bruises and cuts from being tackled and falling to the ground, she was fine.

Convincing the EMTs was another issue. Finally, after putting a butterfly bandage on her head, checking her throat, and making her promise to go to her own doctor to have the stitches replaced, they made her sign a form stating she refused transport to the hospital.

As the ambulance pulled away, it almost crashed into a Cadillac that came barreling into the parking lot, fishtailing and blowing its horn. The Caddy shuddered to a stop, and the door was flung open. Skye's Uncle Charlie emerged from the driver's seat, ran up the steps, and charged through the front door.

He grabbed her in a bear hug, lifting her off the ground. "Baby, are you okay? I heard the call on my scanner."

"I'm fine, Uncle Charlie. Everything is under control." Skye managed a tremulous smile.

May and Jed arrived soon afterward, having heard the dispatches on their scanner as well. They too had to be reassured that Skye was in one piece.

Everyone gathered in the principal's office to wait for Wally. Skye was seated between May and Simon with Charlie and Jed standing behind her. Homer sat at his desk, having sent the teachers and students to wait in the cafeteria until the police searched the building and gave the all clear sign.

It was close to an hour before Wally appeared in the doorway. "The county sheriff and all of my off-duty officers have been searching the building. Cramer is not in the school. I've sent them all out looking for him and notified the state police."

Homer let out a sigh of relief. "Can we go ahead with school?" When Wally nodded, Homer picked up the phone and told his secretary to send the students and teachers to their classrooms.

Wally turned to Skye. "Tell me what happened with Cramer this morning." He flinched when she got to the part about Darleen but this time didn't suggest his ex-wife couldn't or wouldn't do what Skye had described. After Skye described the events up to when she made it to the parking lot, Wally said to the principal, "Your fast thinking in closing off the rest of the school from the gym may have saved us from a hostage situation."

The radio clipped to Wally's shoulder chirped and they all listened as the dispatcher's voice said, "Suspect has been apprehended by state police on I-55 just past the Louis Joliet Mall exit."

They all breathed a sigh of relief.

Wally started to leave but turned back, pinning Skye with a sharp look. "Did it ever occur to you to just come to my door and tell me your suspicions when you couldn't get me on the phone?"

Skye started to explain her reasoning but gave up and said, "Hey, I used to have a handle on life, but since I came back to Scumble River it seems to have broken off."

EPILOGUE

Just the Way You Are

It was the beginning of March. Snow and cold had continued, and cabin fever was at an all-time high in Scumble River. Skye was counting the days until spring break, still several weeks away.

She sat at one of the back tables of the new Brown Bag Banquet Hall with Simon, May, Jed, Charlie, Bunny, Trixie, and Owen. They were watching the dancing and listening to Vince's band. Pink Elephant had changed its name back to Plastic Santa and was once again playing exclusively soft rock. Now it was actually possible to carry on a conversation while the group performed.

Skye took advantage of this to say, "So, what do you think this is all about?"

"To celebrate Wally's fortieth birthday," Simon suggested. "Like the invitation said?"

"But no one seems to know who's throwing the party," May interjected.

"Maybe Wally is throwing it himself," Bunny offered. "Sort of a combination birthday and I-caught-the-murderer party."

Could that be true? Skye had been worried about Wally. He had sunk into a deep depression after learning about

Darleen's perfidy. It had been all Skye could do to talk him out of pressing criminal charges against his ex-wife for her part in Ace Cramer's attempt on Skye's life.

Before Skye could put her thoughts into words, Charlie said, "What I don't understand is why Ace Cramer went back into the gym after he killed Logan and started the fire."

"He had met with Moss Gibson earlier and forgotten some papers regarding their deal in his desk drawer," Skye told him. After she had told Wally about seeing Gibson's car in the school parking lot the night of the dance, Wally had questioned Gibson, who admitted meeting with Ace but disavowed any knowledge of Ace's plan to murder his cousin. "Plus he sold meth out of there, and he wanted to make sure he hadn't left any incriminating evidence in his office."

Trixie added, "Ace was using kids from the teams he coached as pushers. Stars like Nathan Turner would then suck in the kids who were in awe of them, like Elvis Doozier."

"What I never figured out was why the custodian called me to meet Homer in the gym." Skye frowned.

Charlie answered that. "I had a talk with Cal the other day. Turns out, Ace told him this cock-and-bull story about being in love with you and wanting to get you alone. So Cal did him a favor."

"Oh." Skye took a sip of her Diet Coke. "The other thing I'm confused about is Rod Yager. I never did find out how he makes a living."

Owen took a swig of beer before saying, "He buys and sells stuff at flea markets and swap meets."

Skye raised her eyebrows. Trixie's husband rarely spoke. "So, was he or wasn't he a part of the meth business?"

"I know! I know!" Bunny waved her hand like a student with the right answer. "Rod was in love with Ivy, and she used him—at first to get back at Logan for his cheating ways, then after Logan's death to help her with the meth lab.

He bought the raw materials and did some of the heavy work, but he never cooked the meth or sold it."

"Hard to believe he would do even that much." May tsked. "He seemed like such a nice boy."

Bunny shrugged. "Men are like high heels; they're easy to walk on once you get the hang of it."

Before anyone could react to Bunny's assertion, the music stopped and Vince announced, "Moss Gibson has asked to make a statement."

Voices buzzed and there was a smattering of applause as the rotund little man walked up on stage and took the mike from Vince. "Good evening, friends. I have some sad news. Due to circumstances beyond my control, I will not be able to build Pig-In-A-Poke Land in this wonderful community. Instead, I will be locating it about an hour south of here. I hope you will all come to the grand opening next summer."

After he left the stage, Skye leaned over to Trixie and said softly, "I'm so sorry. I know you and Owen were counting on the money from selling your land to Gibson."

Trixie smiled impishly. "Oh, we still have his money, but now we don't have to give up the farm."

Skye's eyes widened. "How did you manage that?"

"He took an option on our property, which means he paid us twenty thousand to say we would sell it to him at a future date."

"That's wonderful!" Skye hugged her friend. "But aren't you still a little short to pay all your mother-in-law's debts?"

"I'll sell my car. My Mustang will bring in the rest of what we need."

"But you love that car." Skye patted Trixie's hand.

"I had my fun with it. There'll be another car. Farmland, on the other hand, is much harder to come by."

Skye nodded and turned her attention back up to the front of the hall.

Wally was now on stage and had hold of the mike. "First,

I want to thank you all for being here. I can't imagine a better way to celebrate my birthday."

The crowd hooted and hollered.

When they quieted he went on, "I also have an important announcement. I am withdrawing from the mayoral race." There was a groan from the audience. "I thought I needed a change from police work, that I needed a bigger challenge, but what I found out was that although politics is supposed to be the second oldest profession, it bears too close a resemblance to the first for my comfort level."

After the laughter died down, Wally concluded, "Regrettably, since the other candidate has also been forced to drop out of the race, the search for a new mayor will have to start all over again. The town council will be meeting Tuesday to restart the nomination process. Again, thank you all for coming and helping me celebrate my birthday."

For a moment, Skye was speechless. Finally she said to Charlie, "I had no idea Wally was dropping out of the mayoral election."

"He told me a couple of days ago but asked me to keep his decision quiet. He wanted to tell everyone at once rather than have the rumor mill grind away at the truth." Charlie leaned back and crossed his arms. "Wally's a great police chief, but I don't think he has the stomach to be a politician."

Skye nodded. "It certainly seemed to change him, and not for the better. He's been mean and distracted and withdrawn. Do you have any idea what's been wrong with him?"

"Yeah. I talked to him about that after he told me he was dropping out of the mayor's race."

"And?"

Charlie sighed. "I don't think there's any one answer. It seems to me that it's a combination of a lot of things that sort of snuck up on him at once. He could handle any one of them alone, but as a bunch he was just overwhelmed."

"What things?" Skye asked.

"Well, mainly the election and Darleen. Both were pulling him in directions he didn't want to go." Charlie shook his head. "He's just too honest for either one."

"You said mainly. What else was wrong?"

"Oh, turning forty, realizing that this was probably what the rest of his life was going to be like." Charlie glanced at Simon, who was busy talking to Owen and Trixie, then lowered his voice and leaned closer to Skye. "And the situation with you."

"My sleuthing?" she asked hopefully.

"No." Charlie gave her a disappointed look. "You know that's not what's bothering him."

"Well, there's nothing I can do about the other." Skye looked at Simon, then over at Wally. She was happy with her decision . . . wasn't she? "You know, Wally's never made any real attempt to change things between us. Did he *say* I was one of the things bothering him?"

"Not exactly, but it's pretty clear."

Skye was silent. There was nothing to talk about. She was with Simon and that was that.

Charlie got up. "I'm going to get another beer. Do you want anything?"

She shook her head, Charlie's words churning in her thoughts. He had to be wrong. Wally was not suffering from unrequited love for her. The idea was too stupid to consider. In order to force herself to think of something else, Skye tuned in on her mother and Bunny's conversation.

Bunny was saying, "I think there's more crime and corruption in Scumble River than there was in Las Vegas."

May shook her head. "Not quite. But we do have more secrets than a locker room full of teenage girls."

Skye nodded in agreement and added, "And more raging hormones than a locker room full of teenage boys.

Turn the page for an excerpt from the Scumble River Mystery

MURDER OF A SMART COOKIE

Cookie Caldwell died the third Sunday in August, and the Scumble River First Annual Route 66 Yard Sale almost died with her. She had lived in town only a few years, and no one seemed to really know her.

Cookie's death raised a lot of questions, the most puzzling ones being: What was she doing at the Denison/Leofanti booth in the middle of the night? And how did a piece of jewelry manage to kill her?

For the next week, until the crime was solved, these questions were asked over and over again on the TV news, while a picture of Cookie stuffed in Grandma Denison's old Art Deco liquor cabinet, one hand thrust out as if she had tried to claw her way to freedom, flickered on the screen.

The Heartland TV channel was on location taping a program about the Route 66 Yard Sale and managed to get exclusive footage of the post-discovery activities. Their news coverage included a much wider angle of the crime scene, which exposed a group of locals who were ignoring the dead woman and arguing among themselves. It was not an attractive depiction of the citizens of Scumble River, Illinois. It was an especially unflattering portrayal of its mayor, Dante Leofanti.

Leofanti's niece, Skye Denison, didn't look much better. The photo of her playing tug-of-war with her uncle over Cookie's purse was not the one she wanted to project as the town school's psychologist.

It was how Skye was spending her summer vacation, not her winter employment, that had got her into her present predicament. And that story started nearly eight weeks before the murder, after she had already lost two summer jobs and started looking for a third. The first loss of employment was due to geese with loose bowels and poor toilet habits, and the second was because of her inability to keep her mouth shut.

Skye stood silently next to her new boss, Cookie Caldwell, the proprietor of Cookie's Collectibles, as the woman carefully examined a ceramic vase. When Cookie turned it upside down, Skye squinted to see the words inscribed on the bottom. They read: "Curtain of the Dawn."

Alma Griggs, the elderly woman on the other side of the counter, twisted the cracked handles of her white patent leather handbag while she anxiously watched Cookie inspect every inch of the vase's surface, then repeat the process with the interior. Finally, the old lady quavered, "Mr. Griggs bought that for me in Texas on our honeymoon in 1932."

Skye did some quick arithmetic in her head—even if Mrs. Griggs had been married at sixteen that would make her eighty-nine years old. Skye snuck a peek at the woman. There was no sign of frailty. Mrs. Griggs was nearly the same height as Skye, about five-foot-seven, and even at thirty pounds lighter, a solidly-built woman. Her white hair was worn in a braided crown on top of her head, and her jewelry consisted of a necklace of red plastic raspberries with matching earrings and bracelet.

Cookie interrupted Skye's inspection of Mrs. Griggs by

placing the vase on the counter and saying, "I'll give you five hundred dollars for it. It is in good shape for its age, but unfortunately there's not a lot of call for this style around here."

The older woman's shoulders slumped under her calico print cotton dress. "Only five hundred? I need at least three thousand to pay the taxes on my house this year. Mr. Griggs always told me it was very valuable."

Skye impulsively reached out and patted her blue-veined hand. "Maybe he meant sentimental value."

Cookie nodded approvingly at Skye, and ran a caressing fingertip around the vase's metal rim. "I'm sorry, Mrs. Griggs, but the market isn't very strong right now, and I'll probably have to hold on to the vase for quite a while before I find a buyer."

"I need to think about it," Mrs. Griggs said. She hesitated before packing the vase back into its box. "I'll let you know tomorrow."

"I won't be here tomorrow, but I'll leave a check with my assistant." Cookie walked the older lady to the door and watched it shut behind her before returning to where Skye stood. "If she doesn't come back by closing tomorrow, I want you to call her and persuade her to sell that vase to me."

"Me? But why?" Skye stammered. "You didn't seem all that interested."

"Oh, I'm interested, all right." Cookie smiled thinly, and smoothed her ash blond chignon. "I just don't want her to know that I'm interested."

Skye frowned. "But you've offered Mrs. Griggs a fair price, haven't you?"

Cookie shrugged. "Fair is such a relative word." She toyed with the sapphire ring on her left hand. "Anyway, that's not your concern."

"But why do you want me to call? Wouldn't it be better for you to talk to her? I'm not sure what to say."

"You're a psychologist, aren't you?" The storeowner narrowed her cool blue eyes. "I'm sure you'll think of something soothing to tell our Mrs. Griggs. I don't care if you hypnotize her. Just get that vase."

Before Skye could explain the abilities of a school psychologist, Cookie glanced at her watch and stated, "It's past noon." She made an impatient face, and added, "I have to attend a luncheon for local business owners at city hall. I'll be back in a couple of hours."

All in all, this was not turning out to be a good summer for Skye. She'd already lost her usual summer job because of goose poop. The Scumble River Recreation Club, where she had worked the past few summers as a lifeguard, had been forced to shut down its beach when an invasion of geese polluted the swimming area. Who knew that bird crap could be so toxic?

As she stood idle, Skye's thoughts returned to Mrs. Griggs, and Cookie's desire for the elderly woman's vase. Skye wondered how much it was really worth. She checked her watch. It was only twelve-thirty; surely her boss wouldn't be back for at least another ninety minutes, maybe more.

Skye moved closer to the window and looked both ways down the sidewalk. The coast was clear. She spun around and headed toward Cookie's office. It was small, but exquisitely decorated in the style that reminded Skye of a Victorian lady's parlor. An ornately-carved walnut settee, upholstered in moss green velvet, faced a delicate porcelain inlaid writing table that served as a desk.

A bookcase full of reference books stood against the far wall. Skye moved a gilt chair out of her way and scanned the shelves. She selected a couple of volumes on ceramics and quickly returned to the sales counter.

Half an hour later, she reached a section on art pottery and there it was. The vase was one of a series made by Frank Klepper, a Dallas-based artist who worked in ceramics during the early 1930s. A similar vase, "Curtain of the Night," had been sold at auction a couple of years ago for eight thousand dollars.

Before Skye could assimilate the fact that her boss was about to cheat a little old lady out of thousands of dollars, the bell above the front door tinkled and a high, thin voice called out, "I'm back."

Skye's heart stopped for a quarter-second, until she recognized the returnee as Mrs. Griggs, not Cookie, but then it started to pound at double speed when she realized she had to decide immediately whether or not to tell the woman about Cookie's deception.

Mrs. Griggs came up to the counter and asked, "Could I see Miss Caldwell please?"

"I'm sorry, she's stepped out for a while." Skye pasted a smile on her face, her thoughts racing. "Can I help you?"

"Well, I went home and thought about it and decided that if my vase was only worth five hundred dollars, I'd better figure out some other way to raise money, so I wondered if Miss Caldwell would be willing to come out to my house and see if there's anything else she'd be interested in buying." The older woman's voice broke. "There has to be something that I can sell to save my house."

Skye felt her face start to burn. How could she not tell this sweet old lady what the vase was really worth? She couldn't let her invite Cookie into her house to cheat her over and over again. Skye took a deep breath, "Mrs. Griggs, that may not be such a good idea."

"Whyever not?"

Should she sugarcoat it or tell it to her straight? Skye struggled to decide the right thing to do. "Well, uh, I think

Miss Caldwell may have made an error earlier when she appraised your vase."

"What do you mean?" Faded blue eyes narrowed suspiciously at Skye.

Skye flipped open the book she had been consulting, pushed it toward Mrs. Griggs, and pointed to the relevant section. "Look here."

The elderly woman clicked open the gold clasp of her pocketbook and drew out a pair of glasses. After adjusting them on her nose, she peered at the part of the page Skye had indicated. The minutes ticked by as she read and re-read the passage. Finally, she picked up the volume and held it close to her face, examining the small picture. Her chest strained the fabric of her dress as she took a deep breath and slammed the book close. "That bitch! She was going to rip me off."

Skye blinked. She wouldn't have been more surprised at Mrs. Griggs' reaction if she'd started to speak Klingon. "Um, maybe it was a genuine mistake."

"When pigs fly." The older woman thumped her purse down on the counter. "When is she coming back?"

Skye looked at her watch. It was nearly two. Cookie would be back any time now, and then the goose poop would surely hit the fan.